Traitorous Lies

JANE BLYTHE

Cover designed by RBA Designs

Formatted with Vellum

Acknowledgments

I'd like to thank everyone who played a part in bringing this story to life. Particularly my mom who is always there to share her thoughts and opinions with me. My wonderful cover designer Letitia who did an amazing job with this stunning cover. My fabulous editor Lisa for all the hard work she puts into polishing my work. My awesome team, Sophie, Robyn, and Clayr, without your help I'd never be able to run my street team. And my fantastic street team members who help share my books with every share, comment, and like!

And of course a big thank you to all of you, my readers! Without you I wouldn't be living my dreams of sharing the stories in my head with the world!

CHAPTER *One*

October 31st
7:57 P.M.

This was the absolute last thing in the world Jax Holloway wanted to be doing right now.

Running through an empty field with no cover while a dozen people were shooting at him, he'd rather be there.

Swimming all the way back Stateside from France wearing nothing but his underwear, he'd rather do that.

Hell, he'd rather jump out of a plane without wearing a parachute, and he had a thing about heights.

Anything but this.

The tuxedo he wore felt too tight against his skin, even though he knew it had been custom-made for him and in fact fitted perfectly. He just wasn't this guy, he didn't get dressed up like this, didn't mix with the rich and famous, and didn't prance around in a suit at charity galas.

But tonight he had no choice.

He had to be there. Had to suck up the uncomfortable feeling of the tux and Jack-o-lantern mask he'd been given to wear when he arrived at the gate of the estate. If he had any other option, he'd snatch it up like a dying man would a cracker, but the truth was he and his family were fresh out of options.

It was this or nothing.

And it couldn't be nothing.

So, he was here, surrounded by men dressed in tuxedos similar to his own, and women in fancy ballgowns that looked like something right out of a fairytale. Classical music played, and he caught sight of a pianist and small string ensemble on the other side of the huge dance floor.

Couples glided across it, laughing and chattering away, and he prayed he didn't have to attempt to dance tonight. It wasn't that he didn't know how to dance, he did, he was actually quite a good dancer, but it was bad enough having to be there. The last thing he wanted to do was take his mark for a spin like he wasn't there to essentially ruin her life.

Monique Kerr.

Twenty-six years old, shoulder-length brown hair, smoky gray eyes, and a dusting of freckles across her nose and cheeks. Only daughter of Samson and Mary Kerr. Mother walked out on her when she was only two years old. Raised by a single father who, from all intents and purposes, sheltered her and spoiled her rotten.

That was his mark.

Truth be told, he wasn't particularly comfortable with having to fly all the way over to France to attend this Halloween ball just to make contact with her. Not just because the whole setup was so far out of his normal life that he had little to nothing in common with the people attending, but because this woman hadn't done a single thing wrong.

While Jax was sure Monique was every bit the spoiled, rich princess he expected her to be, she had committed no crime, and done nothing to facilitate Prey Security's interest in her other than having the misfortune of being related to Samson Kerr.

Her father, on the other hand ...

The crimes the former US Ambassador to Egypt had committed were many and varied.

And they affected Jax's family personally.

Which is why he was there. Sucking up wearing the uncomfortable tux, and the mask that made him feel too hot and like he couldn't breathe. It was why he would make contact with the Kerr princess as soon as he laid eyes on her, and why he'd do his best to charm her into agreeing to leave with him.

Once he got her alone, he wasn't quite sure what his next move would be. He was alone in Europe while his brother, four stepbrothers, stepsister, and all his brothers' girlfriends were tucked safely away with Prey's Delta Team. The men from Delta were ... different. And after the last several months, with his family suffering from attack after attack, it was good to know that the people he loved were somewhere they'd be safe.

But it left him, as the one still single other than his younger stepsister, on his own in France to do a job he didn't feel the least bit qualified for. Sure, he'd served at a SEAL before leaving to join Prey's Charlie Team with the rest of his brothers, taking the spot that had been left empty after a former Prey employee went completely off the rails, but never in either of his careers had he had to seduce a woman for information.

It left him feeling ... dirty.

Spoiled or not, Monique didn't deserve this. While there was a chance she knew her father was the kind of man who would rape a woman, who would ruthlessly go after women and children just to attempt to keep his involvement in a conspiracy to frame two innocent people for treason, that didn't make her complicit in any crimes. And he had no doubt that she wasn't complicit, she was too young to have been involved in the near quarter of a century old rape, and two decades old conspiracy.

There was even a chance she'd been a victim herself of her father's cruel whims.

Seducing her to try to get the location of where her reclusive father was hiding out was wrong on so many levels, and yet, what other choice did he have?

This was more than just about finally clearing his father and stepmother's names, it was more even than getting revenge, it was about literally saving the lives of the people he loved.

Ever since his stepbrother Cooper's trip to Egypt back in July, it had been one assault after another on his family. First, his stepbrother Cole's neighbor had been violently assaulted because these people mistakenly believed her to be Cole's girlfriend. The two were together now, but back then, Cole hadn't even liked Susanna.

Before his family could begin to get their feet beneath them again, his stepbrother Connor's trip to Cambodia to attempt a reconciliation with his ex, Becca, had left the couple fighting for their lives. Immediately after that, his stepbrother Cade's four-year-old daughter, Esther, and the girl's nanny, Gabriella, had been abducted. Thankfully, both had survived and now the three of them were a family and expecting a baby. Then just ten days ago, his brother Jake and Jake's best friend and now girlfriend, Alannah, had almost been killed after being lost at sea.

Enough was enough.

There was no way he could stand by and do nothing when his family kept being threatened repeatedly. Just because they'd been lucky so far and none of them had died, they'd all been left with physical and psychological wounds that couldn't even begin to heal because they were all on edge, wondering when the next assault would come.

If using an innocent woman to try to put a stop to it was the only way, he had to take it. No matter how uneasy it left him feeling.

Besides, it wasn't like he would take things all the way. Jax had no plans on having sex with Monique, would try to keep any touching to a minimum, and would do his best to make sure he didn't even kiss her. The last thing he wanted was for her father's games to add another victim to the tally.

All he had to do was make contact, convince Monique to leave with him, and then get her talking to find out where her father was hiding. After that, he could send her on her way, and she'd walk away with at most a bit of a bruise to her ego. Which he was sure for a woman like Monique, with the entire world at her fingertips, was not going to leave behind any lasting scars.

It sounded so easy in his head, Jax just had to hope it turned out to be that easy in real life.

Behind him, the most exquisite laugh tinkled like bells.

The sound seemed to slam into him with the force of an explosion, leaving him equally as groggy and confused.

Only the pain centered in just one appendage. The one made for pleasure as the sweet, musical sound had him growing rock hard.

No, no, no, no, no.

He absolutely could not allow himself to be attracted to anyone tonight. And he had the most horrible sinking feeling in his stomach that he knew exactly who the magical laugh belonged to.

Still, Jax clung to denial as he slowly turned around, doing his best to shift his pants slightly to make the growing bulge less obvious.

As soon as he turned, he knew this already unwanted mission had just become a whole lot more complicated.

Because the woman with the laugh *was* Monique Kerr.

In person, she was a whole lot more stunning than she'd been in the photos he'd seen as he prepped to fly to France and seduce her. Her pretty gray eyes twinkled like stars, her hair was twisted up into some fancy bun, and she wore an honest-to-goodness tiara with what he was positive were real diamonds. Her ball gown was two shades off white, making her look like a fairy princess getting married.

But it was her smile that hit him the hardest.

It was bright, it was beautiful, and it was aimed at him because she'd very nearly walked right into the back of him.

Their eyes connected, and something passed between them. From the faint blush that stained her cheeks, Jax knew she felt it too, and from the way her smile grew wider, he knew that this op just got a whole lot easier because seducing the pretty Kerr princess was going to be as easy as taking candy from a baby.

That should make him feel better, but instead, it left him feeling sick.

~

October 31st
8:03 P.M.

You can do this.

You've done it before so you can do it again.

The little pep talk did little to ease Monique Kerr's nerves and served only to distract her to the point where she almost walked right into the back of someone.

Trust her to do something so silly.

Despite growing up in a wealthy family where attending social functions just like this one was par for the course, she could never really get used to it. Dressing up had been fun when she was a kid, but now it was more than a little embarrassing. All the time, Monique kept waiting for someone to announce her as the fraud that she was.

While people called her the Kerr princess, and she couldn't deny that growing up she had been given every single advantage money could buy, she wasn't the spoiled, polished girl that everybody thought she was. That Monique was the creation of her family, of who they wanted her to be, but the truth was she was way happier dressed in jeans and a T-shirt, taking care of the animals at her rescue sanctuary, than being all dressed up in silk and frills like she was right now.

In fact, she would much rather spend the evening with her pet hedgehog, Cinderella, than talking to stuffy suits like the one she'd almost bumped into.

A giggle at what he'd think if he knew she'd prefer a hedgehog's company to his own burst out, and it drew the attention of the man in question, and he spun around to face her. Dressed as he was in his tux with the Jack-o-lantern mask covering his face, she didn't know what he looked like, but his eyes ...

They drew her in like magnets, and she couldn't seem to look away.

Something seemed to arc between them, and it made her heart flutter in her chest.

Who was this man?

Without being able to see his face, she couldn't know if she'd met him before. Most of the people there tonight were old family friends, it was the only reason her introverted self had been able to garner enough courage to actually come. That and the fact that her animal rescue could always do with more donations, and the rich families that were friends with her own were always looking for some charity or other to give their money to, so they could convince themselves they were doing their part to give back.

Ask his name.

Tell him yours.

Say something.

Anything.

Don't just stand there and stare at him like you're an idiot.

Sometimes, like right now, her internal voice wasn't particularly helpful.

The problem was, she was shy when it came to interacting with other people, especially strangers. She'd grown up all but sequestered on her paternal grandparents' estate. Her mom had bailed when she was barely two years old, and Monique didn't even remember her, and her dad had been the ambassador to Egypt when she was young. He'd been too busy to deal with her, so he'd left her in her grandparents' care.

They weren't bad people, but they didn't have time for her, so she'd found other ways to form bonds and connections by focusing on animals. Deer, rabbits, birds, foxes, squirrels, bats, raccoons, otters, give her an animal and she was good to go, give her a person and she ...

Stood there staring like a fool, like she was doing right now.

"I'm Jaxon," the man announced, holding out a hand.

Right.

Formalities.

She could do those.

"Umm, Monique," she squeaked, taking his offered hand and intending to shake it, then staring in awe as he brought it to his lips and kissed it.

Whoa.

Who was this guy, and why had she never met him before now?

Something about him was magnetic. All he'd done was tell her his name and kissed her hand, but she couldn't get enough of staring at him, and she couldn't even see his face. Still, if it was anything like his body she was going to lose her mind. The way the black material of his tux showcased his broad shoulders and trim hips was phenomenal, and his legs may as well be tree trunks. This guy was huge, and sexy, and oh so out of her league.

Maybe the Kerr princess could land him, but unfortunately, that woman was only a figment of her grandparents' hard work and the paparazzi's love for a spoiled rich princess even when one didn't exist.

"I-I should p-put this on," she stammered, holding up her own Jack-o-lantern mask, which she was supposed to put on when she entered the house where the Halloween charity gala was being held.

"Don't." The man still held her hand, and she had no intentions of pulling it free from his grip. She liked the way his long, thick fingers felt curled around her own.

After ending several relationships with men who were only interested in her because of her last name and everything that came with that, Monique had kind of sworn off men. It wasn't that she didn't like being in a relationship, because she did. As long as the guy was down to earth. Didn't mind getting dirty and helping her care for her animals, wasn't interested in exclusive postal codes and fancy cars, and didn't want to talk about the stock market or where he planned to go on his next vacation. There was nothing wrong with those things, they just weren't her.

But this guy was there, at the gala, and so she had to assume he was another one of those stuck-up snobs who only saw dollar signs when he looked at her.

Tugging on her hand, she could have sworn he was reluctant to let her go, but he did. He even took a step back, and she had to force herself not to whine a protest and reach out for him.

Not cool, Monique.

Not cool at all.

We don't whine at guys we don't even know just because they're no longer in touching distance.

She would have pouted at her own reminder, but it was right. She didn't know this man and she couldn't assume that he was any different from the men she usually had to put up with flirting with her at these kinds of events.

Whatever magnetic pull she felt toward him, it had to be ignored.

"Can I get you a drink?" Jaxon asked, and she could feel his eyes boring into her even when she blushed and glanced away.

What kind of spell was he putting her under?

How was he doing this? Normally, she'd just say no, easy-peasy, but she couldn't seem to make the word come out of her mouth.

Instead, she actually nodded.

"May I?" he asked, holding out his hand rather than just snatching up hers like most of the men who hit on her would do.

Wait.

Was he hitting on her?

Or was he just being polite?

It would help her to read him if she could actually see his face.

Reaching out to place her hand in his, she paused for a second. "Could you ... take your mask off? So I can see you?"

She could have sworn that now he was the one who hesitated, but then he reached up and pulled off the mask, and she sucked in a breath. This man wasn't just handsome, he was drop-dead gorgeous. Like he should be modeling on the cover of one of her favorite romance books kind of gorgeous. So gorgeous in fact that it took tremendous effort on her part not to reach out and let her hands roam his body to find out just how delectable it was beneath his suit.

One side of his mouth quirked up as though he knew exactly where her thoughts had drifted and thought it was amusing.

"Like what you see, princess?" he drawled, his voice washing over her like a warm breeze, soft and caressing.

Her cheeks heated until they felt like they were on fire, but she wasn't a liar, and he'd asked her a direct question, so she nodded. She absolutely loved what she saw.

Taking a step closer, crowding close, he dipped his head until she felt warm puffs of air against her ear. "I very much feel the same way, princess."

Something about the way he said the word princess made her shiver. There was an intimacy there, even though they'd known each other for mere minutes at the most. Normally, the name would rankle. She might have come from a wealthy family, but she was no spoiled princess. Monique worked hard every day, and she lived only off the money she raised herself to fund her animal rescue.

When Jaxon's fingers curled around hers, and he drew her toward where the drinks were set up, Monique found herself smiling. This night was one she'd been dreading, and now she was excited about it.

With Jaxon for company, how could she fail to have a wonderful evening?

Just because it wasn't normally what she would allow herself didn't mean there was anything wrong with it, or that anything bad was going to happen.

What could it possibly hurt to spend a few hours chatting with this man?

After all, it wasn't like he was the same as all the other men who were interested in her only because they planned on using her.

CHAPTER *Two*

October 31st
8:16 P.M.

When was the last time he'd been around a woman who didn't try to manipulate or hide what she was thinking or feeling?

Jax honestly wasn't sure.

Everything about Monique was so transparent. Her appreciation as her gaze roamed his body, her nervous hesitations, her determination to set aside whatever made her anxious and come with him. Following so trustingly that he knew he was going to feel a whole lot of guilt about using her, even if he had no intention of hurting her.

"Champagne?" he asked when they reached the bar.

"Umm ..."

There was clear hesitation in Monique's voice, and her gaze darted around, surveying the room, although what she was searching for he had no idea. According to his intel, she hadn't come with anyone—neither family nor a date—so she wasn't looking for anyone in particular.

"You don't drink, princess? It's fine if you don't, we can grab something else," he told her. He wouldn't be drinking, he needed a clear head and was pretty sure there would be no need to get Monique drunk to get her talking, not that he would have taken that route anyway. This wasn't about taking advantage of an innocent woman, it was merely about doing an unpleasant but necessary task to clear his dad and stepmom's names and get the targets off his family's back.

"Actually, I don't very often, and never when I'm at one of these," Monique replied.

Anger unfurled inside him at the possibility that something bad had happened to this woman that made her feel like she had to be constantly on her guard. "Someone hurt you, princess?" he growled.

Those gray eyes of hers widened until they were almost impossibly big. "What? No! Course not. I'm okay, no one hurt me," she soothed, and the fingers of the hand he still held tightened. "I just get sick of stuffy, boring, rich guys wanting to drone on and on forever about how rich they are, and all the things they want to do with their money. How they think they're better than everyone else because they have money, and how I'd be so lucky to be with them because they have money. Yuck." Monique made a disgusted face, her body shuddering, but then she whipped up her eyes to meet his.

"What?"

"Sorry," she squeaked.

"For ...?" Whatever she wanted to apologize for, he wasn't following. This woman wasn't anything like he'd expected her to be. He'd thought the Kerr princess was going to be this spoiled, bratty woman who looked down on everyone, but in reality, she was the opposite.

"*You're* one of those guys, right? I mean, you're here." She winced and shot him an apologetic smile, attempting to tug her hand free from his.

Maintaining his hold on her hand was easy enough, and Jax enjoyed the feel of it nestled in his palm. It was so much smaller than his own, her fingers dainty and delicate, her nails polished in a perfect French manicure. Stupid as it was, he wanted to maintain this tenuous connection to her.

There would be no maintaining of a connection.

This was about getting answers.

As soon as he found out where her coward of a father was hiding, he'd be out of her life quicker than she could blink, leaving behind nothing but another type of guy for her to dread running into at these events.

"*You're* here," he countered, not wanting to blow his cover but also not wanting her to lump him in with the rest of the men she clearly disliked.

Monique sighed. "I know. I'd much rather be at home, curled up in front of a fire, reading a book and eating chocolate. Introverts like me don't usually love big gatherings like this. Too noisy, too busy, too many people, too much forced conversation, and too much peopling," she added with an exaggerated shudder and a twinkle in her eyes.

"Then why come?" This woman was like a puzzle wrapped up in silky satin and soft gauze.

"Because I never miss an opportunity to fundraise for my animal rescue."

What caught him by surprise wasn't learning that Monique ran a rescue, he'd already known that, it was the passion in her voice when she said it. He'd assumed that running a rescue really meant she lent her name to the charity so she had an answer when someone asked her what she did and what causes she believed in, not that she actually cared about it. Which, if her tone was anything to go by, she absolutely did.

"A rescue?"

"Yeah, we take any animal, doesn't matter the species, the age, how it came to be in our care," she explained, practically vibrating with enthusiasm. "We once had a tiger. Like an actual tiger. I have no idea how it was even snuck into the country, but the owner quickly realized they were in over their head, so we cared for it for a few weeks before it was taken in by a zoo."

"A tiger, that's cool. I hope it's okay to ask, and I'm not offending you, but why do you need to fundraise for your rescue? You're Monique Kerr, right? The Kerr princess. Don't you have a ton of money already?"

Some of the enthusiasm vibrating through her faded. "I sunk most of my trust fund into buying the land and setting everything up. The rest is set up to pay my personal monthly expenses. I have enough left over to help some animals, but it's not enough. I won't get the rest of the money until my dad and his parents pass. I don't just want to help some animals, I want to help them all. And the people here are always willing to donate to something, which means they can pretend to be good people who care about others and the planet."

"I think that's amazing," Jax answered truthfully, and was rewarded by a pretty blush pinkening Monique's cheeks.

"Thank you. My family … it's not what they had planned for me. They wanted me to marry an appropriate man from an approved family and add to their wealth, so I'm a bit of a disappointment in their eyes."

"Hey." When he squeezed her hand, she looked up at him. "Who cares what they think? You're doing something amazing that you love. That makes you a good person." Unlike him, who was here to use and manipulate her for his own personal reasons.

Big picture.

The reminder strengthened his weakening resolve. It might suck to hurt Monique, but in the end, she didn't even know him so it wasn't like she would mourn his loss or anything. By morning, he'd have the intel he needed and be heading for a plane to fly back home.

"What do you say we get out of here for a while?" Jax suggested. At least with Monique being an introvert who hadn't even wanted to come to the charity ball, she was more likely to open up to him if they were somewhere she felt more comfortable and at ease.

So leaving was more a professional decision and not a personal one.

"Oh, umm, I haven't really done any schmoozing yet, and I had a fundraising goal I wanted to hit before I left." Monique said the words, but she didn't sound all that upset about the possibility of getting out of there.

"Whatever your goal was, I'll match it and add ten percent," he vowed. Since he was there to get intel out of Monique, it seemed only fair that she be compensated. Billionaire former SEAL, founder and CEO of Prey Security Eagle Oswald had more than enough money to pay whatever it was Monique had hoped to raise there tonight, and Jax was confident his boss would be happy to do it, especially since the money was going to a good cause.

"So you really are one of those rich, stuffy, boring guys then," Monique said, sounding disappointed.

"Oh, princess, boring is totally the wrong word to describe me."

When he winked at her, she shivered and her blush deepened. That wasn't a lie, his life was far from boring, but it wasn't like he was rich or stuffy either. Still, for now, she had to believe he had the money to donate to her rescue that she'd been there to raise, so it wasn't like he could blurt out that he made a good living working for Prey, but he was nowhere close to rich, nothing more than comfortable.

"I don't usually leave these kinds of events with guys," she hedged, not an outright no, but she was definitely conflicted.

"No pressure, princess," he assured her. Just because he selfishly wanted to enjoy a little time with her away from the party didn't mean he was going to pressure her. "We can stay, dance a little, talk a little. Pretend you're Cinderella and I'm Prince Charming," he teased with another wink.

One of those cute little tinkling laughs fell from her lips. "Cinderella, huh?"

"Absolutely." Only this time, she wouldn't be the one to disappear at midnight, he would be, and he wouldn't be leaving behind any identifying items.

"I guess a girl can't say no to a prince. Okay, we can get out of here. Let's do this."

~

October 31st

8:39 P.M.

Had she lost her mind?

Monique thought that was the only logical explanation for allowing this man—this *stranger*—to guide her toward the exit.

This wasn't her.

She didn't go anywhere with people she didn't know.

Heck, she barely went anywhere with people she *did* know. Curse of being an introvert. The company of herself and animals had always been enough to satisfy her even when she was a kid. It drove her grandparents crazy because they expected her to be the social, bubbly, life of the party.

Truth was, though, she took after her mother. Which had been a source of much anxiety to her over the years. If she took after her mom, did that mean that if one day she found someone who was happy helping her care for sick and traumatized animals, and understood her need for quiet and solitude, she would wind up ruining it?

Would she walk away from a child as easily as her mom had walked away from her?

Not a worry for today.

As Jaxon led her across the grand entrance hall, his fingertips brushed across the inside of her wrist, making her squirm. How was he managing to turn her on at an event where they were surrounded by people, with just a simple touch?

Cheeks flaming with embarrassment, Monique was convinced every single person there must know the thought running through her mind.

Thoughts very unlike her.

Thoughts of this man crushing his lips to hers in a fiery kiss. His hands roaming her body, tweaking her nipples, his tongue plunging into her, making her scream, then he'd slam home and take her with hard thrusts until she lost the ability to do anything, even breathe. Jaxon wouldn't treat her like spun glass like all her other lovers had. Those boyfriends thought she was fragile, delicate, but she was neither of those things. She wrangled animals every day, some of them weighing close to as much as she did. She could handle a little hot, rough sex.

In fact, she wanted to handle a little hot, rough sex.

With Jaxon.

"Did you drive here yourself?" Jaxon asked as they stepped through the front door and a waft of cool air caressed her skin.

A poor imitation of what it would feel like to have Jaxon's hands or mouth worshipping her skin.

"Monique?"

"Oh, umm, no, a driver brought me," she answered, knowing she was bright red and positive he knew the cause of her blush.

"Can you cancel the car, and I'll take you back to your hotel later?"

"Of course." It was easy enough, although she was sure it would get back to her grandparents that she'd dipped out of the event a mere forty minutes into it. They'd be disappointed, and in return, she'd be upset that she'd let them down. Since her dad had basically disappeared from her life as soon as her mom bailed on them, her grandparents were the closest thing she had to parents, even if she'd mostly been raised by nannies.

"Hey, we don't have to do this if you don't want to. I didn't mean to pressure you." Jaxon's hand lifted to palm her cheek, and nuzzling into it was the easiest thing in the world.

"You didn't pressure me, and I do want to leave with you," she assured him. "I'll text the driver in the car." The cool air was quickly becoming cold, and since she was dressed only in this ridiculous ball gown that couldn't be less her, she wasn't really protected from the icy wind.

"Here." Something warm and soft dropped onto her shoulders, and she realized that Jaxon had taken off his tuxedo jacket and draped it over her. Not only did it cut out the cold wind, and feel delectable against her skin, but it also smelled just like him, and she snuggled it closer and drew in a deep breath.

Feeling Jaxon's eyes on her, Monique lifted her head to meet his gaze. There was something unreadable in his expression, but there were also things she could read. The most prominent being desire.

He was attracted to her. Because of her last name or because of her, she wasn't sure. Then again, he'd seemed impressed that she ran an animal rescue and was there to raise money for it. And she'd been clear she wasn't into stuffy, boring, rich guys. Even though she knew he had to be one of them, he was there after all, he didn't feel like it.

Jaxon felt like ...

She wasn't even sure.

Something cozy, like snuggling up in front of a fire on a freezing winter's night.

Which was insane since she didn't even know his last name. Still, she couldn't deny that something buzzed between them, and if he was willing, she'd like to see where it could go.

"Sir."

They both startled when a valet appeared beside them, holding out a set of keys to Jaxon, who took them, then reclaimed his grip on her hand and guided her down the steps, and to the passenger seat of his car.

Once he was inside, he got the heat going, and Monique supposed she should offer him his jacket back, but she didn't. It would probably be too creepy to ask if she could keep it as a reminder of this magical night, so she pressed her lips together as Jaxon drove them down the long, tree-lined driveway.

"Tell me about yourself," Jaxon's voice rumbled through the dark car as they headed off down the road away from the remote country estate.

"What did you want to know?" Monique shifted slightly in her seat so she could see him better, and she all but melted when he shot her a charming smile.

"Everything."

Laughing, she tugged the jacket tighter around herself, imagining that it was Jaxon's arms around her, and pretending that he wanted to know everything about her because he felt this pull as much as she did. "I'd like to learn about you, too. Maybe we could trade off? Each ask the other a question, one for one?"

For a second his hands tightened on the steering wheel, and she got the uneasy feeling that talking about himself was the last thing he wanted to do.

Had she made a mistake in trusting him?

With her family's money, she should be more careful when it came to her safety, only the thing was, Jaxon *felt* safe. Safer than anything else she'd ever experienced.

His hands relaxed, and he shot her a sheepish smile. "Sorry, it's just weird how much I really want to know the tiniest things about you. Wasn't expecting that to happen."

"Me either," Monique acknowledged as she relaxed. That was why he'd seemed off for a moment, he was overcome by the same feelings she was. She wanted to know literally everything about this man. Big stuff, little stuff, all of it. This might not be love at first sight, but it was certainly a connection at first sight, if that was even a thing.

"You can ask first," he offered.

Since a million questions ran through her head, she picked one at random. "How old are you?"

"Thirty-one."

"So five years older than me, practically an old man," she teased, making him laugh. "Your turn."

"What's your favorite color?"

"This is going to ruin the image I was building of not being this spoiled, rich princess everyone thinks I am, but pink. The bright Barbie kind. Preferably with glitter."

Jaxon laughed again. "Nothing wrong with liking pink, princess."

Normally, when someone called her princess, she interpreted it as an insult. After all, it was what the media had always called her. But when Jaxon said it, the word seemed to roll off his tongue and hit her straight between the legs.

"Your turn."

"Hmm, did you play sports in high school?"

For a second his gaze darted over to her, and she could see the surprise in it, he hadn't expected that question. Along with the surprise was a dose of pain that made her ache to reach out and soothe it away, but they weren't at that point yet.

As his gaze shifted back to the road, Jaxon suddenly froze. It was like his entire body turned to stone, and the joy and excitement she'd been feeling at meeting someone who seemed to like her for her and not just her last name quickly evaporated.

"What's wrong?"

"Maybe nothing," Jaxon replied, but his voice had gone hard, and she doubted that was the truth.

"Tell me. I'm not some wilting little princess who can't handle anything more vigorous than a massage," she snapped, sick of being treated like she was some china doll.

"Never thought you were, princess," Jaxon said, his voice calm and controlled. "Car approaching us from behind, coming at us faster than it should be."

Spinning in her seat, she looked out the back window and immediately spotted the headlights, so much closer than she'd been expecting, and they weren't slowing down. It looked like the other vehicle was flying straight at them.

"It's going to hit us," Jaxon shouted mere seconds before they were slammed into.

The car swerved wildly as Jaxon fought for control, but the other vehicle hit them again and they went spinning wildly toward the trees lining the road.

Monique's last thought was terror that this was a ransom kidnapping attempt and she'd dragged Jaxon into danger, right before pain splintered between her temples, and the world went black.

CHAPTER *Three*

October 31st
8:53 P.M.

Pain ricocheted through his skull, and dark dots danced in front of his eyes.

Jax clung to consciousness only because he knew he had to.

Monique was with him.

Sweet, shy Monique, who had dug her claws into him the moment he laid eyes on her without even realizing she'd done it, or that she possessed the kind of claws that could dig deep inside a man and make it almost impossible to break free.

Knowing he would only be with her for as long as it took to get the location of her reclusive father hadn't seemed to sink in. Nor did the fact he'd never get to crush his mouth to hers and kiss her until neither of them could breathe or fulfil whatever fantasies had been running through her head earlier.

She wasn't his to keep, but for now, she was his to protect.

Which was why it was imperative that he not pass out.

So somehow, he managed to fight off the thick, black sludge attempting to fill up his head and remain awake.

"Monique?" he called out her name, annoyed that his voice didn't come out as strong as he had hoped.

Still, he was going to work with what he had.

Luckily, they were in his vehicle, so he was armed. Taking a weapon into the party had been impossible because guards with metal detector wands were at the front door, but he'd left them in his vehicle just in case. Not that he'd been expecting trouble, but it seemed that someone didn't like that he'd managed to get to Monique.

Further proof if they'd needed any that her father was the final rapist they were looking for.

His pretty passenger didn't answer, so he twisted in his seat to see her hanging limply against her seatbelt.

As much as he wanted to pull her free, check every inch of her body for injuries, and tend to them, the only time he could spare right now was to reach out and press his fingertips to her neck.

It wasn't until he felt the pulse bumping against them that Jax realized how scared he'd been that she'd been killed in the crash. Whatever this strange connection was that seemed to have sprung to life the second their eyes met, it wasn't something they would get the chance to explore.

Unfortunately.

"Sorry, princess, for bringing this mess right to you," he said softly as he unsnapped his seatbelt and dropped to his feet right in front of Monique, since the car had landed on its side, with her closest to the ground, when it rolled down the side of a short hill.

Already above him, Jax heard people approaching. It would be fun to pretend that they were just other motorists there to help, but that would be a stupid assumption to make.

Only one car had been on the road with them and that was the car that had run them right off the road. Deliberately, no way to imagine otherwise. It had hit them twice with enough force to make him lose control.

Now those men were coming to get them.

No doubt killing him was the plan. Samson Kerr didn't really have a choice now that it was obvious they knew his name. Surely the man couldn't be so cold-hearted as to have his daughter murdered, so Jax had to hope that these people were going to take Monique to a hospital. They could pretend to be heroes who had found the Kerr princess alive in her wrecked car and saved her. Monique would likely tell everyone when she woke up that the accident had been intentional, but she'd have a concussion and would be easily discredited.

That was the second-best scenario as far as he was concerned. The best would be both of them walking out of this alive.

Knowing he was weak and off his game, instead of opening fire on the approaching men, Jax instead reached up and opened his window. The engine was still running, and miraculously, whatever damage had been done, the window system was still working. Then he unsnapped Monique's seatbelt and gathered her into his arms.

She didn't stir, and his fear for her rocketed up several notches.

Alive.

At least she's alive.

For now, that would have to be enough.

Draping Monique's unresponsive body over the side of the car, Jax then boosted himself up and over, jumping down to the ground beneath. Snatching Monique back up, he hurried to the closest trees.

A searchlight bounced through the trees, and he could hear voices as the men got closer. Staying in the car would have been signing his death warrant, as that would be where they were expecting to find him, this at least bought him a little time. It was no guarantee that he'd live to see the sunrise. There were at least two other men since he could hear talking, but possibly more. He was injured and a little shaky on his feet, and while he'd kill as many of them as he could, that was all he could do.

The second he fired that first shot, he'd give away his location and they'd return fire, because it was absolutely too much to hope that they weren't armed.

Their boss had realized the second he made contact with Monique, and it was clear somebody had been watching her at the party and reported back to her father that she'd left with him, that the game was over. They had his name, and with the entire might of Prey Security behind them, they would make sure that Samson Kerr paid for his crimes.

Jax was just thankful that the entire rest of his family was sequestered away on Delta Team's remote property. Nobody outside Delta Team other than Eagle Oswald himself knew where the property was located. They'd all been blindfolded as soon as they stepped onto the plane, and those blindfolds were not removed until they were on the property. The relief of knowing no one could get to his family, that even if Samson Kerr had him killed, his brothers would still get justice for their parents, had him breathing easier as he propped Monique up against a tree trunk and got into position.

The light got closer, and the men's voices louder. Listening carefully, he was able to distinguish six distinct voices.

Not great odds.

If he hadn't been injured, Jax was sure he could take them all out without receiving a scratch, but as it was, it was taking half of his energy just to remain awake and on his feet. He'd be lucky if he were able to shoot straight and kill the first man with one shot without that shot going wide.

Forcing every atom of his body to focus on the task at hand, reminding himself of the consequences of failing, Jax let out a breath, shoved the pain away, and lifted his weapon, aiming it at the man who was tentatively approaching the wrecked vehicle.

At least the men were smart enough to know he was a threat. Every other team that had been sent after his family had been decimated, and Jax hoped he wasn't about to ruin that streak.

Monique needs you.

Those words whispering through his mind helped to steady him further, and the grogginess and pain of the head injury faded a little more. His hands stopped shaking, and he lined up ready to take the shot.

If he was quick enough, he could take out at least two, maybe even three of the men before they had a chance to react and do anything about it. Right now, he had the fact that they believed he and Monique were still in the vehicle, dead or at least incapacitated, working to his advantage.

But as soon as he fired that first shot, he lost the element of surprise.

So he had to make the most of these first seconds.

In his career as a SEAL and then with Prey, Jax had killed before, he had no qualms about taking the lives of these men. They were the enemy, and they'd come to kill him, and at the very least hurt Monique.

What kind of father ordered people to run a car off a dangerous mountain road while his daughter was sitting inside it?

Samson Kerr was a rapist and there was every chance he'd laid his dirty hands on his own daughter.

For a second, anger almost claimed the calm he was striving so hard for, but at the last second he was able to shove it away.

Time to even the playing field a little.

Just as the man at the vehicle leaned over the open window to look inside and Jax readied himself to take the first shot, already locking into place in his mind the positions of the other five men, Monique stirred beside him.

"Jaxon!" she screeched, jerking upright in a panic and giving away their location before he had a chance to fire any bullets.

October 31st

8:59 P.M.

Pain and terror mixed and twisted inside her until Monique couldn't fight against it.

With no comprehension of where she was or what had happened beyond the crushing understanding that something was wrong, her shattered mind reached for the first thing it could think of that made it feel safe.

An anchor in the storm of confusion.

Jaxon.

Jerking upright, Monique screamed his name as loud as she could, knowing only that she needed him, that if he was there, everything would somehow manage to be okay.

No sooner had she called out to him than the sounds of something loud rocketed through the air, making her whimper and curl in on herself.

What was going on?

Think, Monique.

The pep talk did little to cut through the fog of fear that had settled around her. It was so thick that she couldn't seem to see through it.

Something bad had happened, of that she was certain. Something to cause the hammering pain inside her head.

She remembered the Halloween ball, remembered meeting Jaxon, remembered leaving with him, talking in his car, and then ...

Nothing.

Just pain and fear and confusion.

"Shh, princess, it's going to be okay."

The words cut through the fog, clearing it a little, and she reached out blindly needing to touch him, feel him, to know that Jaxon was really there.

Her fingertips brushed against something soft, warm, and firm. Jaxon. Here, beside her, safe.

Only the loud bangs didn't stop, and they were quickly washing away any semblance of security, knowing Jaxon was here had given her.

"If you don't want to die tonight, then you better stop shooting," a voice called out when the banging temporarily stopped.

Banging ... shooting?

And that voice, it didn't belong to Jaxon.

Someone else was there.

Someone had ... run them off the road?

The memory tickled the back of her mind, making her squirm as pain spiked behind her closed lids.

Forcing it away, Monique made herself think. If someone was shooting at them, then she had to be sure, had to remember what had happened. But the harder she tried to find the memories, the more they shimmered out of reach.

"Jaxon," she whimpered. Why did she need him so badly? It didn't make sense. They'd only just met and yet he felt like he was ... important.

"We have you surrounded," the other voice called out.

Surrounded?

That meant there was more than one of them.

Against only her and Jaxon.

It wasn't like she was going to be any help, and what could Jaxon possibly know about men shooting at him? After all, he was one of those rich, boring, stuffy men who always attended those charity galas.

Yet ...

That didn't feel like it was true. Jaxon felt capable and confident.

"If you stop shooting back at us, then no one has to die. Don't be stupid now," the other voice cautioned, and it took a few seconds for those words to sink in.

Shooting.

At them.

Someone had been shooting at these people, and since it wasn't her that meant it had to be Jaxon.

"I'm sorry, princess," he whispered, so softly she almost didn't hear him. He sounded so guilty, and yet this was her fault.

Had to be.

Being the only next heir of a family with more wealth than most people could comprehend meant there was always a risk of being kidnapped and used for ransom.

That had to be what was happening now.

Which meant this was all her fault.

She should never have said yes when Jaxon asked her to leave with him, she should have told him they would stay and talk at the ball. That way they both would have been safe, because now they were going to be kidnapped. The voice had said that neither of them had to die, but she wasn't so sure they meant that.

If she was the target of this abduction, then that made Jaxon expendable.

Whimpering, she reached blindly for Jaxon, and the next thing she knew, she was in his arms. His lips touched the top of her head as he tucked her close.

Something went thud on the ground close by, and then she heard

Jaxon's reluctant voice speaking. "I've put my weapon down, we're both unarmed and injured."

Another whimper tumbled from her lips as she felt a rush of people approaching. Too many people. Her head pounded, her body ached, and she was so scared she could hardly breathe. The last thing she wanted was to cause Jaxon pain, and yet that was exactly what she was doing.

Wanting to apologize to him, before she could make the words come out of her mouth, Monique felt hands on her, ripping her away from her only safe place.

"Careful with her, she's hurt," Jaxon snarled, and she was surprised at the ferocity in his words. There was something else there, too, something that said he wasn't as scared as he should be, as she was. It didn't make sense, and Monique chalked it up to the disorientation she felt, making her hear things that weren't there.

Without Jaxon close to her, she needed to see him.

Prying open her eyes, she winced when the light from the flashlights the people around her were holding stabbed through her eyes, making the pain so much worse.

There were six other people besides herself and Jaxon. One was standing behind her, holding her with an arm wrapped around her chest, probably the only thing keeping her standing.

Another two were standing beside Jaxon, who had been forced down to his knees, and were holding weapons on him. Pointed directly at his head.

She didn't think, she just tried to get to him, protect him, and help him.

"Don't hurt him," she cried out, fighting weakly against the man holding her.

Surprise flared in Jaxon's dark eyes as his head snapped up and their gazes clashed. Monique was positive he was trying to tell her something with that look, but she had no idea what it was. Even if she didn't feel like she'd been run over by a truck, she didn't know this man well enough to be able to read in his expressions what he was saying.

"It's okay, princess," he said calmly, far too calmly for her liking.

"No, it's not. Don't hurt him, please. I'll ... I'll do anything," she begged, fully prepared to follow through with that offer.

It wouldn't be the first time she'd sold her body to survive hell.

"She won't," Jaxon roared, moving to fling his body toward hers when the men standing beside him grabbed him and held him still. "She won't. Kill me if you have to, just don't hurt her."

"No!" Killing Jaxon was not an option. She wouldn't survive knowing his death was on her shoulders. "Anything you want, I'll do. I don't care, just don't hurt him, please."

"Monique, don't. Take it back," Jaxon hissed, anger in his tone.

"I won't. If it saves your life, I'm prepared to do anything."

"I'm not worth it."

Ignoring the pain in her head, she stuck her chin out, not allowing his words to pass by without very clearly refuting them. "You are. Everybody is. And if I can save your life, I will, and there's nothing you can do to stop me."

"Want to bet?" Jaxon got this crazy look in his eyes, like he was going to do something stupid, and for one terrifying second, Monique was sure he would get himself killed despite her offers to give these men her body in exchange for his life.

But then the man who had been speaking earlier stepped in. "Enough," he growled. "Take them both and throw them in the back of the van, then clean up down here. I don't want any evidence left behind that we were here."

Apparently, this man was in charge because immediately the two men standing beside Jaxon yanked him to his feet, and the one holding her lifted her so she was thrown over his shoulder. Both of them were taken back up the hill the car had careened down, and the rest of her memories slid into place.

They'd been run off the road, and now these men were kidnapping them. She had no idea who they were or if they were going to take her up on her offer and spare Jaxon's life, but at least for now they were both breathing.

Back up on the road there was a white van, and the man carrying her balanced her, yanked the door open, and tossed her inside. Landing with a bone-shuddering thud, Monique cried out as her already battered body protested, and she barely managed to keep from throwing up. The only thing helping to keep the bile down was the knowledge that if she didn't, they'd be locked up in there with that smell.

Jaxon's body landed beside her, and there was no hesitation on her part. She immediately crawled to him, climbing onto his lap as the van doors slammed shut, sealing them in darkness which actually managed to slightly soothe the pain in her head.

"You shouldn't have done that, princess," Jaxon grumbled, but his arms locked around her, and she could have sworn his face pressed to the top of her head and he breathed in her scent.

"If I can save your life, Jaxon, I absolutely will," she said defiantly.

"Jax."

"What?"

"Everyone calls me Jax."

"Jax," she repeated, liking it. It suited him better than Jaxon. Resting her cheek on his chest, right above his heart, she snuggled closer, savoring the feel of being in his arms. "If I can stop them from killing you, I will. Don't ask me not to. I can handle anything if it means we both live long enough for my father to pay the ransom. I survived once, and I can do it again."

She hoped.

Because she wasn't letting Jax die because of her, which meant she'd already sold her body to the devil.

CHAPTER *Four*

October 31st
10:26 P.M.

Giving Monique his real name was stupid.

Granted, Jax wasn't all that far off from Jaxon, which was exactly why he'd chosen it for this short undercover gig, but it was still wrong giving her his real name when he was deceiving her, and the reason she was currently injured and curled up in his lap in the back of a van.

But that was exactly why he'd had to tell her.

She might not know it, but she'd been kidnapped because of him, and she'd gone and put herself between him and death.

He wasn't sure if the men had planned on killing him then and there. Likely they weren't once they realized he wasn't in the car. No doubt their orders had been to make his death look like an accident, and if Monique wound up collateral damage, then so be it.

His not being in the car when they got there changed things.

Shooting him and Monique, or even just him and leaving her alive, would then make it obvious that someone was the cause of his death, and that would bring in the cops. Given that her father was doing everything he could to remain off law enforcement's radar, that would be the last thing he wanted.

Monique didn't know any of that though. She believed that she was the cause of the abduction, that she'd been kidnapped for ransom, and he had been taken solely because he was unfortunate enough to be with her when they came after her.

But that wasn't what left him feeling sick.

Sicker than the head injury had left him.

After telling him in no uncertain terms that she was absolutely prepared to bargain with her body, she'd said that she could handle it, that she'd survived once and could do it again.

What the hell did that mean?

And why wasn't whatever she was talking about in the dossier that Prey had put together on her?

The van bumped over something, and Jax braced them against the corner of the van so they didn't get bounced about too badly. In his arms, Monique whimpered, and he knew she was in pain, pain he could do nothing about because he was the one who had dragged her into this.

Maybe he should just tell her everything.

He was still holding out hope that her father's orders had included not harming his daughter. Surely the man wasn't sick enough to allow his only claimed child to go through hell just so he could try to desperately hold onto his secrets.

If he died and she somehow survived, if she knew the truth, knew how dangerous her father was, knew what he'd done years ago and more recently, then she could go straight to his family. They'd keep her safe, and if she gave them her father's location, this whole mess would be over, all his family would be free to live their lives, and make their dreams realities.

Including Monique.

Because she deserved the world. He'd already thought that before when he met her, saw how sweetly shy she could be, realized she was nothing like the media made her out to be, that she wasn't into typical rich guys, and loved her animal rescue above all else. But now that she'd quite literally put her body on the line for him, how could he not think she deserved only good things?

"Jax?"

The sound of his real name on her lips made him feel a whole hell of a lot better than it should, given everything he was lying to her about. Tightening his hold on her, he looked down to see she'd tilted her head back a little so she would be meeting his gaze if they could see one another.

"Yeah, princess?"

"It feels like we left the road."

Not only beautiful, compassionate, and brave, but smart too. Monique was right, they were no longer driving on a road, and he had to assume that was because these men were winding their way through the forest looking for a secluded location where they could kill him, possibly both of them, and their bodies would likely never be found.

It would be easy enough to spin that after the car accident, disoriented, the two of them had wandered off into the forest, gotten lost, and perished. There would be a search for their bodies, but both their blood was inside that car, and everyone would assume that because they were injured, they hadn't made it back to the road, eventually succumbing to their injuries or being taken by wild animals.

"Yeah, it does," he agreed, still trying to decide if he should spill all. If he told her everything now he would lose her trust. Once she realized it had been a setup, that he'd been there for her, that asking her to leave with him wasn't innocent, that he'd intended to use her from the very beginning, then there was no way she would trust him ever again, and he might need that trust.

He wasn't giving up.

If an opportunity presented itself, he would take it.

Hell, he intended to make sure there *was* an opportunity to take advantage of.

So, for now, he had to hold onto his secrets and pray that when she did learn the truth, Monique realized that he'd done what he had to do for his family. That it wasn't personal and hurting her hadn't been his intention. If he'd had even a whiff of a plan from her father to take him out, he never would have gone through with this. Putting an innocent person's life on the line to save his family wouldn't have been an option.

"Because they're going to kill us?" Monique asked, going right to the point.

Probably.

Although given she'd offered her body to them, the men might toy with her a little first, pretend that they would keep him alive until she gave them what they wanted.

"Maybe."

"If this is a kidnapping for ransom, my dad will pay," she said, so surely like she believed it one hundred percent, and he believed that if this was a kidnapping for ransom, she'd be right.

But it wasn't.

"He's not the world's best dad, not at all. But he would pay to get us out. If I ..." She squirmed on his lap, clearly embarrassed, he didn't have to be able to see to know that her cheeks had gone red.

"If you what, princess?"

"If I pretend that we're together ... you know a ... couple ... that my dad would pay for both of us then they won't kill you. You won't be a liability anymore, you'll be another bag of money."

"Only your dad would know we weren't a couple."

Monique scoffed. "Yeah, because we're so close that he'd know if I was dating someone."

He all but heard the eyeroll, and Jax realized that he'd likely signed a death sentence for Monique over something she didn't even have. Right now, if he had to play the odds, he would be betting on her not knowing where her father was.

Which meant she was going to die for nothing.

No.

The word roared through his head with a ferocity that had him feeling like a caged tiger who was ready to pounce.

There was no way he was going to allow Monique to become a casualty of his family's war against her father.

As soon as the van stopped and the men got them out, he was going to find a way to get his hands on a weapon. Then he was going to kill every single one of them before Monique had a chance to sacrifice herself for him. No one was putting their hands on her tonight or any other night.

"Listen to me, princess," he said urgently, shifting them so they were both on their knees, with his hands on her shoulders, keeping her steady. Even though it was too dark to make out anything more than the shadowy outline of her body, he leaned in so there was mere millimeters between their faces. "I will get you out of this alive, I swear."

"How?"

Since he couldn't tell her everything and risk her not trusting him when the only way this would work was if she did, he merely touched a kiss to the tip of her nose. "I just need you to trust me. I have some training, and I know what I'm doing. All I need for you to do when we get wherever they're taking us and they drag us out of the van, is to pretend that you're weak and dizzy."

"Easy. I *am* weak and dizzy," she said dryly, and he smiled. Monique was scared, but she was holding it together, being so brave, and now making jokes. She was someone he could become addicted to if he let himself.

"Smart alec," he teased. "But I mean it, Monique. They know we're both injured, and that's our biggest asset right now. They think we're not a threat, but we're going to show them how wrong they are. You with me?" he asked, just as the van came to a stop.

"I'm with you," Monique replied without a single hesitation.

Too bad if she knew the truth about what was happening to them right now, she'd be telling him the opposite.

The only way he could even begin to make it up to her was to ensure that she lived, so this plan of his had better work.

~

October 31st

11:13 P.M.

Who was this man?

One thing Monique was sure of was that Jax was not the usual kind of man she'd meet at one of those events.

Not that that explained who he was.

But it did explain how he could be so calm in the face of danger, how he could come up with a plan he seemed confident with, and maybe even why he'd apologized to her.

Because she would have sworn that she remembered him saying sorry to her after the crash. It was possible she hadn't remembered correctly, or that it was merely a hallucination from the concussion she very obviously was suffering from, but somehow, she didn't think so.

Whoever Jax was, she trusted him.

If anyone could get them out alive, it was him, that was something she believed down to her bones.

So when the doors to the back of the van were thrown open and Jax quickly shoved her down so she was lying on her side, she surreptitiously attempted to move her limbs into something resembling the recovery position. Jax had said to pretend she was weak and dizzy, not at all a stretch given both things were true, so she was going to take that role and run with it.

"Get out," a voice ordered, a different one from the one that had been giving orders earlier, although she suspected that man was around here somewhere, too.

"She's unconscious," Jax said, a tiny hint of reproach in his tone.

"Then bring her out with you," the other man commanded.

Somehow, she couldn't imagine Jax being someone who enjoyed following commands. Then again, he said he'd had some training, so maybe he'd served in the military or something before doing ... whatever it was he did now.

Which she had no clue about because she'd just agreed to get in a car with him and be taken away from a safe place filled with people. A decision she absolutely regretted, even though she didn't place the blame for their current predicament on Jax's shoulders.

"I would, but I'm not feeling that great either. You guys did run us off the road after all," Jax added.

"And if you'd died in the crash like you were supposed to, we wouldn't all be out here in the middle of nowhere in the middle of the night," the man huffed back, clearly not amused about the situation.

Step in line.

If anyone had the right to be unhappy about all of this, it was her and Jax, not these men who wanted them dead.

Only if they wanted them both dead, how did they expect to get paid a ransom?

Was it possible this had nothing to do with someone trying to extort money from her family?

That was the conclusion she'd come to because it seemed like the most logical given her history. But maybe she was wrong. Maybe this was something else, although she couldn't fathom what.

"I'm serious, I think I broke some ribs, you're going to have to get her yourself. But be gentle," Jax growled.

"Fine," the man said with another irritated huff, and the van moved a little as she assumed he was climbing into the back of it.

Fighting against her worry that Jax wasn't lying about the broken ribs and that he might be more seriously injured than he'd let on while they'd been sitting in the back of this van for what felt like hours, Monique forced her limbs to be still and heavy. Since that was absolutely how she felt, and she'd love nothing more than to stay nice and still and possibly be able to get some much-needed rest, it was easy to accomplish even with the terror she felt breathing inside her.

Someone knelt beside her, and she felt hands touch her body.

Not warm, strong hands like Jax's, these ones were cold, and much too rough as they shifted her, ready to pick her up.

But they never did.

There were the sounds of movement, then a small snapping sound, before something went thud.

Her breathing increased.

Was it Jax who had eliminated a threat, or had the man sensed they were up to something and decided to just kill them and get it over with?

"Hey, princess, you did amazing. Perfect," Jax whispered, and his fingers brushed lightly across her temple.

"You're alive?" Blinking open her eyes, she saw him crouched beside her, a tight smile on his handsome face.

"Course I am."

"Your ribs ... were you lying? Or are you hurt?" She wasn't sure why it mattered, given there were still five armed men out there somewhere, assuming the sixth was now dead in here with them. But it did matter. The thought of him hurting made her feel sick.

"Lying. I'm sore and banged up, but nothing broken," he assured her, and she sensed he was telling her the truth. "Now I need you to do something else for me, okay?"

When she gave a small nod, he palmed her cheek, his fingers stroking along her cheekbone in a gentle caress that helped slow both her breathing and her racing heart.

"I want you to stay in here. You're going to go into the back corner and stay there no matter what. I'm going to take the gun and kill the rest of them. There are only five, and I like those odds. But if the worst happens and I don't survive, I need you to make sure you tell those men over and over again who your father is and how he wouldn't want you harmed. That he'll pay anything to get you back alive and in one piece. Can you do that for me?"

Reaching out blindly, Monique grabbed Jax's hands and clutched them to her chest. "I don't want you to die."

"Don't want to die either, princess, but you're my priority."

She'd never been anyone's priority. Not ever. So why now? And why with him?

"Why?" she whispered the plea, knowing they didn't really have time for him to answer.

"I don't know ... I just ... you're special," he explained, for a second sounding flustered before he pulled his armor back on. "Now, stay here. Don't move. Don't make a sound."

Tugging his hands free from her grip, he went to move away but then paused. Turning back to look at her, he had an expression on his face she couldn't read, but when he leaned in and brushed his lips across hers in the quickest yet most emotionally satisfying kiss of her life, she could absolutely read his desire, his attraction to her, and his regret that they both might die out there.

Then he was moving to the edge of the van, and she was shuffling backward into the corner like he'd told her.

"Need some help, girl's unconscious and guy just passed out," he called out in a voice she would have sworn belonged to the man lying dead beside her if she couldn't see Jax's lips moving.

A moment later, she saw two figures moving outside.

Before they could see it was Jax and not their friend talking, he'd fired two shots, dropping both men.

Then he was gone.

Disappeared from view.

The world was suddenly filled with nothing but the sounds of bullets firing.

There were still three other men out there, and they were all united against Jax. Part of her wanted to disobey his orders, climb out of the van, grab one of the weapons from the dead men, and help somehow. But what help would she actually be? She'd never even touched a gun before, let alone used one to kill a person.

When the van suddenly shuddered, and a bullet whizzed through the metal sides, she whimpered and pressed a hand to her mouth to hold in the scream that so desperately wanted to escape.

They were both going to die.

Her and Jax.

And she still couldn't help but believe that this was her fault even with all the doubts swirling inside her mind.

Suddenly, everything went quiet.

Deadly quiet.

Another whimper tumbled from her lips, and Monique scrunched up her eyes, not wanting to see who was going to come for her.

Would it be Jax or the men who had kidnapped them?

The slight rock of the van told her someone was climbing into it, then she could feel them approaching.

"Open your eyes, princess."

That was Jax's voice, but what if it was one of the kidnappers pretending like Jax himself had done just a few moments ago?

Fingers caressed her cheek, the same way they'd done before Jax went on his killing spree, and she knew their touch. There was no way someone could fake how it made her feel.

Whimpering again, she grabbed his hand and held onto it tightly. "Are they dead?"

"All dead."

"So we're ... we're going to be okay? We can go home now?" She hardly dared to hope that might be true. That all they had to do was drive back to the road and then go home.

"Actually, princess, the van got shot up, it's not drivable."

Eyes snapping open, she met Jax's worried gaze. Before pressing him on what he'd just said, her eyes roamed his body searching for the telltale sign of blood that would indicate a wound.

There was none.

"If we can't drive the van, how will we get home?" she asked, hating the wobble in her voice and the tears that blurred her vision, but she was too tired and in too much pain to hide them.

"We'll walk." Jax said it like it was the easiest thing in the world.

But it wasn't.

It was November, and they were deep in the French woods, in one of the largest forests in Europe. She was dressed in a ball gown and heels. Even with Jax's tux jacket on she was going to freeze. They both would. He might be dressed slightly better in his suit pants, shirt, and lace-up shoes, but it was still too cold. They also had no food, no water, and no shelter.

As far as she could see, they were in no better position than they'd been ten minutes ago, now their deaths were just more likely to be slow rather than quick.

CHAPTER *Five*

November 1st
12:02 A.M.

"You doing okay, princess?" Jax glanced sideways as he asked.

Beside him, Monique trudged along through the forest in the pitch dark, cold and hurting, but not a single complaint had fallen from her lips.

Not at all what he would have expected from the Kerr princess before he'd met her.

When he'd gotten on that plane to fly to France, he'd expected to find a spoiled little rich girl. One who was used to getting what she wanted and who would throw her weight around, and her money, using it to manipulate and buy people off.

Only Monique wasn't that way at all. She'd told him she didn't like rich, boring, stuffy guys, and it was clear there was attraction between them.

Attraction that would be easy enough to ignore if it were all there was. But from the second their eyes met, he'd felt something weird settle in his chest. While he was making no claims that it was love at first sight, it was something. Like some primitive part of him had laid a claim on her.

It didn't help that she was sweet and shy yet knew what she wanted and lived her life to the beat of her own drum. If that wasn't enough, the fact that she had been willing to quite literally buy his life with her body would have done it. There was something special about this woman, and he was finding with each passing minute that he didn't want to let her go.

Too bad he wouldn't have a choice.

There was no way he was going to be able to keep from her forever why he'd been at that party, and why he'd made contact with her. Once they found their way out of the forest, he'd contact his brothers, and if they weren't already on a plane after he'd missed the check-in then they'd hop right on one.

When his team didn't come back, Samson Kerr would eventually find out they were all dead, leaving his daughter behind as a witness. Would he allow the only daughter he'd claimed as his live? Or would she now live with a target on her back until they were able to prove that Samson was involved in his stepmom's rape and then subsequent plan to have her and Jax's dad eliminated from the equation by having them branded traitors and killed?

"You know if you're going to ask me a question, the polite thing to do would be to listen to the answer."

The soft, teasing voice drew him out of his head, and he found Monique smiling up at him, her face in the dim light painted with amusement despite the exhaustion clinging to her.

"Sorry, princess," he said sheepishly. "Thoughts are just running a mile a minute."

"I get that. I'm a little in shock, too."

Her big, gray eyes looked up at him with confusion, clearly aware that there was more to him than he'd let on, but there was trust, too. Despite everything they'd been through in the last few hours, she believed in him.

It absolutely gutted him that her trust was misplaced.

He'd keep her alive, protect her with everything that he had, but in the end, he was going to turn out to be just another person who had used her, and Jax had the feeling that was a long list.

"You said you had training, but ... I didn't know you meant you could single-handedly kill six people without breaking a sweat." Her tone was a clear invitation for him to fill in the gaps, and he was trying to figure out how much he could say without telling her everything.

It wasn't like he intended to withhold the information forever, but right now, he was the only thing that was going to get Monique safely back home. If he lost her trust, he had no guarantee she wouldn't go running off and try to do this on her own.

No way was she going to pay the price for his choices any more than she already had.

"Served in the military," he told her, completely honestly. For the moment, she just couldn't know that he worked for Prey. The second that cat was out of the bag, she'd want to know if he was there for work, and once she got that out of him, it would only be a matter of time until she realized she was the job.

Immediately, she stopped walking, moved up onto her tiptoes, the hand he wasn't holding landing on his pecs, above his heart, and pressed a kiss to his cheek. "Thank you for putting your life on the line to keep people like me safe."

If he'd expected her to look down on him because of his career choice, he would have been sorely disappointed. Once again, Monique had shown she was nothing like the public perceived her to be.

"No need for thanks," he said, a little awkwardly.

"Course there is. And I'm going to venture a guess that you were special forces. The way you handled that ..." She waved a hand behind them where a mile away lay the six dead bodies he'd killed. "Says you were one of the best of the best."

"SEAL," he acknowledged. There were women out there who would love to get him into bed just because of what he'd been. While Monique was clearly impressed by his job, she wasn't looking at him like he was a piece of prized meat.

She was looking at him like he was a hero.

Worse, like he was her hero.

Uncomfortable with the secrets he was keeping and the knowledge that as soon as they spilled out he'd lose a chance with Monique he hadn't suspected he would want, he abruptly stopped walking.

"This should do," he announced.

"Do for what?" Monique looked around them, obviously wondering why he'd chosen this particular spot when it looked the same as every other part they'd walked through over the last thirty minutes.

"To spend the night." They'd put some good distance between them and the van, enough to buy them some time.

Sooner or later, someone would realize the team he'd killed never returned and come looking for answers. When they saw six dead bodies and his and Monique's not amongst them, they'd search this forest to try to find them.

When that happened, he wanted Monique far away from danger.

But he wasn't stupid.

They'd both been in a bad car wreck and they were both injured. He'd bet everything he owned Monique had a concussion, and while she'd plugged along without complaint, he knew she needed rest before she crashed.

"I usually enjoy camping," Monique said. "But then again, I usually have a tent, a sleeping bag, and a whole ton of supplies."

"I'll build us a fire. That will keep us warm and keep animals away. Tomorrow, I'll find us something to eat, and at least we have water."

After killing the men who had abducted them, he'd raided the van and come up with nothing other than some bottles of water. It seemed that those men didn't think to be prepared for any situation. His clothes were suitable for walking, but Monique's silk and tulle ball gown and heels were not. Since the first man he'd killed was the only one not covered in blood, he'd told her to wear his clothes. Something she'd reluctantly done, only agreeing if she could wear his suit jacket underneath.

There was no denying that the caveman part of him loved the fact that she wanted to wear his clothes, so agreeing had been no hardship.

Now he tugged on the hand he held and moved her so she was facing him. Not willing to pass up on what could be his only opportunity to touch her before she learned he'd used her and hated him, Jax ran his hands up her arms, loving the way she shivered and her pupils dilated. Settling them on her shoulders with his fingers stroking the base of her neck, he bent his knees so they were eye to eye.

"Between shared body heat and the fire, we won't freeze overnight," he assured her. "I might not be as comfortable as a sleeping bag in a tent, but I'm not the worst thing to sleep on."

"Not the worst," she agreed as her gaze dipped to scan his body. "Definitely not the worst."

Giving her his first real smile in hours, since before they'd been run off the road, Jax pulled her against him and held her in a tight embrace. "I swear to you, Monique. I will take care of you and get you back home safe and sound."

"I believe you," she murmured, nuzzling her face against his neck.

Those simple words, spoken with such a pure heart, wiped the smile from his face. This woman believed in him with zero reason to, and all she was going to get for her blind faith was a heavy dose of betrayal.

~

November 1st
1:12 P.M.

"It is not!" Monique exclaimed, absolutely positive she was right.

There was no way that could be true.

That just wasn't possible.

Nobody could like that.

"Totally is, princess," Jax said, and the corners of his mouth twitched a little, making her doubt that he was telling her the truth. Unfortunately, she didn't know Jax well enough yet to always know when he was teasing her.

Yet.

The word had slipped into her mind without conscious thought on her part. But as she considered it, Monique realized she did want to get to know Jax better. She'd liked him from the first moment she laid eyes on him, and the way he'd killed for her was surprisingly hot, and oh so protective. It definitely appealed to her poor little neglected heart, and she absolutely loved how he was so attentive to her, constantly checking on her and doing little things to make the whole ordeal a little bit easier.

Yep, getting to know him better when they were safe was a must.

Maybe that spark she'd felt at first, the pull toward him that only grew stronger the longer they spent together, was all wrong. Maybe this wouldn't go anywhere. Maybe it would turn out to be nothing.

But maybe it would turn out to be everything.

How could she not give it a chance?

If it turned out to be nothing, no harm, maybe she'd at least wind up with a new friend. That would be something because she didn't have many of those. Most people only saw her last name and thought if they attached themselves to her, some of that wealth and prestige would somehow rub off onto them.

Not Jax though. He seemed to like her more the more he found out she wasn't the Kerr princess she was made out to be.

Narrowing her eyes at him, Monique planted her hands on her hips and studied him closely. "I think you're lying to me, Jax. There is no way in the world that anyone's favorite food could possibly be cheesy pasta with fruit. Fruit! Apples, pears, and oranges. They do not go with pasta. Full stop. It sounds disgusting!"

His laugh rang out through the quiet forest, and the sound seemed to lodge inside her, unfurling with warmth through her limbs until she was sure she was staring at him with an almost lovestruck smile.

"You should laugh more," she said without thinking, that was probably way overstepping, but it was true. He had a great laugh, so strong and carefree, and she sensed it wasn't something he allowed himself the freedom to do very often.

"I think you're right," he said. The smile fell from his face, but it wasn't replaced with a frown, merely a look of contemplation, like he was truly considering her words. "I think that maybe I'll have more to laugh about from here on out."

Did he mean ...?

It was probably way too much to hope that he could mean he'd have more to laugh about because she'd be part of his life going forward.

Yet she hoped for it anyway.

Because the air between them seemed to be growing hot and heavy,

Monique steered the conversation back to safer ground, not wanting to push too hard too fast just because Jax was the first man she'd found herself truly interested in in a long time. "So are you just trying to trick me, or do you really eat pasta with fruit?"

"Day for tricks was yesterday if I'm not mistaken, princess," Jax told her, amusement dancing in his dark eyes.

They were nice eyes.

Set in a nice face.

Chiseled jaw, just the right amount of stubble, and thick, long lashes. Beneath his white shirt and suit pants she would bet anything that his body was spectacular. Most of the men she'd dated might go to the gym on occasion, but they didn't really work out, and they hadn't served in special forces. Jax's body would be a work of art, all hard planes and defined muscles.

"Do I want to know what thoughts are running through your head right now, princess? You're blushing," he added when her brow furrowed.

"Uh, it was nothing. So you really weren't messing with me? What possessed you to even think up the idea of cutting up oranges and putting them in your cheesy pasta?" she asked as they started walking again. As exhausting as it was traipsing through the forest, neither of them with any idea of which direction they should be heading in, talking helped to keep her distracted enough that the pain and fear swimming inside her didn't take over.

Jax was there.

Jax would keep her safe.

Already he'd killed for her, and made a fire to keep them warm, he wore the weapons he'd taken from the dead guards confidently, and he had in fact been a surprisingly comfortable bed as they'd slept tangled in each other's arms.

For warmth, nothing else.

Totally nothing else.

"I guess it was when I was around six or seven. My mom died when I was four and my brother Jake was six. Our dad served as well, in Delta Force, and after Mom died, he didn't want to leave the job he loved. That meant that Jake and I had to be bumped around from relative to relative, and all of them made it pretty clear that caring for two little boys who were grieving their mom and just wanted love and stability was the last thing they were interested in doing."

Reaching for Jax's hand was as instinctual as breathing, and this time it had nothing to do with needing a steady hand to help keep her balanced with the dizziness. She knew exactly how Jax and his brother had felt. The same way she felt growing up without a mom, with a dad who was never there, and grandparents who thought raising her was the nanny's job.

"I'm sorry you had to go through that. I'm glad you had a brother to be there for you." Maybe she wouldn't have been so lonely if she'd had a sibling. Monique had always wanted a little brother or sister, but her dad had never remarried after divorcing her mom, so siblings hadn't been in the cards for her.

"Yeah, me too. Since we knew no one wanted to care for us when Dad was away, we learned pretty young to start doing things for ourselves. Including cooking."

"I always wanted to cook when I was a kid, but apparently that was not an appropriate interest for a Kerr." She and her grandparents had had drastically different ideas of what her life was going to look like, and she was so glad she'd managed to break away from them and make her own way. "So you decided to try thinking up the most disgusting ideas you could?"

Jax laughed again. "Actually, it was a bet. One night, I complained that I had missed a snack and I was hungry. Jake was making cheesy pasta for our dinner, and he dared me to put my fruit in it. We were stupid kids doing stupid things, but turns out that fruit with pasta is actually delicious."

"There is no way I am ever going to buy that. I think you're crazy." It was one thing to be silly as a kid, but to still eat that as an adult ... ugh.

"I bet I could convert you."

"Not in a million lifetimes," she assured him. She loved cooking, was always up for trying something new, but there was zero percent chance she was going to eat pasta with cut-up pieces of apple, pears, or oranges in it.

Zero.

"I can be very persistent," he teased, arching a brow, and she felt that look right between her legs. She didn't have a doubt he could convince her to do a whole lot in the bedroom, all the things she'd always wanted to do but never found a lover she was comfortable enough with to ask.

Before things could get awkward, her stomach let out the loudest gurgle.

"Food time," Jax said immediately, snapping right back into protector mode. "I don't have much to hunt with, I'd rather not use the guns unless we're desperate, but I can probably catch us something to eat."

"No," Monique said quickly. "I don't eat meat. I hate the thought of animals dying to feed me. Don't worry, I'm not one of those vegetarians who is always trying to convince others. Other people can eat whatever they want, I'm fine with it and don't look down on them or anything. I just love animals too much to ever eat one."

"I understand having principles, princess, and I would never judge you for them. But we're in a survival situation here, we're going to need fuel, and we have to take what we can find."

"Couldn't agree more." Jax had been her white knight, riding in and saving her life, and taking care of her in the aftermath. But now it was time for their roles to reverse. "So I told you that I'm an introverted homebody, and you know I love animals. Well, I have another hobby, and it turns out that it's one that's actually going to wind up saving our lives."

CHAPTER *Six*

November 2nd
10:54 A.M.

The excitement on Monique's face as she found some berries that she deemed safe for consumption was well and truly worth the slight hunger pains and the desire for a more filling meal of meat.

Jax was quickly devolving into an addict where this woman was concerned.

Every time she smiled at him, he lost a little more resistance, gave in a little more, fell a little harder.

There was just something about her sweet, sunny smile, and contagious amounts of energy that was hard to resist. Add in knowing that she had the strength and backbone to put her life on the line for someone she didn't even know, and it was no wonder he was swimming in an ever-deepening sea of guilt.

It was like a carousel in his head, constantly spinning, an argument that just went on and on. Tell her to ease his own burden and possibly lose her trust, making it harder for him to get her out of there especially if the men her father had sent after him tracked them. Or keep his secrets and know that while he might be keeping her safe in the short term, he was only digging himself deeper into a hole he wouldn't be able to climb back out of.

They hadn't talked much about her family, but from what little she had said, he knew she didn't have a close relationship with her father. That after her mom bailed on them when she was two, he'd basically dumped her with his parents and gone on about his life like she didn't exist.

Monique seemed to have carved out her own place in the world. She didn't deny her family or who they were, even used the perks of being a Kerr to her advantage, going to events she was uncomfortable at to leverage her connections and raise money for her animal rescue. But other than that, it seemed she lived a mostly solitary life out on her animal sanctuary in Vermont, on her fifty-acre property that she rarely left. She'd told him she felt more comfortable with animals than people, but there was an ease between them that would have indicated to anyone who saw them together that they'd known one another a whole hell of a lot longer than two days.

Felt like it too.

Not something he could easily explain to anyone else, but it felt like he'd known her forever. She was everything he would have looked for in a partner if he'd ever had the inclination to look.

Ever since he was twelve years old, his entire life had focused on the determination that he and his siblings were going to find out the truth about what happened to their parents. That left little time for anything else.

Of course, he'd dated women over the years, from high school, and while he was in the military, and again while he'd been at Prey. He'd always made it clear he didn't have the time for anything serious and always picked women who were happy with just the occasional hook-up for dinner and some hot sex.

But none of those women could hold a candle to his princess.

"Why are you smiling at me like that?" Monique asked, a slight pinkish tinge to her cheeks, her nose scrunched up in that adorable way it did when she was confused and trying to figure something out.

"Because I think you're beautiful, and the way you keep finding us food to eat makes you even more beautiful," Jax answered honestly. While he was keeping a pretty major secret from her, he was trying to be as truthful as he could be about everything else. All the stories he'd told her about his childhood, about his brother Jake, and stepbrothers, Cade, Cooper, Connor, and Cole, were all true.

The only thing he hadn't mentioned was Cassandra.

If they were correct—and he believed they were—that Monique's father was the final rapist and biological father of his stepsister, then she was soon going to learn that she had a little half-sister.

"Oh." Her blush deepened, but her smile grew, and she looked pleased with the compliment. "I know you could hunt for food for us, so I know I'm not doing anything you couldn't do, but I appreciate you giving up meat and eating the leaves and berries."

Not bothering to fight the urge to reach out to her, touch her, take these moments while he could because he knew there was a finite end to them, Jax reached out and palmed her cheek. Like she did every time he did this, she immediately nuzzled into it, her smile turning soft and dreamy.

Even he was having a hard time believing they hadn't known each other for eternity.

He would have sworn it wasn't possible to form a bond with someone this quickly, and yet everything about being around Monique felt natural. Right.

"I'll catch meat if we need it so there are enough berries for you, but for now, you're keeping us fed. It doesn't matter if I could do it, too, you're doing it, that's what counts." His fingertips swept across her skin, marveling at how soft it was.

Didn't matter that they'd been traipsing through the forest for over twenty-four hours, that they'd been sleeping on the ground, that there was dark bruising on the side of her face where she'd hit her head, or that she was wearing clothes borrowed from one of their dead abductors. Monique was without a doubt the most beautiful woman he'd ever had the pleasure of laying eyes on. He loved everything about her, her smoky gray eyes, the smattering of freckles across her nose and cheeks, her chocolate locks with the faintest of red highlights when the sun hit them.

Without thinking, his thumb brushed across her bottom lip. He'd so much rather be touching her lips with his own, but this was better than nothing.

From the way her pupils dilated, it was pretty clear Monique wished it was his lips on hers rather than his thumb as well.

Since both of them wanted it ...

Jax leaned in and feathered a light kiss to the softest lips he'd ever had the pleasure of kissing. It wasn't enough, but it would be taking advantage to do more given he'd been lying to her since they met.

Forcing that thought into his mind, he managed to cling to control and pull back before he headed down a road there was no coming back from.

Disappointment was obvious in Monique's expression, but she didn't pull away from him when he reached for her hand and guided her over to a broken tree trunk that would serve as a bench to sit on.

"What are we doing?" she asked.

"Taking a break," he replied, kneeling in front of her. "Follow my finger."

When he held it up in front of her face, he got an eyeroll out of Monique, but she dutifully followed it as he moved it up and down and side to side. Her pupils were equal and reactive. He knew she still had a headache, even if she hadn't said it aloud, he could tell by the tight lines around her mouth when she thought he wasn't looking, but he thought the worst of her concussion symptoms had passed.

"I'm okay, Jax." Monique's much smaller hand curled around the finger he held up, and she brought it to her lips, touching a kiss to the pad. "I feel like garbage, my body aches, my feet have blisters, I'm covered in cuts and bruises, my head feels like it got crushed in a vice, but I'm alive. Not only alive, but you've kept me warm at night with a fire, you've kept me sane by telling me about you and your life. You've even gone above and beyond, heating the water from the river a little so it wasn't ice cold when you cleaned the blood off me. You've been literally perfect."

Those words were meant to encourage him, convey her gratefulness for what he'd done, but they only made the guilt he was battling so much worse.

Jax knew he was only doing what he had to do to find answers and keep his family safe. He hadn't known much about Monique other than that she was Samson Kerr's daughter and what the media portrayed her to be. This decision to come and meet her hadn't been made maliciously or with the intent of hurting her.

But he was going to.

She was a genuinely sweet person, and he was using that against her.

It wasn't right and it wasn't fair, but there was no way to go back in time and do things differently. What was done was done, and they were both going to have to live with the consequences.

"Here, let me see if I can do a little something about your body aching," he said, settling down into a more comfortable position and grabbing one of Monique's legs, massaging out the tightness in her muscles, needing to do something to alleviate his guilt before it choked him.

~

November 2nd
3:44 P.M.

Exhaustion was pressing down on her this afternoon.

So far, she'd been doing okay, managing the headache and the slight dizziness. The leaves and berries she'd been foraging for them had been good for her stomach, and the nausea had subsided. The massage Jax had given her earlier had helped ease the tightness in her sore, overused muscles.

But the last hour or so she'd gotten so tired it was getting harder and harder to put one foot in front of the other.

Not that Monique had any plans to tell Jax that.

If she did, she knew he would stop immediately. Build them a camp and let her rest for as long as she needed to.

The problem with that plan was that it kept them right where they were.

Lost.

In the middle of one of the largest forests in Europe.

With the temperatures getting colder by the day as winter approached.

They needed to be out of there sooner rather than later, and any delay could cost them their lives.

She was well aware of the fact that they might not be able to find their way out of the forest. They had no idea which way the van had driven, or how deep into the forest it had gone. There was no road to follow, and it had quickly become impossible to follow the path the van had made through the trees.

People got lost and died in the wilderness, and she and Jax could soon be two of them.

Shivering at the thought of never making it home to all her animals, as much as her heart hurt at never seeing them again, it hurt worse for Jax. While she had a family who wouldn't really care if she died, not that they'd outright wish it on her, more that they were just ambivalent, Jax had five brothers who loved him and would miss him if he were gone. Miss him, the person, not the lack of an heir to a fortune she didn't even want.

"You okay, princess?" Jax asked, obviously noticing her shiver.

It wasn't just fear and sadness making her shudder, but the cold seemed to be really hitting her hard this afternoon. Probably because of the exhaustion draped over her like a heavy cloud, because they were walking almost nonstop, which should in theory keep her body temperature up enough to hold off the cold.

Managing a smile, she nodded.

Slowly, his gaze roamed her body, and then Jax took a step closer, crowding into her personal space. Not that she minded in the least. In fact, she'd love to have more of him in her personal space. That kiss earlier hadn't been nearly enough, she wanted so much more with this man.

So much it would have scared her if she didn't feel so unexplainably safe with him.

Capturing her chin between his thumb and forefinger, he tilted her head back so she had no choice but to meet his gaze. Where she couldn't help but feel he was reading every nuance of her expression and looking right down inside her to her very soul.

"You're lying to me, princess," he murmured. "Tell me the truth."

There was something so compelling about Jax's tone that the words were spilling out of her mouth without conscious thought. "Just everything catching up with me, I think. I don't know why I just feel so tired."

"Why didn't you say something?"

"Because I know you'd insist we stop and rest, and we have to keep going. We have to find our way out of here and back home."

"We can spare an afternoon."

Lifting a hand to grip his wrist, Monique shook her head, hardly able to move it since Jax still held her chin. "No, Jax, we can't. It's going to keep getting colder, and we're not dressed to be out in the cold. Neither of us is getting enough sleep or enough food. And by now, the bodies have probably been found, which means people are out here looking for us. I don't want to be here when they find us."

Jax's mouth opened, and she was sure he was going to offer her some platitude. It wasn't that she didn't believe Jax could protect her and keep her safe, she did, and he had. But they would know he'd killed six of their men and they'd send more this time. Jax was good but numbers were numbers, and they didn't lie. There was a limit to how many he could take on and still come out on top.

Before the platitude could come out, a loud scream pierced the air.

Not a human scream.

"What the hell was that?" Jax demanded, releasing her and spinning in a slow circle, searching for the source of the scream.

"Fox," she answered immediately. "What?" she said with a shrug when he looked over his shoulder at her. "I love animals, and I've cared for plenty of foxes before. That was a fox."

"Monique, wait." He grabbed at her as she darted around him, heading in the direction the sound had come from, but she easily dodged out of the way, suddenly reenergized.

An animal needed her.

This was her purpose in life.

Caring for those that couldn't care for themselves.

It didn't take her long to locate the little ball of red and white fur tangled in a fallen branch. Poor little baby must have gotten stuck as it ran, and now it was huddling against the ground like it was in pain. Had it hurt itself?

A hand snapped around her bicep, stilling her as she went to move toward the possibly injured animal. "You can't go up to it," Jax hissed.

"Why not?"

"Because it's a wild animal."

"Dealt with plenty of them since I opened my rescue," she reminded him.

"*After* someone else has already caught it and brought it to you to heal and be nursed back to health."

Rolling her eyes at him, Monique planted her hands on her hips. "I didn't tell you how to do your job, I just trusted you. Now you can trust me to know how to do my job."

With that, she broke free of his hold and approached the terrified animal slowly.

Just because most of the animals at her rescue had been brought to her didn't mean she hadn't rescued lots in her lifetime. Plenty as a kid, and sometimes she was called out to rescue the animal that would be put in her care. Besides that, most of her days were spent dealing with animals who were hurting and scared, she knew what she was doing.

"Shh, baby, I'm not going to hurt you," she crooned as she knelt beside the branch where the animal was trapped. "It's okay. It's okay. I'm just going to help you, all right? I'm going to get you all untangled, and then I'm going to see if you're hurt. If you are, I'll make it all better, I promise."

Her soft and soothing tone worked, and while it still cowered, the little fox didn't move a muscle as she quickly untangled one of its legs from where it had gotten stuck between two smaller branches.

"There you go, baby, all free," she murmured as she yanked off the sweater from the dead guard that she was wearing over Jax's suit jacket. She'd be colder without it on, but the little fox needed it more.

Reaching out with a steady hand, knowing how she approached the animal would fuel how it reacted, she stroked a single fingertip down its chest, then rubbed lightly under its chin, making sure to keep her hand where it could see it at all times.

"Can I pick you up now, baby?" she asked, as she wrapped the sweater around the trembling creature then when it didn't fight against her, scooped it up and sat down, settling the fox on her lap.

When she looked up, she found Jax staring at her incredulously. "What the heck are you? Some sort of animal whisperer?"

"Told you that you should trust me to do my job. I know how to get an animal's trust, how else could I run the best animal rescue in the country?" Monique wasn't trying to brag, she was just being honest. The reason she wound up with such an array of animals was because she was so good at what she did, and she only hired the best of the best.

Animals were innocents, they didn't hurt on purpose to be cruel or malicious, and they deserved the very best care she could give them when they were at their most vulnerable.

"You are just full of surprises," Jax said.

There was something odd in his tone that she didn't focus on figuring out. She had a little fox who needed help and her attention focused on it. "I'm not leaving it behind," she warned Jax, better to let him know that now. The fox's foot was injured, possibly broken, leaving it alone was basically a death sentence. Not only would it not be able to hunt for food, but it was also perfect prey for a predator. "I'm sure Cinderella will be thrilled to have a companion when I get you home."

"Cinderella? Do I even want to ask?" Jax asked in amused exasperation.

"My pet."

"Like a dog, or a cat, or a bunny rabbit?"

"Like a hedgehog," she answered with a grin.

"Why am I not surprised you have a pet hedgehog?"

Stroking the soft fur of the little fox, who settled sleepily in her arms, Monique's grin widened. "Because I'm full of surprises and you can't wait to uncover every single one of them."

At least she hoped that was how he felt because it was absolutely how she felt. She was falling hard and fast, and she prayed she wasn't falling alone because if she was, it was going to be a hard landing.

CHAPTER *Seven*

November 3rd
9:23 A.M.

This had to go down in history as the craziest mission he'd ever gone on.

Flying to France with the intention of putting the final nail in the coffin of the conspiracy to frame his dad and stepmom for treason, he never would have envisioned it turning out like this.

Traipsing through the forest, lost with no idea which direction they should be heading in, with the target of his op trailing along beside him, an injured young fox snuggled in her arms.

Crazy.

Totally crazy.

And yet he was actually enjoying his time with Monique. Not being lost and injured in the forest with no idea if they were heading toward civilization or further away from it and deeper into the forest. But the part where they talked and laughed and he got to know her better, that part he loved.

Sensing Monique's exhaustion, Jax stopped and held out his arms. They hadn't seen any predators, human or animal, the entire time they'd been out there, so he felt safe enough not to have his weapon in his hands. It was still hanging on a strap around his chest so it wasn't like it wasn't still on his person.

"Here," he said to her.

"What?"

Nose scrunched in confusion, it took everything he had not to lean in and touch a kiss to it.

But he was trying to do the honorable thing.

Kissing her under these circumstances was wrong, and he shouldn't have done it earlier, and had determined he wasn't going to do it again. Until there were no more secrets between them he wasn't going to lay another hand on Monique in a sexual way.

"I'll carry the fox," he explained.

"Thought you told me that if I wanted to keep him, he was my responsibility," she said, arching a brow at him, but amusement danced in her gray eyes.

"Guess I finally realized how serious you were about keeping it." When she'd first insisted that she was going to take it home with her and keep it on her animal rescue along with her pet hedgehog, he'd thought the weight of having to carry it would wear her out sooner or later.

Wrong.

No matter how exhausted he knew she was, she'd carried her little bundle without a complaint. It was obvious how deeply she cared about animals, and he knew trying to talk her into leaving the fox behind would be impossible.

In the end, did he even really want to?

She was right when she said that with an injury to its leg, there was no way it would be able to hunt properly, and it wouldn't be able to move easily if at all, making it ideal prey. It was take the creature with them or let it die, he just didn't want its presence to wind up making Monique die.

"Let me carry your baby for a while. I hear water up ahead. When we get to it, we'll stop and rest for a bit." With the way she'd snuggled the little animal to her chest as they slept last night and kept it on her lap every time they stopped, Jax was pretty sure that was about as long as she'd let him keep possession of her newest baby anyway.

There was slight hesitation before she nodded and passed the bundle over. "He is getting kind of heavy."

"Yeah, *getting*," he scoffed. They both knew the little guy had been too much for her to carry for more than the first hour or so after they found him. Still, if the young fox made her happy, and it was clear it did, then he wasn't going to take that away from her.

Surprisingly, Monique had calmed the fox easily yesterday, and ever since, it had been docile as though it had been raised a pet surrounded by people all its little life, instead of a wild animal. While it eyed him a little suspiciously, the fox then quickly settled down into his arms and closed its eyes.

"Is Cinderella going to like having a little brother?" he asked as they walked side by side.

Monique laughed, and the sound was prettier than any music he'd ever heard before. "I'm not sure. She's kind of spoiled and used to getting all my attention when I come home at night."

"Of course she's spoiled. I bet every single animal in your rescue is."

"They deserve it, you know? They'd already been hurt or traumatized, taken out of their natural environment, and trying to adjust. I want them to know that they're loved and cared about."

There was no mistaking the wistfulness in her tone.

What she was really saying was she never wanted an animal to feel like she had growing up. Unloved and uncared for.

As much as Jax wanted to push to learn what she'd meant when she told him she'd already survived hell once before and could do it again, he'd been respectful of her desire to hold onto her secrets. It was bad enough he'd met her under false pretenses, he at least owed her respect for her privacy.

"I hate you grew up feeling that way," he said softly.

"I hate that you grew up feeling that way, too," she told him.

Once again, he heard the words she didn't say aloud.

Together, they could make sure that neither of them ever felt that way again.

It was so tempting. He'd fallen hard and fast for the woman he was only supposed to spend a couple of hours with, and a huge part of him would love to ask her out on a date when they got home. To keep getting to know her, and maybe one day fall in love with her.

But he was lying to her, and when she found out, the spell would be broken, and he'd lose her.

"Here's the river," he said as they stepped through the trees and it came into sight. It wasn't what he wanted to say, but every time he felt emotions building too strongly between them he had to take a step back.

Not wanted to, *had* to.

"Give your little guy a drink," he ordered as he passed the creature back into her arms.

"He's sleeping," she said, dropping to her knees and tucking her bundle onto the ground at the base of a tree.

Then she looked up at him with the sweetest pair of eyes, and he knew that he'd be powerless to say no to her.

"Sit with me for a bit?" she asked, and since he couldn't see the harm in that, he nodded and took a seat on the hard ground beside her.

As soon as he sat, he realized his mistake.

Because Monique shifted immediately to straddle his thighs. Even through the layers of clothes separating them, he could feel the heat of her center drawing him in, almost making him lose his ability to cling to rational thought.

When her lips crashed into his, that last thread of rationality fled.

All he could do was feel.

The tip of her tongue brushed against his lips and opening them to her felt far too natural. Their tongues danced together, and her hands, which had been resting on his shoulders, drifted lower.

Trailing a path down his chest, her fingertips seemed to be everywhere at once as though she wanted to memorize how he felt beneath her.

Of their own accord, his hands gripped her hips and ground her down against his growing erection. Monique moaned into his mouth, and it sent every last drop of blood in his body south, and he grew almost impossibly hard.

Grinding her against him again, he couldn't have stopped his hips thrusting if his very life depended on it. This woman had burst into his life like a breath of fresh air he hadn't even known he needed. For so long his life had been focused on only one thing. But his family's quest for answers was almost over, and he was starting to think more about what his life would look like after they'd proved their parents weren't traitors but victims.

Monique.

His soul screamed at him that that's what his life should look like.

She was everything he needed and more than he ever could have hoped for.

The problem was, she was also more than he deserved.

When her hands fumbled at his waistband, Jax finally snapped to his senses. He couldn't do this. It would be an even worse betrayal than the one he was already committing. While it was easy to say it now, days later, he knew what he should have done was tell her everything when they'd been in that van. It would have been before feelings started to develop, and given that they were being abducted, she might have believed what he told her about her father.

Now he'd missed that opportunity, but if he didn't want to permanently lose a chance with her, he had to stop this before it went too far. Before he did something he couldn't take back and violated her trust.

"Princess, we can't," he murmured as he tore his lips away from hers.

Heavy-lidded eyes burning with desire slowly morphed into confusion. "You don't want to?" she asked, vulnerability creeping into her tone.

"We shouldn't," he answered, not willing to lie and say he didn't want to because he absolutely did. Since he wasn't strong enough to keep touching her and not take what she was offering, he used his grip on her hips to lift her and set her down on the ground beside him.

"I'm sorry."

Her whisper burned inside him like acid. She shouldn't be apologizing to him, he should be the one apologizing to her. He was the one lying to her, keeping secrets. Monique had done nothing wrong, and yet he could see her curling in on herself, shutting down, erecting barriers between them.

Pushing her away was the right thing to do, yet he'd hurt her.

Being stuck between a rock and a hard place sucked.

~

November 3rd
5:29 P.M.

She was such an idiot.

Monique had been drowning in embarrassment ever since that disaster of a seduction attempt this morning.

Okay, sure, being flirty and sexy had never really been her strong suit. It kind of went against the whole introvert thing. Or maybe it was just because she'd never really felt safe with any of her previous partners. She'd known but not wanted to acknowledge that those men had only really been with her because of her last name and the advantages they thought they'd get by attaching themselves to her.

It wasn't like that with Jax.

She just felt connected to him, and thought he felt the same way.

Only it was obvious that he didn't.

Maybe he felt something, but it wasn't the same as what she was feeling. What she was feeling was all-consuming enough to give her confidence she never would have thought herself possible of.

Sex had been a touchy subject for her, given that her first experiences weren't what they were supposed to be. But she'd come a long way in the last twelve years, and she'd gotten to a point where sex was enjoyable even if it wasn't mind-blowing.

With Jax it would be mind-blowing. That she was absolutely certain of.

Too bad he hadn't felt the same way.

For the first time since she met him at the Halloween gala, things were awkward between them. It was disconcerting even if given the fact that she'd only met Jax a few days ago and things should have been awkward between them all along.

But they hadn't been, and she'd been reveling in that fact. It was so amazing to meet someone who you just immediately connected with, and she didn't want that to change. Why had she stupidly thought that he'd want to have sex with her?

Especially out there when their lives were on the line.

Her timing couldn't have been worse, and she couldn't really blame him for not wanting to sleep with her on the dirty forest floor. And looking back and trying to take her emotions out of it, when she'd asked him if he didn't want to have sex with her, he hadn't said yes. What he'd said was that they shouldn't, not that he didn't want to.

Was she being ridiculous in holding onto that tiny distinction?

Just because he hadn't said he didn't want to didn't mean he actually wasn't interested in sex with her. Maybe he just wanted to wait until they were safe and back home and he could do it all romantic. She bet that under all the muscle, Jax was a romantic at heart.

Maybe she was blowing this whole thing out of proportion. Just because she'd stepped out of her comfort zone and tried to instigate something she really didn't have any right doing under these circumstances, didn't mean that he was rejecting her. And just because being rejected was a sore spot for her didn't mean she should be taking her frustration and hurt out on him.

He had every right to say no, just like she would have if things had been reversed.

"Jax?" she said tentatively, breaking the oppressive silence that had smothered them all day. That wasn't what she wanted. Her feelings had been hurt, sure, but she still liked Jax and didn't want to lose him. At the very least, she hoped they could walk away from this whole ordeal as friends.

"Yeah?" He stopped walking and turned to face her. There was hope in his dark eyes as well as relief, and it helped to know he hadn't liked the tension simmering between them either.

"I'm sorry about earlier." Monique really was. She wished she could go back and undo it, but she couldn't. Humiliating herself in front of the man she had a crush on was not something she was going to repeat, but she also didn't want it to ruin things.

"Damn, princess, don't be sorry. I wanted to. Badly. I just can't ... not like this. It wouldn't be right, it would be taking advantage." There was a plea in his voice that was echoed in his expression, begging her to believe that it hadn't been a rejection.

She wanted to believe that.

After all, Jax didn't seem to care about her last name, so he wasn't using her for anything, and he had kissed her back. In the end, she had two choices. She could believe him and they could move forward, or she could not and things would remain tense.

Put like that, it was an easy choice.

"Okay," she agreed. While she didn't see how it could be taking advantage when she was the one to initiate it, it was clear he saw it that way, and who was she to argue with how he interpreted things?

"Okay?" he repeated like he hardly dared to hope that she was letting him off the hook.

"Yeah. I mean, I still feel embarrassed, but I get why I'm not the most attractive woman you've met right now." Giving a self-deprecating laugh, Monique looked down at herself, at the too-big borrowed shoes, the pants that were rolled up too many times to look fashionable, at the suit jacket that looked silly with the tactical pants from the dead guard. She was dirty, smelled bad, her hair was a mess, and there were bruises and swelling on her face. Why would he want to have sex with her right now?

A growl rumbled through Jax's chest. Startling both her and her new little fox baby.

Setting the little bundle down, he grabbed her roughly, yanking her off her feet and up against his hard body. Pure instinct had her wrapping her legs around his hips, bringing the bulge in his pants right up against her needy center.

"You better not say that again," he snarled.

"S-say what?" she stammered. It was hard to think when she was this close to him. When she could feel his chest heaving as it pressed against hers, his warm breath puffing against her lips, because held like this, they were eye to eye, which meant they were also lips to lips.

Don't embarrass yourself again.

Don't be stupid.

Remember what he said.

Respect his boundaries.

If she didn't remind herself of that, she was likely to humiliate herself all over again by grinding against his thickening length and begging him to let her touch him, to have him touch her.

"That you aren't the most attractive woman I've ever laid eyes on. Hell, you're the most beautiful woman in the entire world. It doesn't matter what you're wearing, it doesn't matter if you're dirty and injured. You. Are. Stunning. Do you know why you're so beautiful?"

His words still swirling around inside her head, leaving her dumbfounded, all Monique could do was shake her head.

"Because of this." Leaning down, he touched a light kiss to her chest, right above where her heart was pounding wildly. "You have the biggest heart I've ever seen. You care about people and animals. You were prepared to put yourself on the line for me. You are unapologetically you, and you don't let the fact that others see you differently influence you or make you act differently."

"They don't know me, it doesn't matter what they think," she whispered, mesmerized by his words and the passion with which he spoke them.

"Damn right. They don't know you. But you're letting me get to know you and that's such a privilege, princess. You have no idea how badly I want to make love to you, but not here, not now. Do you understand? It has absolutely nothing to do with you, and I don't want you to waste a single second feeling embarrassed when the fact that you want me makes me feel like king of the world. Get it?"

All she could do was nod.

How could she not believe him when he spoke from his heart?

"Got it," she murmured.

"Good."

Pressing his lips to hers in a featherlight kiss, she then felt another growl rumble through his chest before Jax kissed her like he was consumed with need. She was, too, and her fingers lifted to tangle in his short hair as she took everything he had to offer.

In that kiss was a promise.

Once they were back home, all bets were off, and he was going to pursue her. She felt it vibrating through him, his need, his desire, his attraction to her. It all poured out of him in the kiss, and she clutched at it, using it to soothe the sting of rejection she'd felt earlier.

Jax was a good man, one who cared deeply about the people in his life, who had taken on a job that could get him killed because he wanted to follow in his dad's footsteps and make the world a safer place. He was loyal and protective, sweet and funny, and for some crazy reason he'd focused on her.

If they could just find their way out of the forest, they could explore these feelings, nurture them, and let them grow, and maybe one day fall in love and start a life together.

The only thing stopping her from having that future was the fact that they were lost. Nothing else could ever come between them.

CHAPTER *Eight*

November 4th
6:18 P.M.

The temperature had dropped dramatically.

Worryingly.

Jax knew they were both getting weaker. While they'd been able to replenish their water bottles every time they found a river so they weren't dehydrated, and Monique had continued to find them sources of food so they weren't starving, neither, was her little fox friend, but they weren't replenishing their bodies' supplies quickly enough.

Add in the fact they'd both been injured before they even started walking, and they'd just wrapped up day four of hiking through the French forest, and he wasn't sure how much longer they'd be able to keep going.

Of course, Monique never complained, but she needed more regular breaks and he could tell she found it harder and harder to get back up on her feet. Feet that were a mess, covered in blisters, some of which he was becoming worried about.

If an infection set in and they couldn't find their way out of the forest in time ...

The last thing he wanted was to sit by helplessly and watch Monique wither away and die while he could do nothing about it.

"Sorry, this is going to be cold," he told her as he held the water bottle above her feet.

"It's okay, I know we need to wash them so they don't get infected," Monique assured him. There were dark circles under her eyes, and he was sure she was getting paler as the days went by. Leaning back against the tree trunk, she looked utterly wiped out. But she was hanging in there.

In her lap, she clutched her little fox, bundled in the sweater from the dead guard. With the temperature dropping the way it was, they would have to have a conversation about that. She needed the added warmth more than the fox did. It was made to live out there, and its fur would keep it warm enough. Monique didn't have the same ability.

Pouring a little of the cold water on her feet, he felt Monique tense even as she didn't make a sound. Taking the handkerchief he'd happened to have with him in his back pocket when he went to the ball, he wiped her feet down, removing all the bits of dirt and stick that had managed to get inside the shoes as she walked. The handkerchief was still stained with some of their blood from that first day when he'd cleaned them both down after they'd fled the scene of their would-be murders, and now more blood stains were being added to it.

The more he dabbed and cleaned, the tenser Monique became until she finally winced and hissed as he touched a particularly big blister.

"Sorry," she murmured.

"Why are you sorry, princess?" She had to know he didn't expect her to be anything other than human. She was holding it together, doing everything he asked of her, doing her part in keeping them going, but she was allowed to hurt, to be in pain, to need a moment to fall apart.

"Don't want to complain."

"Hardly complaining to be in pain," he reminded her, sure there was an underlying reason for her hesitation to show even the slightest bit of discomfort. Hell, he'd complained more than she had over the last four days, and he had training and experience in being in situations like this.

Her gaze skittered away until it was fixated on something over his shoulder. "Don't want to make you mad," she whispered.

"Why the hell would I be mad at you for being in pain when your feet look like this?" Jax lifted the foot balanced on his knee that he'd been cleaning to remind her that she wasn't whining about nothing. Her feet were beat up and had to be extremely painful just resting there let alone walking on them.

Monique shrugged and didn't answer, but he wasn't letting that slide.

So far, he'd been working hard not to push her, fighting against his instincts to find out all her demons so he could slay them one by one. But not any longer. She'd opened the door by apologizing for something she hadn't done wrong, and he was going to walk through it.

Barge through it if necessary.

"Tell me," he said, firmly but gently.

Ever so slowly, her gaze crept back to his, tears shimmering in her gray eyes. He could feel her resistance, but he also sensed a desire to share her pain, allowing someone else to shoulder it with her.

"I'm here for you, princess. This is a safe place. No judgement." From what little she'd said, he could put the pieces together and come up with a vague idea of what she'd been through, but he wanted—needed—to hear it from her. Even if listening to the words cut him up inside.

"When I was fourteen, I was abducted from my school," she began, her voice taking on that faraway tone that told him she was reliving this while speaking the words. "It was a kidnapping for ransom. One of the teachers had a gambling problem, was in deep with several loan sharks, and thought I'd be an easy target since I was introverted and didn't have a lot of friends. He kept me for three days before my dad paid the ransom, and he let me go. Since I knew who had taken me, I told the cops, and he was arrested. I don't know why he didn't do a better job of hiding his identity. He got sloppy, and it led to his downfall."

The story all sounded so neat and tidy, but her words from earlier, telling him she'd sold her body, told him that a lot more had happened in those three days than she was letting on.

Reaching out, Jax scooped up the sleeping fox and set it in

Monique's lap. The little creature stirred but quickly settled, and he gathered them both and put them on his lap, circling his arms around Monique, trying to create a bubble of safety for her.

Giving her time to get herself together, he didn't push, just smoothed his palm the length of her spine, offering her comfort and he hoped strength. Not because Monique didn't have strength in spades, but because every now and then, everybody needed a little boost.

"There was another girl. He didn't mean to take her. She was in the wrong place at the wrong time. Saw him shoving me in the back of his car. He didn't have a choice. Had to take her or she'd tell. She was younger than me by a couple of years and so scared. He said she was expendable, not worth anything because she was a scholarship student and didn't come from a family with money, but she was a human being, *that* made her worth something. It's not money that gives us worth. When he got the money, he was going to kill her and let me go, but I begged and pleaded, and in the end, he asked what I was willing to pay to secure her life."

Monique didn't have to say what she'd paid for the other girl's life with.

Her own body.

Raped when she was only fourteen.

"When I got home, my dad and grandparents wanted me to act like it never even happened. They said I was alive, and dwelling on what I'd gone through wouldn't be productive. Any time I cried or had a panic attack, they acted like I was being unreasonable. So over time, I learned to bury my feelings, let them out only when I was in private."

Trauma on top of trauma.

By not letting her deal with her ordeal and getting her help, they'd only compounded things. Things like that never just went away, and you didn't just get over them, especially when you were only fourteen years old.

"That night, when we were run off the road, I thought it was because of me. That they were taking me for ransom, and you were going to be collateral damage." Tilting her head up she met his gaze squarely. It was still swimming with tears but so far she'd held them in. "I don't think this was a ransom abduction."

The urge to tell her everything was on the tip of his tongue, but instead, Jax just shook his head. "I don't believe it was."

"And I don't think it was because of me, was it? These were your enemies. You said sorry to me in the car after the crash. Everything is blurry, but I remember that."

"My enemies," he agreed, offering her what truths he could without piling on more pain when she was already so emotionally vulnerable.

"The weather is getting colder. Soon it's going to be too cold for us to survive even with the fire, isn't it?"

"Yes."

"And we're still lost."

"Still lost."

Shifting the sleeping fox back to the ground, Monique shifted until she was facing him, her hands framing his face. "I don't think we're going to survive."

"I'm going to do everything—"

She cut off his words by crushing her mouth to his. "I know you'll do your best, and I don't blame you," she whispered against his lips. "But if we're going to die out here, I don't want it to be without having made love to you. Please don't say no this time."

~

November 4th

6:40 P.M.

If Jax said no this time, Monique wasn't sure what she was going to do.

Despite the freezing air around them, inside she was burning with fiery desire and only Jax could quell that dizzying need.

"Please only say no if you don't want me," she murmured. "I don't care about any other reason, I just want you. Need you. So unless you don't want me then please say yes. Please give me what I need."

Monique couldn't explain it, she just knew she needed him.

Rejection—again—would shatter the thread of trust that had been there immediately upon meeting him and only grown in the last several days. That thread was already almost unbreakable, and she wanted to feel it solidify, the connection between them acknowledged and acted upon.

Especially if they were going to die out there.

While it was way too soon to say that she was in love with this man, what she felt for Jax was unlike anything she'd ever felt for another man. It was the beginning of what could one day turn into love if it was nurtured and cared for.

Something she might never get a chance to do.

Dying was a real possibility, more real with each passing hour, so if she didn't have the time to fall in love with him, then she at least wanted to feel him inside her.

Those dark eyes of his studied her carefully, searching for the truth, to see if this was what she truly wanted.

It was, and Monique allowed him to see that. The only reason she could think of that she wouldn't want to make love to him was if he was using her for her last name, but that wasn't the case. In fact, it was almost like Jax liked her in spite of her last name.

"You really want this, princess?" His hands on her hips reminded her of the last time she'd tried this, and she found herself almost waiting for him to lift her off him.

But he didn't.

Instead, his grip on her tightened until it was just shy of painful, and he pulled her tighter down against him until she could feel his thick erection pressed into her wet center.

"I really want this. I'm falling for you, so fast it's scary, and yet at the same time it's not. It's the safest feeling in the world. I'm clean, and I'm on birth control even though it's been almost eighteen months since my last relationship ended. I just ... I know things can happen ... against your will ... and I like to know I'm at least protected against pregnancy if the worst happens."

Something flared in his eyes that she assumed was the anger she'd felt tightly coiled inside him as she told him her story. But there was tenderness and affection in them, too, and she knew.

Jax was going to say yes.

"I'm clean too."

"Then we don't have to worry about not having a condom," she said, grinning as she rocked her hips against the bulge in his pants. If it felt this good with layers of clothes between them, how amazing would it feel when he finally slid inside her?

"We don't have to worry about a condom, but *you* have to worry about how many times I'm going to make you come," he told her with a smug smile, his dark eyes now burning with desire. "I think I'm going to start with my tongue."

Before she could utter a word, Monique squeaked as he grabbed her knees and flipped her so she was lying on her back on his legs, with her legs thrown over his shoulders.

"Oops, should have gotten these out of the way first," Jax said as he put her legs back down long enough only to strip her out of her borrowed pants and her panties. "You make me so crazy I can't even think straight," he told her as he hooked her knees back over his shoulders, leaving her spread wide before him.

Maybe if it were anyone else, she'd feel embarrassed but with the hungry expression on Jax's face there was no room for embarrassment.

No room to feel like anything other than the princess Jax kept calling her.

"So beautiful, spread out before me like this, princess, so perfect," Jax murmured as he touched the lightest of kisses to the inside of her right thigh. "Do you know how lucky I feel that you want me?" Another kiss, this time to her left thigh.

Her bare center was practically begging to feel his lips, and she wasn't ashamed that she whimpered as her hips pressed closer, trying to find what they so desperately sought.

A chuckle rumbled through Jax. "So anxious, so greedy, aren't you, princess?"

"Y-yes," she murmured, her cheeks flushing, and she wasn't sure if it was because of desire or slight embarrassment at how greedy to take everything he could give her she really was.

"So desperate to be touched here." Finally, his lips brushed her center, but they were gone far too quickly, making her whimper again.

"Jax," she pleaded.

"Yes, princess?" He arched a brow at her as he looked at her from between her spread legs. "Tell me what you want. Beg for it."

"Please, I need you."

"You need me to do what?"

"To t-touch me."

"Touch you how?"

His mouth was so close to her center that she felt each puff of air from every word he spoke, and it stoked the fire already raging inside her. "With your mouth. I want to feel your lips, and your tongue, your teeth."

"My teeth, huh? My princess isn't all sweet and vanilla, is she?"

"No. She doesn't want to be treated like a princess right now, she wants to be devoured."

Like her words were a match that took the fire inside her and set it alight in Jax, he groaned and then his mouth was on her.

That first touch of his tongue had her gasping, and then all she could do was absorb everything he was doing to her as his mouth was all over her, suckling her bundle of nerves, scraping his teeth over the sensitive bud, his tongue teasing her entrance. His palms pressed against her thighs, somehow opening her further, and his thumbs circled her entrance while his mouth went back to her bud, lavishing it with attention.

"Jax, more, more," she whimpered.

Slowly, his thumbs slipped inside her, both at the same time. After stroking a few times, he pressed against her walls, opening her so his tongue could delve deeper.

Her eyes rolled back in her head, as without even thinking, her hips rocked against his mouth.

"That's right, princess, ride my face, take what you need," Jax praised as his mouth alternated between thrusting his tongue into her and claiming her bundle of nerves, sucking it harder and harder while the tip of his tongue swirled around it.

Something powerful began to build.

It started low in her belly, a slight tingle.

It grew quickly.

Quicker than she could process.

Claiming each cell of her body as it spread.

Crescendoing into something stronger than she'd ever felt before, when it finally burst, it felt like fireworks had gone off inside her. Pleasure fired along every nerve ending, making stars burst behind her closed lids, and through it all, Jax licked and stroked her, giving her every drop of pleasure that he could.

Finally, it began to ebb, leaving little aftershocks in its wake.

"I want you inside me now, Jax," Monique said as he lowered her legs from their perch on his shoulders, and she reached down to free his impressive length from his pants and boxers. "But I don't want soft and sweet. I don't want to be a princess right now. I want hard, fast, and passionate like you can't get enough of me. I want bruises and teeth marks because you're so crazy for me you can't control yourself."

It's what she'd always wanted but never been brave enough to ask for.

Jax made her feel brave.

Made her feel invincible.

"My princess has a wild side," Jax said as he leaned in to nip at her bottom lip.

"Not a princess right now," she reminded him.

"You'll always be my princess."

The words didn't have time to sink in before he gripped her hips and lifted her, burying himself inside her in one smooth thrust. For a second there was a small sting as her body accommodated his size, but it quickly morphed into pleasure as he gave her everything she asked for.

Setting an almost frantic pace, one of Jax's hands stayed on her hip, the hold he had on her definitely hard enough to leave a few bruises behind. His other hand shoved her clothes up, baring her breasts, and after touching kisses to each nipple, making them both pebble, his lips found hers, and his hand took over teasing her breasts. Each tweak of her nipples as he rolled them between his thumb and forefinger sent sparks straight between her legs.

The bruising kisses, the rough way he massaged her breasts, the feel of the rough callouses on his fingertips as they brushed over her hardened nipples all felt so amazing that pleasure quickly spiraled to life inside her.

"You need to come now, princess," he ordered, voice tight as he was obviously restraining himself, holding in his orgasm so they could come together. "Touch yourself," he ordered.

Powerless to do anything but obey, Monique reached between where their bodies joined and touched her sensitive bud.

"Harder, faster," Jax growled, then the hand that had been on her breast gripped hers, and he forced her to work her bundle of nerves at the same pace that he was relentlessly thrusting into her.

The spirals of pleasure grew stronger.

Unfurling through her body.

Then his mouth claimed one of her nipples, sucking hard, before his teeth sank into her breast and the unexpected burst of pain detonated a bomb of ecstasy that claimed her in a fiery burst that had her screaming his name into the otherwise quiet forest.

She felt him come inside her as he found his release, and the combination of that and his tongue now lapping at the bitemark on her breast had her feel well and truly claimed.

Exactly like she'd wanted.

With a sleepy smile, Monique sank down to rest against Jax, keeping him buried inside her, not ready to lose that connection yet.

"Was that everything you wanted, princess?" he asked as he tugged her clothes back down to cover her chest, then tucked her head under his chin.

"Everything. It was perfect. Thank you for not treating me like I'm a fragile china doll."

"You're not, princess. You're a strong, brave, powerful warrior, fighting for those who need you, like your little buddy there. We put on quite the show for him."

Monique laughed as she looked over at the fox. "He slept through the whole thing."

Jax hugged her tightly, then touched a kiss to the top of her head. "Do you want me to clean you up before we try to get some sleep?"

"No. I don't want to move yet, I'm not ready to let you go. I don't think I'll ever be ready to let you go," she murmured, clenching her internal muscles around his softening length still buried inside her, maybe giving too much away about how she was already feeling, but not caring in the least.

She'd found her person, her other half, her soulmate, she was sure of it, and she couldn't imagine a single thing ever being big enough to come between them. Jax was her forever, whether that be until they were old and gray or until they perished out there in the forest.

CHAPTER *Nine*

November 5th
11:25 A.M.

It definitely made him a bad person that he couldn't regret having sex with Monique even though he was lying to her.

Jax knew the smarter option would have been to say no and find a way to let her down gently, but she'd been so open with him, allowed herself to be so vulnerable, and she'd begged and pleaded with him not to reject her.

How was he supposed to say no to that?

It didn't matter how smart it was, telling her no would have snapped the bond growing between them.

Just as surely as telling her the truth would.

Only ...

Maybe she would understand.

She'd been raped when she was fourteen, bargained with her body to save another girl, so she would understand why his family had to do whatever it took to get justice. She'd get that coming to France to meet up with her at that Halloween ball wasn't about hurting her, it was just about trying to use anything they could to get answers.

Monique would understand. She had to.

At least that's what he kept trying to convince himself of.

Because the alternative was that he would lose her.

It shouldn't have been him who came to France to make contact. One of his brothers would never have developed feelings for Monique, they were all madly in love with their girlfriends. They would have been able to keep clear heads, keep focused on the mission, and not allowed themselves to get distracted by falling for her.

Only at the time, one of them falling for her wasn't even a consideration.

His brothers hadn't felt comfortable leaving the women they loved after the ordeals of the last couple of months, and Jax had wholeheartedly agreed.

It made sense for him to come, being the only single one, and no one, certainly not himself, could have foreseen what would happen the moment he laid eyes on the beautiful inside and out Monique Kerr.

Falling for her was a blessing and a curse because she was everything he'd never considered wanting, and everything he was going to lose when the truth came out.

"You seem so lost in thought today," Monique's voice pulled him out of his head. "Are you having regrets about what we did last night?"

Stopping abruptly, he grabbed Monique around the biceps and hauled her off the ground and into his arms. Giving out a little squeak, her legs automatically wrapped around his waist. Since she had the fox in her arms and couldn't hold onto him, Jax made sure he had one arm under her bottom, supporting her weight, the other curled around her back, anchoring her to him.

When he looked at Monique, at the doubt in her big gray eyes, it was hard to believe this was the same woman who had asked for hard and rough, not to be treated like a china doll. Monique was not a fragile, breakable doll, and he'd never come harder in his life than when he sank his teeth into her soft flesh and she screamed, her internal muscles clamping around him.

But beneath her strength was a vulnerability that came with having to navigate the world alone. Without a team to have her back. How exhausting that must be. While his life had been rough in a lot of ways, he'd always had Jake beside him, and then later Cade, Cooper, Connor, and Cole. He always had a purpose and people to work toward it with.

Monique had no one.

"Don't regret a single second of it. Never could," he said fiercely. No matter what happened next, whether they died of exposure and hypothermia in the French forest, or made it back home where he'd be forced to tell her the truth, he could never regret what they shared.

If anyone was going to regret them having sex, it was going to be Monique.

It gutted him to know that she would as soon as she learned their meeting at the gala was no accident, even as he knew he had no one to blame for his predicament but himself. Telling her right after they'd gotten away from the men and the van would have been best. The danger of what had almost happened would have been fresh, and they hadn't bonded too deeply at that point. Knowing what he did about her now, he wouldn't have worried about her running from him. Maybe she would have kept an emotional barrier between them, but she'd just witnessed him kill to protect her so she would have stuck close to him even if she didn't like it.

Should haves.

Would haves.

Could haves.

None of them mattered now.

What was done was done, and he had to make the most out of it and hope for the best.

"Do you regret it?" he asked, forcing himself not to hold his breath as he waited for her answer. Knowing she would regret it when she learned the truth was one thing, but if she regretted it now, a piece of him would shrivel up and die. Jax had never given this much of himself to a woman. Never given this much of himself to anyone who wasn't family.

Crushing her mouth to his was her answer, and it wiped away any fears he had.

He hadn't lost her.

Yet.

And he was prepared to fight for her.

Just because she was going to be hurt when she learned the truth about why he'd been in France didn't mean he was just going to give up. He'd find a way to prove to her that he'd never meant to hurt her, that he and his family had been desperate. The alternative was losing her, and he wasn't sure he could survive that. Not emotionally anyway.

This woman had turned up in his life at a time when falling for a woman was the last thing on his mind, even though he'd just watched all five of his brothers partner up. He hadn't been interested, hadn't thought he was ready, but Monique was everything, and he'd fight for her with everything that he had.

"Guess that answers my question," he said with a chuckle as he reluctantly set her back on her feet. The temperature was dropping further, and they needed to keep walking to maintain their body temperatures.

"Mine too," she told him with one of those charming smiles that managed to be both shy and confident all at the same time.

Just as he was reaching out to take a turn carrying the fox, Jax saw it.

Footprints.

About three yards from where they were standing.

Someone had been there, and recently.

"What?" Monique asked, looking around them, instantly picking up on his change in demeanor.

"There," he said, pointing as he stepped closer to try to determine how many sets of prints there were.

"Looks like ... footprints?" Monique asked as she followed close behind him.

"Yeah."

"Someone is out here." The thread of fear in her voice was obvious, and he wished there was something he could do about it. But until he knew who the prints belonged to he couldn't.

"At least four someone's."

"Do you think we're near a house, or a road, or a village, or something?" she asked hopefully.

"Could be. Or it could be ..." Jax trailed off, not needing to finish the sentence. It could be more of her father's men, sent out to find them. If it was, he wasn't going to look for them with Monique and the fox in tow. "I want you to hide."

"Hide?"

"Up a tree. Should keep you out of sight until I know what's going on."

"I don't want to leave you." Her eyes pleaded with him, but this was the safest option. If it was help and safety he'd come back for her, but if it wasn't then he at least bought her some more time, which was about the best he could hope for right now.

"Don't want to leave you either, princess." Leaning in, he touched a kiss to her forehead, then took the fox from her arms. There was no way she was going to leave it behind so he may as well help her out with it. "If it's them then as soon as you hear gunshots, I want you to wait up here for as long as you can, then climb down and keep walking. I'll tell them that you died, and I left your body behind days ago. They'll want to confirm that so they'll head off in the opposite direction. That should buy you enough time to keep walking in the direction we were heading."

"You're talking like you're not coming back. Jax, I don't want you to trade your life for mine."

"I absolutely will if I have to," he told her honestly. Since he didn't want to waste time arguing, the men could be nearby still and hear them, he wrapped an arm around her waist and boosted her up to a branch on the closest tree. "Since you'll have to get down on your own, I'm going to give you the little guy now. Don't go too high, just a few more branches and you'll be hidden. Here, take this as well," he added, shoving one of the weapons into her arms.

Doing as he asked, when she and the fox were another three branches up, he took one last look at her, aware that this could be it. The end of what could have been the best thing to ever happen to him. Cut short far too soon.

"Be careful, Jax," she whispered. "Come back to me."

"I'll do everything I can to make that happen, princess."

With that, he turned and crept away, a weapon in his hands, keeping his steps as light as he could to make the minimal amount of noise.

Failure wasn't an option, not when Monique's life was dependent on him.

He had no plan, he couldn't until he knew what he was up against. All he had was a fierce determination to protect his girl. Because, hell yeah, she was his, and he'd do anything he had to prove it to her.

But first, he had to find out if this was a threat or the break they'd been praying for.

Jax got his answer a moment later when he passed a tree, only to come face to face with the barrel of a weapon.

~

November 5th
12:03 P.M.

How long was she supposed to stay there?

Not only was Monique freezing just sitting up there in the tree in the middle of the forest, but she was hurting and uncomfortable. Balancing herself on the branch would have been hard enough, but keeping hold of the wriggling little bundle in her arms, plus a weapon, made it almost impossible.

Already, she'd almost tumbled off her perch three times.

Of all the times for the fox to decide he was ready to move about on his own, which was a good thing because it meant his injury was healing, it had to be now.

Now when there could be people with guns hunting her.

Now when Jax had gone off to try to stop them from hurting her.

Now when she was so terrified for him, she could barely breathe.

Even though she understood why he didn't want her to follow him when they didn't know who those footprints belonged to, and knew it could be the people after him, it didn't make it any easier being left behind to wait.

Monique was finding that she didn't like the idea of not having Jax close. How was that going to work exactly if they did make it out of this and get back home?

It wasn't like they were ready to move in together. They still had a lot to learn about each other, and while she felt a bond with Jax and absolutely one hundred percent wanted to nourish it and help it grow, she also didn't just want to jump headlong into something. She had to meet his family, and unfortunately, at some point he would have to meet hers. They'd have to find out how their lives and jobs would mesh. It wasn't like she could just move away from her animal rescue, but she also couldn't expect him to uproot himself from his family.

So many things to talk through.

Things they'd avoided for now because they were both focusing on just trying to survive, and maybe they were both a little nervous about how quickly they'd developed feelings.

At least Monique knew she was.

It was crazy, and yet she couldn't deny it was happening.

From the first second she laid eyes on him, she'd felt a pull, urging her toward him, and the more she learned about him, the more time she spent with him, the more she believed nothing could make her not like Jax.

He was out there right now, putting his life on the line for her, just like he'd done when they were abducted. He could have left her behind in that car, made a run for it, she was unconscious, might have been dead before she even knew what was happening.

But he hadn't left.

He'd stayed.

Protected her.

Killed for her.

Now he was doing it again, and she couldn't sit there a moment longer.

"Try not to squiggle too much and get us both killed," she warned her little fox, who whined at her, but stayed still in her arms as she awkwardly made her way down the tree.

Thankfully, her feet hit the ground without incident, and then she was sneaking off in the same direction Jax had gone. She was well aware this could be a huge mistake she was making, but she'd waited for what felt like hours and hadn't heard any gunshots.

What if there were none?

It wasn't like she could stay there forever.

They might be beating Jax to get him to tell them where she was. She had to go and help him.

It wasn't safety he'd found. If the footprints led to houses or a village, or just people out for a walk, then he would be back for her already.

With zero plan in mind, she followed the prints in the ground until she heard voices up ahead.

Multiple men, having what sounded like a hushed conversation.

No screaming.

That had to be a good sign.

Maybe Jax had found help after all, and it was just taking him a while to sort things out before coming back for her. He wouldn't leave her alone in the tree, cold and scared, worrying about him, just for fun while he relaxed and chatted with whoever had been out there.

Just in case Jax hadn't found the men yet and it was just whoever had been out there wandering around, Monique approached quietly, moving slowly, so that her steps barely made a sound, clutching the gun tightly, although she wasn't sure she would have the guts to use it. Through the trees ahead, she could see several figures dressed in black. They looked just like the men who had attacked and kidnapped them, they even had weapons slung on their shoulders.

Had they already killed Jax?

It wasn't like shooting someone was the only way to kill them.

But if they had shot at him, why hadn't Jax shot back?

He had the other five weapons from their abductors. He could have killed at least a couple of them before they got to him.

The voices got louder the closer she got, and her anxiety continued to climb.

Please be okay, Jax.

I don't want to lose you when I just found you.

Just then, she saw him.

Standing right there with the four men in black, he looked completely calm and at ease, and she wondered if these were his brothers come looking for him.

Relief almost had her calling out and running forward. He might be mad that she hadn't stayed in the tree until he came back for her, but she didn't care, she just wanted to be close to him.

Then she heard him speak, and she froze.

"No, I didn't ask her," Jax said.

Ask her?

Ask who?

Herself?

What did he need to ask her?

And why was he talking with his brothers instead of backtracking to her? If he'd ascertained that these men were no threat, he should have come right back. What was more important in that moment than making sure she knew he was alive and they weren't about to be captured again?

Knowing eavesdropping was wrong, and that you never heard anything good, Monique pressed herself against the nearest tree trunk and listened in.

"What do you mean you didn't ask her?" a man spoke.

"Time was never right," Jax muttered.

"Time was never right?" a different man repeated. "You've been out here for five days, I think that's enough time to see what she knows."

See what she knows?

They had to be talking about her, right?

Who else could they mean?

But what was Jax supposed to ask her? And why hadn't he asked her this question over the last five days?

"I needed her to trust me," Jax said, slightly sullenly, sounding nothing like the man she'd been getting to know.

Why wouldn't she trust him?

He'd done nothing to indicate that he didn't have her best interests at heart, had stuck by her when he didn't have to, and survived along with her these last few days.

"If she knew I was at the Halloween gala for work, she might not have been inclined to stick close to me," Jax continued, obviously completely unaware she was listening to his every word.

Jax was at the charity ball for work?

Wait, that didn't make any sense.

She'd almost crashed into him right at the beginning of the event, and they'd left almost immediately. If he was there for work, although what work he'd be doing at a charity Halloween gala she had no idea, then why would he leave? If he left, he couldn't do whatever work it was that he'd gone for.

Oh ...

For a moment, it felt like her heart stopped beating in her chest as reality sank in.

She was the job.

He was supposed to be there to ask her something, which he hadn't yet done because he wanted her trust.

Trust she'd given freely and without reservation.

While she didn't recall doing it, she must have made some sort of noise because the next thing she knew, she was surrounded by big men in black, including Jax. Five weapons pointed at her, but when they saw it was her and not a threat they all lowered them.

Anger and humiliation warred inside her now that she knew the truth.

Jax was nothing but a liar and a user just like everybody else. No matter how much she wanted to be seen for herself, for who she was and not what people thought she was, it never seemed to work out for her.

This betrayal hurt worse than all the others combined, because she hadn't just trusted Jax, she'd allowed herself to develop feelings for him.

"Monique, you were supposed to wait in the tree for me to come and get you," Jax said, taking a step toward her, care and concern on his face that added fuel to her anger.

How could he pretend that he wasn't using her? That nothing about their interactions had been real?

He was a good enough actor to fool her before, but no longer.

"Yeah, you would have liked that, wouldn't you?" she snarled in a voice she'd never heard herself use. No matter how angry she got, she always bottled it up, never unleashed it, it wasn't ladylike according to her grandmother, but more than that, she just always believed nobody cared so what was the point in yelling. Wouldn't change anything.

Now she was the one who didn't care.

Jax had taken her feelings, twisted them, and used them to his advantage, and she wasn't just angry about it she was downright livid.

"Would have liked continuing to play your little game, using me, toying with me, just like everybody always does. Well, you can just go to hell, Jax, all of you can. I don't care what question you came all the way to France to ask me, you don't deserve an answer."

With that, she held her head up high, hugged her little fox tight, and brushed past all five men to stalk away. She didn't know where she was going, and quite frankly, she didn't care. It would suit her perfectly if the earth just opened up and swallowed her whole to put her out of her misery.

CHAPTER *Ten*

November 5th
12:34 P.M.

This was not how it was supposed to go, Jax thought in a panic as he watched Monique walk away from him.

She was supposed to wait in the tree until he came to get her. He would have thought up how he was going to approach things on the way, but instead, she'd overheard enough for her to lose all trust in him.

For him to lose her.

All the secrets he'd been keeping were falling like a house of cards and he didn't know how to stop it from happening.

"You and her ...?" Jake asked, the others moving with him as he went to follow her.

"It's complicated," he muttered, not ready yet to admit to his brothers that not only had he slept with the target, but he'd committed the most grievous of sins possible on an op. He'd fallen for the target.

After coming face to face with a weapon, he'd been prepared to open fire, kill as many of them as he could, and keep killing until every threat toward Monique was eliminated. But then he'd seen Cole's face and knew that it was his brothers who had come to find him. The relief had been instantaneous as he'd seen Cole, Connor, Cooper, and Jake, they were safe, rescued, and Monique wasn't going to die out there.

Now he hated that they were there.

Their presence was going to cost him the woman he was falling for.

If he'd been able to find a way out for them, he would have used the journey home to tell her everything, hoping that he could explain it in a way she understood. But now, having overheard that she was the op, that she was being used, everything that could have been was slipping through his fingers.

"Monique, wait," he pleaded as he darted around so he was in front of her.

The fury, hurt, and betrayal in the gray eyes that looked back at him made him stagger back a step. Of course, he knew she was going to be upset learning the truth, but he hadn't expected to feel like he was witnessing the storm of the century brewing in her gray eyes.

"I'd rather take my chances finding my own way out of here," she ground out through clenched teeth.

"I'm not going to let that happen, princess," he told her, gently but firmly. She could hate him, but he wasn't leaving her alone at the mercy of the weather, the environment, and the men who would be searching the forest for them. "Can I explain what you think you heard?"

"Don't treat me like I'm an idiot. I know what I heard, Jax ... if that's even your real name."

It hurt to know she was doubting everything, even down to the small things like his name. But Jax had to remind himself that he *had* lied to her about his name. From the moment he told her his name was Jaxon, he'd been setting himself up for this very moment, only back then he'd had no way to know he'd fall so hard and fast.

"My name is Jax," he assured her. "Not Jaxon. I couldn't stand hearing that fake name coming from your lips, so I gave you my real name."

If he'd hoped that small admission was enough to soften her a little toward him, he was sorely disappointed. Monique looked like she'd been carved from stone. She was standing so still, her body so obviously tense, that he wished he could reach out and massage that tension right out of her.

"These are my brothers," he added when she didn't yell at him to get away from her or order him not to explain.

Not that he would have obeyed the order, he needed her to know this wasn't about her, that his family had been desperate for her father's location because until they had it and him in custody, they weren't going to be safe.

"This is Jake," he said, pointing to his biological brother. "Then Cole, Connor, and Cooper," he said, pointing out each of his stepbrothers in turn.

Monique made no attempt to greet any of them, and wisely, they all remained silent. Jax could sense their disapproval. Not of Monique, but of him and how he'd allowed this to play out. He couldn't deny how badly he'd messed things up, but there wasn't anything he could do about it now.

One thing he was certain of, though, was that Monique wasn't a spiteful person. Despite what he'd done, if she knew where her father was, he was positive she would tell them.

"I told you about all of them," he reminded her. While yes, of course, he had been lying to her about why he was in France, everything else he'd told her was true. He'd just kept some important details to himself. "I also have a stepsister."

Her eyes widened at the revelation, and fury flared in them, along with the betrayal she wasn't bothering to hide.

Good.

He didn't deserve any concession from her, he deserved to know how deeply he'd hurt her.

"Her name is Cassandra. She's in trouble and she needs help. We all do. If you overheard that I went to the Halloween gala as part of a job, then you're right, but it's not how it seems. It's not you. At least not specifically."

"Just spit it out, Jax, so I can get as far away from you as possible," she snapped, her tone so much harder than he was used to. This was Monique Kerr with her guard up, and he didn't know how to get her to lower it.

Nodding, he stopped beating around the bush and just told her everything and prayed for the best. "I told you mine and Jake's mom died when we were small. That was true. I also told you our dad wasn't around much and that no relatives wanted to take us in and care for us. That was also true. And I told you that our dad remarried when I was twelve and Jake was fourteen. He remarried the widow of one of his Delta Force teammates, almost immediately after his team was ambushed. They all died except for our dad."

"Oh, I'm sorry." Sympathy flickered in her gaze, and she looked to his brothers who were standing around him. "That must have been hard to lose your dad that way."

"It was," Cooper told her, gently and offering her an encouraging smile.

"They weren't happy about their mom remarrying, but one night, not long after, agents raided our house in the middle of the night. They took their mom and our dad into custody and claimed they were traitors, but none of us believed it. Then they claimed they both committed suicide in custody, but we didn't believe that either. We found out they weren't sharing a bed, and we believed the marriage was a sham."

"I don't get it, why would it be a sham? And how do you know they weren't traitors?" Monique winced as she realized how bluntly she'd phrased the question and shot them all an apologetic look, but didn't take her words back.

"We believed in them back then and wanted answers. A few months ago, we started to get them. It turns out that my stepmom was raped," he said softly.

Monique visibly shuddered at the word, and he could see her clutch tighter at the little bundle in her arms. "I'm sorry she went through that."

"The product of that rape is alive and well."

"Cassandra?"

"Yeah. My stepsister, who was only five when our parents were arrested on false charges. Over the last few months, we've learned that my stepmom was in the CIA, and she was raped by four men while on an assignment in Egypt. When they learned there was living proof of that assault, we believed they tried to take her out of the equation. My dad and the rest of his team were collateral damage. One of the men involved is a world-renowned Egyptologist, he's dead. Another two died before we knew about them. But the son of one of the men, and this final rapist have been trying to silence my family for months. Trying to kill us."

The tension in the air was so thick you wouldn't just need a knife to cut it but a power saw.

"So far, we've survived every one of their assaults as we kept searching for names. Monique, we believe your dad is the last remaining rapist," he informed her as gently as he could.

She gasped and staggered back.

Instinct had him reaching out a hand to steady her, but the look she shot him had him stopping before making contact.

"My dad isn't a rapist," she hissed.

"Isn't he? How do you know that? You've barely had any contact with him your entire life," he reminded her, not to be unkind, just because she had no idea who her father really was. "He left you with his parents to raise after your mom left. He doesn't check in with you. You speak to him twice a year on your birthdays. He could be anything and you wouldn't know."

"This op wasn't about hurting you," Jake said, stepping closer. "We sent Jax in because he's the only one who's single, and after everything we've all been through these last few months, the rest of us wanted to stay home with our partners."

"We were hoping you would be able to give us the address of where your dad is hiding out since we've been unable to locate him," Connor added.

"We were desperate," Cole said, and Monique's stance softened.

"Look, I can understand that, and while I don't believe my dad is a rapist, if I knew where he was I would give you the address so he could prove it by giving you a DNA sample. In fact, *I'll* give you a DNA sample to prove that your sister isn't my sister. But I don't know where he is. Jax is right, I don't have anything to do with him and never have. I'm sorry."

Her words were everything he'd hoped to hear but hadn't allowed himself to believe she would ever utter, and Jax felt relief knock most of his remaining energy right out of him. She understood. Now he could take Monique home, and they could figure out what happened next.

But when he took a step toward her, she quickly backed up.

"I understand why you were desperate, Jax, but that doesn't make it okay what you did to me. I'm not all right with being used and treated like I don't matter. I'm sick of being treated that way. I'm not really stupid enough to walk off and stay out here when I have a way to get home, and I'll give you the DNA sample and even try to find out where my dad is so he can help you clear up this mess, but I don't ever want to see you or hear from you again."

With those firm words, that relief vanished, and he realized he'd lost her.

Whatever could have been was over.

And somehow, he had to find a way to live with the consequences of his decisions.

~

November 6th
4:46 A.M.

Finally.

The plane started its descent, and Monique let out what felt like her first real breath since the future she had been starting to picture in her mind completely fell apart.

All she wanted to do was get as far away from Jax and the rest of his family as possible so she was free to lick her wounds in peace. Here on the private jet with all of them watching her, she had to keep her game face on.

For once in her life, she was thankful for the lessons her grandmother had taught her as a young girl. One of them was how to keep her emotions to herself, something a lady should always do, according to her grandmother. While Monique didn't agree that she wasn't allowed to show her emotions, she was grateful that she knew how to paint on her mask of indifference.

Without it she'd only be adding to her humiliation.

She was absolutely gutted to know that while she'd been dreaming about this wonderful future, opening herself up, sharing parts of her past she usually kept hidden, and falling for him, Jax was only there to use her.

How stupid was she?

Why hadn't she seen the truth?

After all, what kind of man wanted to leave a fancy party just to hang out with her?

None of them.

That was the answer, and when Jax had been different and taken an instant liking to her, she should have known better. Should have been more cynical. Other than her name and all that went with it, why else would anyone ever think to look at her?

Letting out a sigh as the plane hit the runway, signaling the end of the ordeal the last several hours had been, she looked out the window at the dark early morning. It was weird to be back home, even though she should have returned a couple of days ago.

France had not turned out the way she'd envisioned, and in the worst possible way.

She hadn't just allowed Jax to have sex with her, she'd asked for the things she'd always wanted. Now those memories, which should have been badges of courage for her finally standing up for herself and her desires, felt dirty and tainted.

How would she ever be able to trust a man with what she needed again?

How would she trust anyone again?

It seemed this was a lesson she was doomed to have to learn repeatedly because she couldn't seem to get it through her head. The only way she was ever going to get a relationship where she didn't have to second-guess the person's reasons for being with her was if she married one of the men her grandmother was always trying to set her up with.

The problem was, if she married any of them she was basically pimping herself out as part of a business contract where her family could expand its wealth along with the family of whoever she married. It wouldn't be for love, and there was a good chance her husband would cheat on her as it would be a marriage in name only.

That wasn't the life she wanted either.

All she wanted was to just be her.

Just be Monique who loved animals and was a little shy and introverted unless she felt comfortable with the people she was with. No Kerr. Just take her last name right out of the equation so she could just be herself.

Too bad all that could ever be was a wish.

The plane stopped moving, and she unclicked her seatbelt and grabbed the bag someone had packed for her. She was grateful that Jax's brothers had assumed she would be with him when they found him and brought along a few outfits for her, so she wasn't stuck in the clothes borrowed from the dead guard. The jeans were comfortable, and the sweater soft and pink, the material brushing lightly against the bite wound on her breast.

Yesterday, that wound had been something she was proud of, now it was nothing but a slightly painful reminder of the biggest mistake of her life.

At least it would fade.

Unlike the emotional scars of opening herself up to a man who was only using her. Not just using her but had singled her out and traveled the globe to arrange a meeting. If he'd just asked her about her dad and explained his family's situation from the beginning, she would have been happy to donate a sample of blood for DNA testing. There had been no need for the whole charade.

Ignoring the guys—who had thankfully left her alone once they got on the plane to fly home—she headed out of the plane, dragging in a breath of fresh air. They'd all be flying on to Maine, but they'd dropped her off in Vermont first. Another thing she was grateful for.

Rifling through her purse, which Jax's brothers had collected from the crashed car, she pulled out her cell phone. Apparently, the small private airfield they'd landed in was about an hour away from her property, so she might have a bit of a wait for an Uber to come get her, but at least she'd be home soon.

"There's a car waiting to take you home."

Startling at the unexpected voice behind her, her hand flew to her chest where her heart was racing, and she spun around to find Jax standing just behind her. Unfortunately, her hand rested right above the bite mark he'd left behind, and she felt her anger surging.

Why couldn't he have just been honest with her?

Why play her like a fool?

Why have sex with her when he was only there to try to get intel from her?

It was such a violation of her trust, and it left her feeling dirty and used.

"Oh, uh, thanks," she mumbled. It wasn't that she didn't appreciate being able to get home quicker, it was just that everything felt awkward with Jax now. The amazing thing with him had been that from the very beginning, everything felt so natural, like she'd known him her entire life. Now she realized she'd never really known him at all.

How much of the last few days was real, and how much of it had been an act?

The problem was, she honestly didn't know, and that made none of it feel real even as she knew some of the things he'd told her had been true.

Because as far as she was concerned, there was nothing left to say, Monique turned and headed for the small building she assumed would lead to an exit, only to be stopped when Jax darted out a hand to circle her wrist.

"Wait, please, can we talk?" he asked, his voice lacking its usual confidence.

"I don't see what else there is to talk about." Nothing was going to change that their whole relationship, extremely brief though it had been, was a lie. Not because it had to be, but because he'd chosen to play things out that way.

"We were desperate, Monique."

"I told you I got it, I understand. Your family has been targeted over and over again, and I hate that you've all been in danger. I agreed to send you a swab so that you can do a DNA test and prove your stepsister isn't related to me. I don't know what else you want from me, Jax," she said wearily. As angry as she was and as much as she'd love to rant and scream at him, reality was she was tired, embarrassed, humiliated, and feeling stupid. All she wanted was to go home.

"I just want you to know I *never* meant to hurt you."

He was so imploring, his voice so sincere, his dark eyes practically begging her to believe him, but the problem was she wasn't sure what to believe when it came to this man anymore. Her trust in him had been obliterated.

Maybe if she hadn't been used because of who she was in the past it would be easier to get over. Jax's way of using her might be different than the other men who had hurt her, and she wasn't lying when she said she got why he'd done it, but in the end, it made her feel the same way.

Like she wasn't a real person.

She was only something to be used for what value she could offer.

It wasn't okay to treat her that way, and she wasn't going to allow herself to be put in that situation. Jax might be sorry now that he'd hurt her, but that didn't undo that hurt. Neither did understanding where he'd been coming from.

If she was overreacting, then that was her prerogative. Protecting her feelings was also her prerogative, after all, it wasn't like she had anyone else there to do it.

"Whether you meant to or not, you *did* hurt me," she told him. "You used me, reduced me to nothing more than my last name, and I'm so sick of that happening. I meant what I said in France, Jax. I don't want to see or hear from you again."

With that, Monique straightened her spine, turned around, and walked away.

It was the hardest thing she'd ever had to do, but it was the right thing to do for herself.

CHAPTER Eleven

November 6th
5:05 A.M.

"You just going to let her walk away?" Connor asked from behind him.

"Hell, no," Jax said, spinning around to find that all four of his brothers had followed him off the plane. "I'm not going to make the same mistake you did with Becca all those years ago."

When Connor's eyebrows all but flew to the top of his head, Jax winced, that hadn't come out the way he meant it.

The problem was, he was so messed up over losing Monique that he couldn't think straight.

No excuse, though. His brothers had hopped on a plane the second they lost contact with him, leaving behind the women they loved who had all been through traumatic ordeals these last few months. The absolute least he owed them was some respect and gratitude.

"Sorry, man, that came out wrong. I just meant that I learned from your mistakes, and I don't intend to repeat them," he explained.

"It's okay, Jax, I get it, and I'm glad you're not going to repeat the mistakes I made. But ..." Connor trailed off looking around at the others as though to ascertain that they were all on the same page before continuing. "Isn't it kind of fast to have developed feelings for her? You only met her six days ago."

"Cooper fell for Willow in Egypt in a matter of days," he reminded them, looking to Cooper who nodded.

"I did. We spent a lot of intense moments together, and seeing how brave and strong Willow was no matter what Tarek threw at her made it almost impossible not to fall for her."

He hadn't had much of a chance to talk through what happened with his brothers in detail before Monique found them in the forest, one thing his girl did not have was a good sense of time, he'd left her alone for no more than thirty minutes or so before she came after him. They also hadn't had a chance to talk on the plane because Monique was right there, and he wasn't comfortable sharing the details of what they'd gone through while she was able to overhear.

"Monique and I also spent a lot of intense moments together," he reminded Cooper and the rest of his brothers. "And she's every bit as brave and strong as Willow, or any of the rest of the women you all love, and I respect the hell out of all of them."

"She's the Kerr princess," Jake told him doubtfully, and Jax found himself getting annoyed.

This was exactly why Monique was angry with him. She was so used to being used and judged based on who her family was—something she had zero control over—that she just couldn't allow people in her life who did that to her.

"You know nothing about the real Monique," he growled at them, daring any one of his brothers to disagree.

"Thing is, do you? Do you know who the real Monique Kerr is, or was she fooling you every bit as much as you were fooling her because she needed you to stay alive?" Cole asked, not unkindly, more like he was just looking out for a brother, and Jax couldn't be angry at him for that.

"Look, it's not like that, okay? She's not like she's portrayed to be. She's sweet, shy, and introverted. She's funny and I enjoyed talking to her. She also shared some stuff that happened to her when she was a kid, allowing me to see her vulnerabilities."

Sighing, he dragged his fingers through his hair. This wasn't how he'd expected their homecoming to be. He'd pictured taking Monique back home with him, washing every inch of her beautiful body, then falling asleep in a proper bed with her in his arms.

Instead, she'd gone home alone, and she never wanted to see him again.

To make it worse, his brothers seemed to want to talk him out of caring about Monique, and he wasn't about to let that happen.

Any of it.

But he had to fight this battle first. If he was going to win over Monique, apologize to her and make it up to her for keeping secrets, then he needed his family on his side. Without their support, Monique would never feel comfortable with any of them.

"Since she didn't know about her father's involvement in all of this, she thought when we were run off the road that it was a kidnapping for ransom attempt. That those men were after her and not me. She believed that since it was her they wanted, because she's been through something like that before. Thought I was collateral damage, so she tried to make a deal for them to keep me alive." Once again, he raked his fingers through his hair, tugging enough to feel a sting in an attempt to let out a little of the raging emotions inside him every time he thought of her doing that for him. "She offered to let them use her body however they wanted if they didn't kill me."

For a long moment his brothers just stared at him in shock.

He got it. That didn't vibe with the image the media had of the young heiress, but that was just all it was. An image. Not the real Monique. Not the woman who hated being judged because of who she was and treated accordingly, even though none of the things she was portrayed as were true.

Monique deserved to be seen.

Not just by him, but by everyone and that started with his family.

There was no way in hell he was going to allow them to judge her when they didn't even know a thing about her. The fact that she'd offered them a DNA sample after he'd lied to her and she didn't even believe them should be enough to convince them she was not just a decent human being but an amazing one.

"I'm sorry she went through that," Cole said softly. None of them had to ask to know that he was thinking about how Susanna had been raped because Monique's father and the other men involved in this had thought she was Cole's girlfriend, and that hurting her would get them to back off in their search for answers. Susanna was now Cole's girlfriend, but at the time, she'd been nothing more than his neighbor who he hated.

"Yeah, me too," Connor added as he rubbed at his chest. His girlfriend Becca had been raped while they were in college and in the aftermath their relationship had crumbled until he tracked her down a couple of months ago and they rebuilt what they'd lost.

"She was prepared to go through that again to save me. I think she deserves your respect," he told them firmly. If there was any possible way for him to win Monique back, he would. He wasn't giving up on her, and if he was successful, his family would become her family. A family he wanted to love and care about her, give her what her biological one hadn't.

"No one is disrespecting her, Jax, we're all just surprised she's not what we expected," Jake assured him.

"And she's ... she's Cassandra's half-sister," Cole added.

"Half-sister who didn't have a great childhood, who doesn't have the same support system that Cassandra does, who isn't responsible in the least for her father's actions. She's just a woman looking to be loved and accepted, nothing more and nothing less. I don't want to have to choose sides, especially between two women who have done nothing wrong, but I won't allow anyone to disparage Monique for any reason," he warned, prepared and ready to draw his line in the sand. It was the least he owed Monique.

"You saying you'd pick her over your family?" Jake asked, eyes widening in shock.

"No. I'm saying I don't want to have to choose, but I can't explain how I feel about Monique, it was quick, but it was powerful. She's all alone, and I lied to her, I won't let her down again."

"We wouldn't ask you to," Cooper assured him. "You're right, Monique is already family. She might not believe it, but she's Cassandra's half-sister which means she's one of us."

"One of us," Connor repeated with a firm nod.

"We've got your back and hers," Cole added.

Jax looked to Jake, needing his big brother to get how important this was to him. They might not have set out to hurt Monique, but they had, and she didn't deserve that.

"I'm with you, brother," Jake promised. "You say she's important to you, and that's all I need to know. Everything we've seen over the last few hours supports that she's not the spoiled, pampered princess we were expecting. Whatever you need from us you have it."

"Right now, all I need is your prayers for a miracle. I'm not letting Monique go without a fight. She needs space and I'll give it to her. I'm going to watch over her and make sure her father doesn't decide she's become a liability. Then I'm going to figure out how to prove to her how sorry I am and that I'll never let her down again."

For which he would definitely need a miracle.

~

November 7th
6:52 P.M.

"Aww, thanks, my little cutie pie."

The first smile in days finally settled on Monique's lips as Cinderella came wriggling out of her specially designed crate that lived in the small sectioned-off backyard of the property. Since she'd been away, some of her staff had been tending to her favorite little creature in the whole world, and yesterday she'd gotten back too early in the morning to say hi.

Now it was evening again, and finally her little baby was waking up and ready to play.

Which was exactly what she needed.

She needed to do something to stop herself from thinking about the whole mess France had been. Maybe if she could stop thinking about it, she could finally ease the knot of emptiness clawing at her insides.

It was no way to live, but she didn't know how to make it stop.

When she thought about it now, it all sounded so stupid and fanciful, like she was Cinderella and she'd gone to the ball, met Prince Charming, and instantly fallen in love. Logically, she knew it didn't happen like that, not really, or at least not very often. Why would she think that she would be lucky enough to find a prince and fall in love in a matter of days?

Not really in *love* but there were feelings, strong feelings, and the whole time they'd been wandering that forest in France, trying to find their way out, she'd thought they were going to get a real chance to explore them if they lived.

Well, they lived, and now all she wanted to do was forget.

Because she was no Cinderella and Jax was no Prince Charming.

He was nothing but another liar who didn't really see her. All he saw when he looked at her was her last name and what he could get out of it.

Now granted, his reasons for wanting to use her were definitely unique, not like any of the other men who had used her, but in the end the result was the same.

She was nothing, not a real person, just a tool.

Just something to be used and discarded.

And that was exactly how she felt, all wrung out and empty, unsure of her place again. Something she'd worked so hard to overcome so many times before.

"You know what hurts the most?" she asked Cinderella as the hedgehog excitedly scrambled into her lap and then scurried up her arm to her shoulder, the little creature's favorite spot to snuggle.

It was silly to talk to an animal about her problems, but who else did she have?

It wasn't like her grandparents cared that she'd gotten her feelings hurt. If anything, they'd be annoyed that she'd left the Halloween gala with anyone who wasn't a billionaire. After all, they never gave up hope that she would finally do what they wanted and agree to marry an eligible—by which they meant man approved by them—bachelor and fulfill what they believed was her legacy.

While she was friendly with the people who worked with her at the rescue, she genuinely liked them and spending time with them, they weren't really friends. Certainly not people she could talk to.

So her options were to talk to no one or talk to Cinderella.

The little hedgehog was for sure better than nothing.

"It's the fact that he didn't see me. I thought ... I thought that he did. I thought that my last name didn't matter to him. In fact, I got the feeling that he liked me in spite of my last name, and that was so refreshing. I'm so tired of being nothing but the Kerr princess. I'm not that woman, and all I want is for someone to finally see *me*. Is that really so crazy?"

Her hedgie nuzzled into her neck, and she smiled and lifted a hand to stroke Cinderella's quills. Nudging the little one into her palm, she shifted Cinderella off her shoulder, touched a soft kiss to her little head, and then set her down on the grass and grabbed a small ball, rolling it and watching with another smile as Cinderella scampered off after it. Well as much as a hedgehog could scamper.

"I think that's something I have to stop hoping for. The facts are, my family is well known and has way too much money, that's always going to be all someone sees when they look at me. It's stupid to keep thinking differently. I'm not Cinderella, I'm just a regular old girl with a family name she doesn't want, and nothing is ever going to change that. There is no Prince Charming in my future. Well, at least not a human one," she said with a giggle that only sounded a little forced to her own ears.

Her little fox was there with her at the rescue. She hadn't introduced him to Cinderella yet, but she intended to because she wasn't going to rehabilitate and release the fox, she was going to keep him. The thought of not having him close led her to almost a panic attack.

Unexplainable though it was, she needed that animal.

So since he was staying, she was going to give him a name to match with Cinderella, and she'd settled on Prince Charming.

That definitely had nothing to do with the man she'd wondered if he could be the real-life answer to her fairytale dreams.

Jax was no prince, and she didn't mean that in regard to his level of wealth.

Those were things she'd never cared about. Of course, she wasn't naïve and knew that having money alleviated a lot of problems, but it also created a whole set of new ones. Especially when you were the shy girl at your expensive and exclusive private school who wasn't into makeup and clothes. Even as a kid, she'd known the only reason the other girls didn't bully her was because her family was wealthier than their own, and they wanted to keep her as an in.

"I'm so sick of being used," she shouted into the quiet evening, startling Cinderella, who came hurrying back over to her and nudged her hand for pets. It had taken her a long time to earn the trust of the orphaned baby, but now the little creature was so empathetic, a true friend, her little baby.

Complaining about Jax and his family was pointless. What was done was done, and she'd been truthful when she told them she understood they'd acted out of desperation and not with a malicious desire to hurt her.

But she'd also been truthful when she said using her wasn't okay.

Just because it was hard for her didn't mean that she didn't enforce her boundaries. Over the years, she'd become an expert at it. If she hadn't, she'd be living under the thumb of her grandparents and have been effectively sold off in a business partnership marriage as soon as she was legal.

Boundaries were important, but Monique longed to be able to lower them and let people in.

Like she'd done with Jax.

No one else other than the cops who had worked her kidnapping case, the doctors who had treated her, and the counsellor who worked with her in the immediate aftermath knew about the rape. For once in their lives, her grandparents had actually done the right thing for her and made every single one of them sign detailed NDAs.

More than a decade later, almost half her life, she had never found a person she was comfortable sharing those details with.

Until Jax.

She hadn't just given him her secrets, and she hadn't just given him her body. She'd also given him her heart.

Which had to make her the stupidest woman on the planet.

What kind of idiot gave out their heart to a man they didn't even know within days of meeting them?

Obviously, that answer was her.

She was that idiot.

Worse still was that Monique knew herself well enough to know that she would now close herself off even more as another man shattered a piece of her trust. How many pieces of trust did you have before you ran out?

It felt like she was dangerously close to running empty.

That wasn't what she wanted. She wanted a big family filled with love and laughter, the opposite of what she'd grown up with. She wanted people she could go to when she was sad, or angry, or happy. She wanted people who would share the ups and downs of life with her. She wanted to be loved and accepted for who she was as a person and not because she'd happened to be born into one of the wealthiest families in the world.

She just wanted to be seen.

Wasn't that what everybody wanted?

To be seen and accepted.

It sounded so simple, and for billions of people around the world, it was.

For Jax it was.

While she sat alone in her backyard, playing with her little hedgehog, he was at home surrounded by his family without the ache of loneliness in his chest that she had in hers.

An ache she was starting to wonder if it would forever be a part of her.

After all, she'd handed over a piece of her heart to Jax, so there was a piece missing now, one that she could never find and replace.

CHAPTER *Twelve*

November 7th
8:38 P.M.

The light shining from the simple cabin sitting in a small clearing in the trees called to him like a lighthouse, guiding him safely through the storm.

It was a beacon calling him in, and ignoring the call left his heart aching.

There was nothing in the world Jax would rather do than go storming into that cabin, sit Monique down, make sure she'd received the medical care she needed, cook her a nice hot meal, swaddle her in enough blankets so she'd never be cold again, and then make her listen to him.

Too bad life wasn't that simple.

The only thing that was even going to give him a chance at getting her to listen to his apologies was giving her a little space. It was the opposite of what he wanted to do, and it went against every instinct he had, but she'd told him no several times when he'd asked to talk, and the very least he owed her after lying to her was respecting her boundaries.

He just wished there was a way to sneak around them without upsetting her more.

But there wasn't, and he accepted that.

For now, he was focusing on what he could do for her rather than what he wanted to be doing.

Just because Monique didn't believe that her father was the fourth and final rapist who had set this entire mess into motion, he and the rest of his family did believe it. Believed it enough to act on it.

Which meant ensuring Monique was protected.

While he would love to believe that her father wasn't so cruel and heartless that he'd have his own daughter murdered just to keep his secrets, he had to accept it as a possibility. It certainly seemed like the men who had run them off the road and then driven them out into the forest had intended to kill them both. Even if they hadn't, Monique had been injured in that assault, so at the very least, he had to believe that her dad was okay with hurting her even if he wasn't okay with killing her.

Not something Jax planned on allowing to happen.

So after giving the car they'd hired to drive her home a head start, so neither she nor the driver noticed they were being followed, he'd said goodbye to his brothers, hopped in a car, and driven to her animal rescue.

It was set in a beautiful landscape, nestled deep in the woods. The fifty acres were divided into several sections, including one for her cabin and a backyard, one for a veterinarian clinic, one for an office block, and then several paddocks and buildings where they kept the animals they were caring for and rehabilitating.

From what he'd learned by looking up her rescue's website, it was that they were a no-kill shelter for dogs and cats. They also cared for and rehabilitated wildlife that were injured or abused, as well as some more exotic animals, that had been confiscated from people who had bought them on the black market. She had a great reputation and did a wonderful thing, saving the lives of hundreds of innocent animals over the years.

But there was one other thing he'd noticed about her rescue.

She didn't take safety and security seriously.

Well, not hers.

The animals were all afforded that care, but she didn't have a system in place to keep herself safe in the event that her rescue was attacked. Most likely she thought that was never going to happen, but with her father desperate, Jax wasn't going to take that risk.

So while she'd pottered around the rescue today, checking on how things had been running while she'd been away, he'd roamed the perimeter putting up security cameras. So far, he had about a third of the property monitored, and over the next couple of days he'd finish that off. While he'd prefer to know her house and the offices were being monitored around the clock, at least knowing he had the perimeter secured would help.

A little.

But not as much as being able to have eyes on Monique twenty-four-seven.

Now he was settled back in his car, parked close to the beginning of the driveway, hidden by the trees on the other side of the small road just in case someone should spot him. The last thing he wanted was to scare Monique after she'd just lived through a traumatic ordeal and should be resting and recovering.

Not that it looked like she'd done much of that today. The glimpses he'd caught of her had shown her moving slowly like she was in pain, not a surprise given the blisters he knew littered her feet. She also seemed to be curled in on herself, and he hated that he'd once again made her doubt her worth by judging her only on the basis of her last name.

How was he supposed to undo the damage he'd caused if she wouldn't give him a chance?

Frustration burned in his gut, but it wasn't directed at Monique, it was squarely aimed at himself. He was the one to blame, but he wanted a chance to put things right. And if she'd have him to make sure she never doubted herself again. No matter what her last name, she was a human being worthy of love, affection, and admiration.

When his phone began to ring, he glanced down at it, and it was only because he saw it was Cade's name on the screen that he answered. His oldest stepbrother was the only one of them with kids—not only did he have a recently turned five-year-old daughter, but a baby on the way—even though Jax wasn't sure that would be the case much longer.

His brothers were all in love, and he knew they were hanging out for this nightmare to end so they could begin their futures with the women who had stolen their hearts.

If Cade was calling, it meant Essie wanted to check in with him. The little girl was doing well after her own ordeal, but she'd become clingier to all of them, worrying about them all the time, whether they'd get hurt, and the last thing he was going to do was worry her further.

"Hey," he said when he answered the video call, immediately seeing that it wasn't just his niece who wanted to talk but his entire family gathered together. Monique's family, too, if she could let herself believe it.

"Uncle Jax, you have a booboo," Essie said, sounding dismayed as she moved closer to where the phone must have been set up to fit them all in the camera.

"Just a few small ones, I'm fine," he assured the child.

"How come you didn't come back here with everybody else?" Essie asked with just the tiniest hint of a pout.

"Because I have a friend who I didn't want to leave alone," he answered honestly.

Essie's eyes lit up. "A friend who's a girl?"

"Yes, my friend is a girl," he replied, already knowing where this was going.

"A girl you're gonna marry?" the little girl asked hopefully.

If ever there was a time to downplay what he felt for Monique, it would be now. It would also be kind of ridiculous after he'd all but drawn a line in the sand earlier. Besides, he didn't want to downplay things, he wanted to scream from the rooftops that Monique had barreled into his heart and lodged there.

"I don't know, but I do like her a lot."

"That means you're gonna marry her and I can be the flower girl," Essie said delightedly as she clapped her hands. She'd gotten a real bee in her bonnet about weddings and being a flower girl lately, even before her dad proposed to Gabriella, Essie's former nanny.

"Enough wedding talk for today, snuggle bug," Gabriella told the child. "Why don't you go read a little before bed, and your dad and I will be in to tuck you in soon."

"'Kay, Mommy," Essie agreed. "I miss you, Uncle Jax. Come home soon, 'kay?"

"Okay," he promised. Once the child had disappeared from view he looked at the others. From their expressions he knew they were worried about him, and while he appreciated their concern it wasn't warranted.

"I'm sorry for pushing you to be the one to go to France," Cade said. As the oldest he'd always taken on a heavy burden of responsibility for all of them, so it made sense that he would do it for this as well.

"I should have gone," Jake said.

"Right, sure, of course you should have, Alannah wasn't just out of the hospital or anything," Jax said with an eyeroll, catching the grin his one-day sister-in-law shot him.

"I could have gone," Cooper piped up. "Willow was all healed from what happened in Egypt."

"Becca and I talked about me being the one to go," Connor added.

"Susanna insisted that I do it," Cole said. "After all, I am the most charming."

The declaration made them all laugh, even as it was true. It was nice his brothers were all wishing they'd gone in his place so things hadn't gotten so messed up, but reality was he'd been the best choice then since he was the only single one, and none of them could have predicted that he'd fall for his target.

"I wish I'd gone," Cassandra whispered softly. "I'm the cause of all of this, and she's my sister. I know I could have convinced her that her dad—our dad—is dangerous. What if he tries to hurt her? I'm safe here with all of you, but Monique is all alone."

"Not alone, I'm here, and I'm not going to let her get hurt," he assured his stepsister. Sometimes it was hard to remember that Cassandra wasn't still that little girl he'd first met almost twenty years ago. She was such a beautiful, bright, strong, resilient young woman, and ever since they learned she'd been conceived via rape, she'd been carrying such a heavy burden.

"I just want this all to be over," Cassandra murmured.

"And it will be. Soon," he promised. "Truth is, as much as things are messed up right now, I'm glad I'm the one who went to France, because if I didn't, I never would have connected with Monique the way I did.

I'm not giving up on her, and as soon as we get her DNA sample and compare it to yours, we'll be one step closer to ending this."

Which meant that they were all in the most danger they'd ever been in.

They had Monique, and while she didn't know it, her father knew that her DNA would prove to the world that Cassandra was her half-sister. After that, it was only a matter of time before the dominoes came crashing down and they could prove Samson Kerr's involvement in everything and clear his dad and stepmom's names.

After that, they'd all be free, no longer bound by their long-ago promise to find the truth. Free to live their lives however they wanted.

His brothers and their partners were all safe, but he and Monique were alone out there, easy targets if her father decided to act. He wanted to believe he had what it took to protect Monique, but he didn't even have eyes on her, and they were surrounded by miles of uninhabited woods.

~

November 8th
2:17 P.M.

Fresh air was supposed to be good for the body.

Good for the soul, too.

And the air out there was fresh, clean, and full of the scents of nature. But it also reminded Monique too much of France and being with Jax in the forest.

Everything reminded her of him.

Her plan to just forget about him, mark him off as a mistake, didn't seem to be working out too well. It had been a whole forty-eight hours since she'd last seen him, and yet he consumed her every waking second.

When she ate, she thought of how he'd followed her lead and gone along with her finding them edible plants and berries to sustain them instead of hunting like his plan had been. When she took a step and felt the stinging burn in her feet from the blisters, she thought of walking for hours side by side, filling the silence with chatter and laughter as they got to know one another.

When she took a shower, she thought of how gently he'd used his handkerchief to clean away the blood on her face when they'd run away from the van after he'd killed all the men who had kidnapped them. When she climbed into bed last night, she thought of how he'd built them a fire to keep warm, then taken the side away from it when they slept so she'd have the benefit of both his body heat and the fire. She also thought of what a comfortable pillow he'd turned out to be and how safe she'd felt sleeping in his arms.

Every time she talked to one of her employees, she found her mind flashing back to sneaking up on Jax and the men he'd been talking to and overhearing him say that he was there for a job and had been using her.

Then there was her little foxy Prince Charming. Jax hadn't wanted her to carry the injured animal around with them, and she got why, it was an added burden to her already flagging strength. But she couldn't leave the fox behind, and now every time she looked at him, she'd be forced to remember Jax.

Jax, who hadn't turned out to be her Prince Charming.

It shouldn't matter, she shouldn't even *need* a prince charming. After all, she was doing a pretty good job of taking care of her life and herself without the help of anyone else. She worked hard, doing something she loved, contributing to society instead of living off her family's wealth. She shouldn't need saving, and she didn't, not in the Cinderella story kind of way.

What she just needed was for someone to see her.

For someone to care enough to search the ends of the kingdom to find her, just because they couldn't imagine their life without her in it.

Instead, she was alone, like she always was, wandering from area to area across her property, checking in on all her animals, making sure they knew without a shadow of a doubt that they were safe and cared for.

And if she never found anyone who made her feel that way, then she'd survive. Maybe she wouldn't find the happiness she craved, not everybody did, but that didn't mean she couldn't find another kind of happiness. Having a partner and family weren't the only ways to feel like you belonged.

Yet they were the ways she craved.

They were what she'd always wanted.

Her fairytale didn't have a prince, a castle, and a kingdom—she could already have all of those if she wanted—hers just had people. Lots of people. Lots of laughter. Lots of love.

That's what her fairytale dream was.

But that was the thing with dreams, they didn't always become realities, and she had to stop acting like they did.

With a sigh, she closed the stable door behind her, leaving behind the two little donkeys that had been rescued in a police raid on a meth lab and delivered into her care. They were healing well now that they had proper food and medical care, and one day soon they'd be ready to find a forever home.

Forever home.

Too bad nobody ever talked about that for people.

What she wouldn't give to find her own forever home. She'd thought that it might be with Jax, but that was clearly no longer on the cards. That didn't mean she couldn't find it with someone else, though. Dating was hard for her as an introvert, even harder because as soon as men found out who she was, their attitude toward her changed. But that didn't mean she shouldn't try.

There had to be a good man out there who wouldn't use her.

And if the thought of anyone other than Jax running their hands all over her naked body made her feel a little queasy, she was sure that feeling would pass over time.

As she walked through the trees toward her next stop, Monique suddenly felt like she was being watched.

Freezing, she spun in a slow circle, searching the trees for any signs that she wasn't alone.

There didn't appear to be anyone, she couldn't spot any shadows or any movement. The woods were quiet and peaceful like they usually were, nothing seemed different, and yet the feeling of eyes tracking her every move didn't fade.

"Brad? Angela?" she called out, wondering if one of the two workers there today had just been crossing paths with her and that was why she suddenly felt like she was being watched.

Nobody answered her calls, and she shrugged off the sensation.

More than likely, it was just leftover trauma from last week. After being run off the road, kidnapped, and forced to walk for days through the forest, it was no wonder she was on edge. After she'd been abducted when she was fourteen, she'd spent months living with the fallout. The constant paranoia, fear of the dark, fear of strangers, of being alone, the phantom feel of the man's hands touching her, of him inside her. She'd struggled to eat and sleep, she'd wanted to stay locked in her bedroom because nowhere else felt safe, and she'd lived in a constant state of waiting for someone to jump out of the shadows and grab her.

Just because things hadn't been as bad as they could have been this time around didn't mean she was going to walk away from the ordeal without consequences.

Forcing herself to brush off the feeling of eyes on her, she changed direction. She'd been going to check on a cow and her newborn calf who had arrived while she was away, but instead, she felt the need to go and check on her fox.

As badly as she didn't want to think about Jax, there was a sick sort of security in remembering how he'd killed for her. She believed that his intention had never been to hurt her, but he'd had so many opportunities to tell her the truth, and he hadn't taken any one of them. That was what was confusing. He'd had her alone. Why hadn't he just asked her his questions? Was it because he'd been afraid of losing her if he told her the truth? Believing that he hadn't meant to hurt her was one thing, but if she allowed herself to believe that he hadn't been lying about developing feelings for her, then she'd have to push too deeply to figure out if she'd made the right choice in not letting him talk to her.

It was easier to just cut him out of her life and work on pretending the whole thing hadn't happened. But that was easier said than done when she had the fox there. It was a permanent reminder of the ordeal, of Jax, of how he'd taken more than his fair share of turns carrying the little guy to give her a break.

Every word he'd spoken, every choice he'd made, every action he'd performed while they'd been together said that he felt that same pull between them that she did. It said that he wasn't lying, but the facts were, he *had* been lying, which left her all confused and emotionally strung out.

She didn't want to think about it, but she couldn't stop.

There it was again.

That feeling of being watched.

Was it possible the men who had attacked them in France had followed her home?

Just because she didn't believe that her dad was involved didn't mean that someone hadn't come after them. Her dad might not be a good dad, but that didn't make him a rapist and would be murderer. It didn't mean he had sent those men after Jax to silence him.

If she believed he was behind the attack, she'd have to believe that not only had he been absent from her life for almost its entirety, but that he was actually okay with her being caught in the crossfire so long as he protected himself.

Her dad wasn't that cold and selfish, was he?

Approaching the smallest of the barns on the property, which was where she'd set up her healing fox after having him thoroughly checked out by the vet she employed on a full-time basis, Monique slipped inside.

Scanning the space for a weapon, she found a rake leaning against the wall and picked it up, then positioned herself where the door would shield her when it opened. If it never opened, then she'd know it was only her overactive imagination causing her trouble, but if it did open, and she was right and someone had been watching her, then she wasn't going to go down without a fight.

CHAPTER *Thirteen*

November 8th
2:34 P.M.

This was a bad idea, and yet Jax couldn't seem to stop himself from doing it.

Monique obliterated all his common sense, leaving him a slave to his instincts, and his instincts screamed at him to go to her. To be closer. To watch her every move from a distance that was small enough that he could get between her and any threat that presented itself.

Last night, after ending the call with his siblings, he'd been unable to sleep in his car. It was too far away from Monique's cabin, and he couldn't get out of his head how remote her rescue was. It would be far too easy for a team to infiltrate it through the dense woods and spring an attack before he even knew there was a problem.

Since she was the only one who lived on the property, it would make it even easier for a team to slip in and grab her, or kill her, or do whatever they wanted to her and from his position across the street at the end of the driveway he'd be powerless to stop it.

So he'd slept on her porch, sneaking back to his car when he heard her get up in the morning. Then he'd spent the day following her around her rescue, watching with pride as she checked in with every animal who was staying there, even though she had staff members who were tending to them.

While he hadn't wanted her to realize that he was watching over her, didn't want to upset her, and she thought he'd gone back home with his brothers, it seemed she was onto him. He'd hated the fear on her face as she spun in a circle searching for something, for him, even though she didn't know it.

She was scared.

Of course, he'd known she couldn't walk away from their ordeal unscathed, but he'd hoped that being back home would make her feel safe again. From the look on her face, he'd been wrong, and he knew he had to let her know he was there and he wanted to install a top-of-the-line security system. Between following her around like a lovesick puppy, he'd been putting up more cameras, but it wasn't enough. He needed the whole place to be under surveillance so he knew the moment anything breached it.

Slipping into the building she'd entered, another barn, although this one quite small, and he already knew from watching her yesterday that this was where she was housing her little fox from France, he wasn't prepared for something to come swinging at him the second the door closed.

There was a grin on his face as he dodged at the last second, managing to avoid being struck with whatever his princess was wielding.

"Whoa there, wildcat," he said as he spun around and managed to dodge around her as she tried to swing the object—which turned out to be a rake—at him again. It was too long and too difficult to use as a proper weapon, and he was able to shift so he was behind her.

"Jax?" she asked incredulously as she froze.

"It's me, you're safe, no need to be swinging a weapon. Although we will need to have a conversation about your weapon choice. That is not a good one. While it keeps a bit of distance between you and an attacker, it also makes it easier for them to dodge your blows. Especially since it's hard to keep control of something long like a rake. You want something smaller in the future, although the move to stand behind the door where you wouldn't be immediately spotted and then act without hesitation was a good one."

"You're here to give me a lesson in self-defense?" She stared at him with wide eyes, and seeing her in her natural habitat, with her shoulder length brown locks in two pigtails, and comfortable jeans and a sweater clothing her, worn boots in what he could still make out was a soft shade of pink, had him grinning at her despite the angry look she was shooting his way.

"No, princess, not to give you a lesson." Although it wasn't a bad idea. She probably wouldn't go for him being her teacher, but he could have someone from Prey there before the end of the day to run through the basics with her.

"Don't call me that," she snapped.

The bite to her tone wasn't what he was used to hearing from her. She was so sweet and softly spoken, and yet she oozed passion and sincerity with every word that fell from her perfect lips. He'd heard fear and pain in her voice, but he'd only heard anger when she realized that there had been ulterior motives for his being at that charity ball.

"What are you even doing here? I thought you went home with your brothers after you dropped me off at the airfield." She still gripped the handle of the rake, her hold so tight that her knuckles had blanched white, and if she wasn't such a sweetheart, he would likely have thought that it was his neck she was imagining her hands wrapped around.

"No way in hell I was leaving you alone and vulnerable," he informed her. "And besides, my brothers didn't go home. They went back to where my family is hiding out until we can end this mess."

Straightening her spine, Monique let the rake drop, then crossed her arms over her chest. A defense mechanism, he knew that. She wasn't ready to accept the truth yet, and that he got. There had been a lot of times over the years when he or one of his brothers had been struck down by moments of doubt. Moments where they wondered if believing their parents were innocent was just because they couldn't handle the truth. Those doubts ate away at you over time, because deep down they all knew that neither his and Jake's dad, or Cade, Cooper, Connor, Cole, and Cassandra's mom would betray their country.

But those moments existed. And if it wasn't for the tangible proof that they clung to in the knowledge that their parents hadn't been sharing a bed, which meant the marriage was nothing more than a sham, then he could see the doubts overtaking things until he believed what everybody else did.

"By end this mess I assume you mean destroying my father," Monique said.

"If we don't take him out, he'll wipe out my entire family," he told her. "I can't let that happen. We've done nothing wrong. All we ever wanted was to clear our parents' names. They deserve that much. Now we just want to be free from the past, so we can focus on the future."

Her stance softened slightly. "I understand that. I truly do. I told you, Jax, I don't have a problem with you all protecting yourselves or wanting to find answers. All you had to do was ask me, and I would have helped in any way I could."

"I wish I'd told you the truth from the beginning," he told her honestly. If he had, there wouldn't be this gaping distance between them even as she stood three feet away.

"Me too. But you didn't. And because you didn't, you've just become another person who didn't see *me.* I know it's silly to be worrying about that when your family is in danger, but I can't help it. I've never been seen and ... I thought you were different. I thought you liked me. Me. Just me. Not the rich, spoiled heiress everyone thinks I am."

"Princess, I see you, I swear I do. I know you're not ready to talk, but I can't stay away. I'm sorry. I want more than anything to be able to respect your boundaries, but whether you're ready to believe it or not, I think your dad is involved. If I'm right and he is, then you're in danger. You've gotten too close, and I believe that his sense of self-preservation will override everything else. Including the fact that you're his daughter."

"I said I'd give you a DNA sample, then you can prove that you're wrong."

The fact that she hadn't already provided said sample, told him everything he needed to know. She had doubts. However small, they were there. A part of her was worried that the DNA test would prove that Cassandra was her half-sister. That alone wasn't enough for his family to prove that her father was a rapist, but it was something. Another step forward. Sooner or later, all these little steps would get them where they needed to be.

"I know you did, and I believe you will, but again, that's not why I'm here. I'm here because I can't stay away from you. I think about you every second. Dream about you in what little sleep I get. You're vulnerable out here, and the one thing I can do for you right now is protect you. I've already started putting up cameras around your property."

The blurted confession had her eyebrows almost jumping off the top of her head. "You did what?"

"On the perimeter, but I'm worried it's not enough. I want to put them around all the buildings and scattered throughout the trees."

"You want to be able to watch my every move?"

"Yes," he answered honestly. "I want to know without a shadow of a doubt that you're safe, and if you're not, I want to be able to get to you before anyone else lays a hand on you."

Taking a big chance, Jax closed the distance between them, standing close enough that she had to tip her head back to maintain eye contact. As badly as he wanted to touch her, he didn't, just soaked in the fact that she was right there, alive, and healthy, and so beautiful it hurt.

"I messed up. I didn't know I was going to fall for you when I agreed to do this. I thought at worst I'd dent your ego a little, get close, get a location on your dad, and disappear. I never thought I would fall for you."

"Fall for me?" she whispered, a delicate hope in her soft gray eyes.

"Fell so hard and so deep I won't ever be able to climb my way back out. Don't want to either. I'm sorry, Monique. For hurting you, for betraying your trust, for making you feel unseen. I know it's asking a lot for you to forgive me, and I understand maybe you won't be able to ever trust me again. But regardless of what the future holds, this world needs you in it, so I will do everything in my power to keep you safe."

Lifting a hand, he reached out and brushed his fingertips along her jaw, his thumb feathering over her bottom lip.

Then because he knew if he didn't go now, he'd have her in his arms, kissing her senseless until she had no choice but to forgive him, Jax turned and walked out of the barn, still clinging to the idea that he'd get his miracle and have his girl back soon.

~

November 9th
11:21 A.M.

Why did Jax have to say such sweet things?

It was so much easier to be angry with him when he wasn't standing before her, all strength and determination and sincerity, taking responsibility for his actions, and apologizing for them, and telling her he was going to protect her.

Whether she wanted him to or not was implied, even though he hadn't said those words out loud.

Hadn't needed to.

She heard them anyway.

And what did it say about her that a part of her absolutely wanted him to protect her?

Was she really that desperate to be loved that she would give a second chance to a man who had already shown her once before that he didn't really see her?

Yet that wasn't quite true.

Yes, he'd gone to France to meet up with her by "chance" at the Halloween gala, but back then, he hadn't known her. All he could know was the things the press said about her, and they never missed an opportunity to paint her as a silly, spoiled little rich girl. It wasn't like she could be angry with him for not being a mind reader.

It was that he hadn't told her the truth once he felt that connection. There had been plenty of time for him to. Even before they left the party, which she wouldn't have done had she known who he was, but she would have given him the DNA.

DNA.

She'd been putting off doing the swab and having it sent to the Prey lab they'd given her the address for.

Silly, but ... once she did this, there would be no going back. What if they were right? After all, they seemed pretty sure of themselves. If it turned out that Jax's stepsister was her half-sister, it would mean her dad had been lying to her practically her entire life.

According to Jax and his family, Cassandra was two years younger than her, which would mean that the time she was conceived was right before her mom walked out. Had her mom known about the pregnancy somehow, and left because her husband had been unfaithful?

That would certainly ease a little of the pain Monique had always felt about the abandonment. Although it wouldn't get rid of it entirely, after all, her mom had still left her behind even if she had reason to leave.

But a DNA test would only prove her dad had been a cheater, it didn't prove he was a rapist. While she'd had little to do with him, she just couldn't picture the stuffy man in the suit she rarely saw raping a woman. Her dad was always so ... bland. Quiet, withdrawn, never showing any emotion, joy, anger, or sadness, it was like they didn't exist for him. He'd never even cried when she'd been returned after being ransomed. Just patted her on the head once and then left her in the care of her grandparents like he always did.

She just couldn't picture him having enough interest in anything at all to do something so vile.

A knock at her front door had her shoving up from the couch where she'd been curled up thinking and watching the flames dance in her open fireplace. Of course, the fire made her think of Jax, but in the end, she was thinking about him anyway, she hardly needed the reminder.

It was like he'd permanently taken up residence in her head, and she didn't know how to get rid of him.

Or if she wanted to.

Her anger and hurt said she did, but the rest of her ... well, it wasn't so sure.

Since she'd clearly understood the whether or not she wanted him to part of Jax's speech yesterday afternoon in the barn, she hadn't objected to him putting up the security cameras. Truth be told, they would make her feel safer, and it was probably something she should have done when she first bought the place and was setting up the rescue. Her last name was still a threat, and she had employees she didn't want getting hurt because someone thought they could use her to make a quick buck.

Opening the door, expecting to find one of her employees come to check on her, or possibly even Jax, who she was pretty sure had slept in a car in her driveway last night, instead she was greeted by the sight of a woman.

A pretty young woman around her age.

With long, light brown hair hanging down her back, red and gold highlights glinting in the fall sunlight, and piercing green eyes, the woman stared silently at her.

It was her.

Cassandra.

And as she stared back at the woman, also in silence, she knew. The shape of her nose, the angle of her chin, and the small birthmark there. Those features combined with the unusual highlights of her hair, told her the same thing a DNA test was going to.

This woman was her father's daughter.

"Y-you look l-like ..." Monique stammered, a whirlwind of emotions raging inside her. "I look like my mom, but you take ... you take after him."

Cassandra gave a solemn nod. "May I come in?"

Almost tripping over her own feet, her body feeling like it had gone completely numb, Monique stepped back to allow the other woman to enter. Meeting a sister she'd never even known existed felt so weird. A part of her was excited, she'd always wanted a sibling, especially a sister, but the other part of her couldn't believe that her dad would cheat on her mom and create another child.

"It was my fault Jax went to France to find you," Cassandra said, guilt and regret in her pretty green eyes. "I was desperate. We all were, are, but I'm the one who put this all in motion. If I hadn't been conceived, none of this would have happened. None of it. My dad—at least the man I always thought was my dad—wouldn't have been killed along with his team. My mom wouldn't have been arrested as a traitor. She'd still be alive, they both would, and my brothers wouldn't have spent their whole lives focusing on clearing their names. My existence ... it ruined everything. Ruined all their lives."

When Cassandra burst into tears, Monique didn't even hesitate. She quickly wrapped the other woman in a hug and guided her over to sit on the couch.

They might not know each other, but Cassandra didn't hesitate to cling to her as she sobbed, and Monique just let her get it all out. Holding onto her little sister, because she was convinced that was what the woman was, she stroked her back and murmured reassuringly in her ear that she wasn't alone.

"None of that is true," she told Cassandra when the other woman's tears began to ease. "None of it is your fault. You being born didn't hurt anyone, you're not responsible for other people's actions. You have six brothers who love you, who would do anything for you. Do you know what I would give to have that?"

"But you have money, and power, and—"

"And that's all I have. Had. Well, no power, but money, sure. I also had a mom who walked out on me, a dad who was quite literally never around. Grandparents who wanted to mold me into a high-society socialite who was only good for being married off to someone who would add more unneeded money to the family. I would have traded it all for what you have in a heartbeat. You had a mom who loved you unconditionally, a dad who loved you even though you weren't biologically his, and six brothers who would go to the end of the earth for you. I can't say what's happened to your family is fair, it's not, it sucks big time. But you're not alone, and that's the one thing I've always been."

"I know I'm lucky to have such an amazing family, I don't mean to sound ungrateful," Cassandra said, and Monique quickly shook her head.

"I know you're not. I know you know the value of family."

"It's just ... ever since I learned how I was conceived, I just ... I feel so dirty."

They were sisters, yes, it was hard to deny it when Cassandra looked so much like Monique's father, but that didn't make her dad a rapist. She still couldn't believe he would do that.

"My dad ... our dad ... I can't ... I don't think he would do that. To your mom, I mean. I'm still not sure that it wasn't consensual." Wincing because she knew that sounded harsh, Monique offered an apologetic smile. "I know you don't want to think your mom would be unfaithful, but honestly, I think my mom left because my dad was so coldly disinterested."

"Or maybe she left because she knew the truth about what he'd done and fled for her life," Cassandra said softly, also offering an apologetic smile to soften her words.

Only those words felt like they had opened up a trapdoor beneath her, and she was plummeting into a new depth of hell she hadn't known existed.

CHAPTER Fourteen

November 9th
4:06 P.M.

Cassandra had been in there for hours.

Had it been a mistake to allow her to go and see Monique?

Both women were vulnerable right now but were also working at cross purposes. Cassandra wanted proof of who had fathered her and then for that man to be punished for raping her mom. Monique wanted to prove that her father didn't have any other children and that he was no rapist.

Yet the two of them had been holed up inside Monique's cabin for almost five hours. Hopefully, that meant they were bonding, getting to know one another as sisters. Regardless of whether or not Monique was able to forgive him and trust him enough to give him a second chance, he wanted her to have a family. And his family was already hers. She and Cassandra were sisters, which meant she would always be one of them.

Even as he held on for his miracle that she would be part of them because she was his as well as Cassandra's half-sister.

Watching the cabin from outside instead of being in there with her was torture, but he was still grateful to be in a better position than he'd been the day before. Monique had agreed to the security system, and she hadn't said anything about him sleeping in her driveway. He knew she knew because he'd seen her standing in the window looking out at him.

Progress.

Baby steps, but steps all the same.

If he wanted to prove to Monique that she could trust him, that he wouldn't let her down again, then he had to just keep doing what he was doing. Show her that he would be there for her, would put her safety above all else, and was serious about finding ways to make amends. Show her that she was seen. That he understood she was more than the world was shown.

As much as he wanted to be the one in there talking with her, he couldn't deny he was jealous as hell of his baby sister, he was glad that Monique wasn't alone. If she wasn't ready for his company, at least she and Cassandra were getting to know one another, and she was learning that she had a family who would love and accept her and want nothing in return except her happiness.

When the door to the cabin finally opened, he was out of his vehicle before he even realized he was moving. In the doorway, he could see both Monique and Cassandra, and the two women shared a hug before Cassandra waved and headed down the porch steps.

For a moment, his gaze connected with Monique's, and when it didn't immediately skitter away, he held it and allowed every drop of what he was feeling for her to shine through. Jax didn't care that it was fast, didn't care that it should be impossible to feel so strongly about someone he'd known for a week. He and Monique had bonded during those days in the forest, and they'd gotten to know a lot about one another.

Besides that, he knew her deep down in his soul in some primitive place he hadn't even known existed. What he felt for her was raw and primal. It was his instincts recognizing a soulmate. Whether he believed in those or not before he'd met Monique, it was irrelevant now, because the second their eyes met in that ballroom it felt like the other half of his being had snapped into place.

Finally, after giving a small nod to acknowledge she saw everything he was trying to tell her, Monique closed the door.

It felt like they'd just taken another baby step back toward each other.

"She gave me the sample," Cassandra told him, holding up the swab. "Although it kind of feels like a moot point. I look like her dad, and she thinks so too. Besides, I just ... feel like she's my sister. It's hard to explain."

"Not in the least," he assured her as he opened his arms and Cassandra stepped right into them. "There's something about her that just immediately puts you at ease, isn't there?"

"There is," Cassandra acknowledged as she rested her cheek on his chest. "She's like a princess in so many ways, but not the stuck-up kind, she's like a Disney princess, all sunshiny and full of life. Do you know she has a pet hedgehog named Cinderella?"

Jax chuckled. "Yeah, she told me about it when we were in France."

"I know you said I don't have to be, but I'm sorry that things got messed up between you two because of me." Cassandra tilted her head back to look up at him.

"Not because of you, boo," he contradicted, making her scowl at the use of the old nickname. "Knowing your mom was raped and you were conceived as a result might have added to our determination to find answers, but we were looking long before that. You have to stop blaming yourself, yeah?"

It hurt to know that the woman he absolutely considered family, even if they weren't biologically related, was bearing a burden that wasn't hers to carry.

Cassandra was struggling with the revelation of where she came from, and none of them knew how to help her with it. Of course, they knew it must feel awful to learn that you existed only because your mother had been taken against her will, but it was like Cassandra thought that they would all think less of her now. That it would change how they saw her.

"I don't know how," Cassandra admitted, her voice soft and so full of pain that Jax pulled her tightly against him.

"You'll figure it out. Because you deserve only great things, Cassandra. This isn't always going to be our lives, you're not always going to be in hiding, and we're not always going to be focusing on getting answers. One day we'll all be free. That's when we'll all start really living. Those men, they've taken enough from us, they don't get to take our futures as well."

"Does your future include her?" Cassandra asked, looking over her shoulder at the cabin she'd just left. "Because I don't want to see her hurt. I like her. She's sweet and fun, and she was pretty mad at me for blaming myself for everything that's happened to our family, just like the rest of my siblings. She deserves to be happy, Jax. She's right, I'm so lucky to have so many people in my corner, and she's sitting here all alone, hurting and scared, with nobody to have her back."

"Not nobody. She has me," he assured her. "I don't want to hurt her, because you're right, she deserves all the happiness in the world, and I don't ever want her to feel alone again. I don't know how to fix it, but I'm not giving up."

"Good, she deserves to have someone fight for her."

"She's got it. In fact, I think she has it from more than just me."

"She definitely has me too," Cassandra agreed. "And since she's my sister, and hopefully one day your girlfriend, and then maybe wife, she has all of our brothers as well. She's not going to know what hit her when she jumps from pretty much no family to a huge, loud, bossy one."

Jax laughed and gave Cassandra another squeeze before guiding her toward his vehicle. He hadn't been sure her going there was a good idea, not that he'd known about it until Cole dropped her off there this morning, but he was glad she'd insisted. It was exactly what both Cassandra and Monique needed.

"Time to get you back home. I'll drive you to the airport and Cole will fly back with you. I'm sure those Delta guys are sick of having to secretly fly people in and out of their hideout."

"Those guys are pretty sweet when you get to know them," Monique said as she rounded the car and climbed into the passenger seat.

Was that a hint of affection he heard in her voice?

Had she gone and fallen for one of the Delta Team guys?

Those men were ... different. Not all in a bad way, and he knew they were loyal as well as being fierce warriors, but they also carried an air of danger and a whole lot of barely hidden anger.

"Any one of them sweeter than the others?" he asked, aiming for nonchalance as he followed her into the vehicle.

"If you're fishing for information, I'm not going to give you any," she taunted, a sparkle in her eyes reminding him of the old Cassandra, the one who hadn't yet learned about her parentage.

Honestly, if one of the Delta Team guys were responsible for putting that look back on her face, then he was all for whatever it was Cassandra was clearly hiding from him.

"Should I bring up a feed to the cameras pointed at Monique's cabin so you can watch her like the stalker that you are?" Cassandra asked, all teasing innocence, and Jax found he felt lighter than he had for a long time.

"You definitely should," he answered with a grin as he started up the car and reversed down the driveway.

Finally, they were nearing the end of this decades-long nightmare, and so long as they all came out the other side alive and unscathed he couldn't wait to see what the future held for them.

November 10th
9:37 A.M

Monique already knew what the email was going to say, so why was she hesitating to open it?

She liked Cassandra Charleston, would love to have a woman like that for a sister. They got along great, and she'd enjoyed every second of the time she'd spent with the other woman the day before.

It had only taken one look at Cassandra to know the truth.

They were half-sisters.

So why was reading the results in an email so difficult?

Sitting on her couch, in front of the fire, phone in hand, Monique felt paralyzed. Knowing what was likely the truth and seeing it written out in front of her seemed to be two different things.

Maybe she just needed more time to adjust to the idea that her dad had cheated on her mom and she had a sister.

Only time wouldn't change things.

They were what they were, and whether she read the email now or put it off until later, the results would still be the same.

"Stop being a baby," she told herself aloud, needing something to break the silence in the suddenly too quiet cabin. The only sounds were her ragged breathing and the crackling of the fire that reminded her so much of Jax that it hurt, only she couldn't stop herself from building one and sitting mesmerized, watching the flames dance about.

All her life she'd wanted a sibling, and while this was not the way she expected it to happen, she wasn't sad about it. If her dad had cheated on her mom, she didn't like that, but neither of her parents had really been a part of her life so it wasn't like this would ruin her ideal of their marriage.

Despite the assertions of Cassandra, Jax, and the rest of their family, she still didn't believe that her dad had raped anyone. Not that she wanted to push the idea that Cassandra's mom had been unfaithful, she just didn't see another option. Her dad was the least emotional person she'd met, and she just couldn't see him doing anything that would require any sort of passion, good or bad.

"Just do it. Get it over with."

The urging was the last little push she needed, and Monique stopped letting her finger hover over the unread email from the Prey lab, which was doing a rush on the DNA testing, and opened it.

Probability of the two samples being related was listed as 99.9%.

Sisters.

Well, half-sisters, but that seemed like a total technicality.

Cassandra was really her sister.

Which meant her dad really had had sex with another woman while still married to her mom.

It felt ...

Surreal.

Stumbling to her feet, Monique didn't even know where she was going until she pushed open her front door and staggered down the porch steps toward the car parked in her driveway.

Pure instinct.

She was in shock and knew where to go to find something—some*one*—to ground her.

"Princess?" Jax was suddenly there before her, and she didn't overthink it, just stepped up to him and rested her cheek on his broad chest.

The second she made contact with his warmth, tension oozed out of her body, and if he hadn't wrapped his arms around her waist she probably would have sunk to the ground, suddenly boneless and weightless.

"What's wrong?" Jax asked, one arm holding her securely against him while the other drifted up and down her spine, the touch soothing, and she snuggled deeper against him.

"I got the results," she murmured.

For a second his hand stilled before resuming its path, trailing the length of her back. "And how do you feel about it?"

"Do you know?" Not lifting her cheek from his chest, Monique tilted her head back so she could see his face.

It was serious as he looked down at her and he nodded. "Cassandra called to tell me as soon as she got the email. She wanted to call you, too, knowing you'd have gotten the results as well, but she wanted to give you space to process."

"I just ... it's ... I'm ..."

"Struggling to comprehend it all," Jax finished for her, and she nodded, then closed her eyes and tucked her face into the warmth of his body.

"It's not like my parents had a great marriage, I mean, my mom bailed on us when I was a toddler. So it's not as though I feel like this revelation destroyed my family or anything. It just ... it changes things. Changes everything. My dad cheated on my mom. I guess that's why she left. Cassandra's probably right and she found out about it. I wish she'd taken me with her, but what's done is done. My grandparents are going to freak, but I think they'll want to meet Cassandra, she's family, and while I won't say they *care* about family, they are *obsessed* with it. I just ... I don't know if that's what she wants. I mean she already has a family and I ... don't know where I fit into that."

"Where do you want to fit into it?"

"I always wanted a sister," she answered honestly. Despite the shock of finding all of this out, there was a definite spark of excitement inside her. Now she was a big sister instead of an only child, and she wanted to spend more time getting to know Cassandra. Maybe one day they'd feel like a real family, and she'd have someone to spend the holidays with, and confide in, and she wouldn't feel so alone anymore.

But what did Cassandra want?

Their situations weren't the same.

While she learned her absent dad betrayed her abandoning mom, Cassandra had learned that her beloved mom had cheated on the dad she adored, and had six overprotective brothers who adored her.

Did she have space in her life for anyone else?

Especially someone who would be a constant reminder of what happened to her family?

"I can hear you thinking from here," Jax said, his voice rumbling through his chest. "What are you worried about?"

"Does Cassandra want ... how does she feel about the results?"

"Are you asking me if she's happy to have a sister?"

"Yes," she whispered the word, hating that once again she was feeling disposable, good only for her last name and not herself. Yesterday, Cassandra had been delightful, but she'd also been there to get the DNA sample. Now that she had it and the results, there was no reason for her to be nice and act like they got along.

"All of this has been a huge shock to her, but she likes you a lot, and she thinks you're the silver lining from this whole ordeal."

Opening her eyes, because she needed to be able to judge Jax's sincerity and her faith in him had already taken a hit, she looked up at him. "If she's not comfortable with me, I understand that. I can live without my fairytale, I've been doing it all my life anyway. I understand it must be terrible to find out you're an affair baby."

"Princess," Jax drew the word out, and she heard the pain and sadness in his voice.

"Don't, Jax," she pleaded before he could bring up again that his family believed that his stepmom was raped and that was how

Cassandra was conceived. She still didn't believe that was what had happened. "I know what you all believe, but I ... I just can't accept that."

The arm around her tightened, and the hand stroking her back paused to palm her head, tilting it further back. "I understand that, I get where you're coming from. I exploded into your life and brought nothing but danger and trouble, and a story that's hard for you to believe. I'm so sorry for how everything happened. I wish I could go back and do it differently, but I can't. All I can do now is try to fix what I damaged."

She so badly wanted to believe that, but the facts were that he'd gone to that Halloween ball with the intention of gathering intel from her. Intel he was yet to get. Was he only hanging around now, pretending to want to make amends, so that she would tell him where her father was staying?

If he was, he was going to be disappointed because she honestly had no idea.

The problem with trust was that once it was broken it was so hard to fix because it made you doubt everything.

That was exactly how she felt.

More than anything, she wanted to believe that the connection she'd felt to Jax from that first second when their gazes connected was real. That he regretted not telling her the truth earlier, and he was there with only one goal in mind, to fix things.

But she'd been burned before chasing down fairytales that didn't exist in the real world. She didn't want to get hurt again.

Maybe what she needed was to hear everything that had led to them believing that her dad was a crazy rapist intent on destroying their family. If she knew why they thought it, she would know how to refute it.

Opening her mouth to tell Jax they needed to sit down and really talk, before she could get a word out, a loud crack sounded through the air, and she was falling toward the ground.

CHAPTER *Fifteen*

November 10th
10:00 A.M.

Fear gripped him as Jax shoved Monique to the ground and flung his body protectively over hers, covering as much of it as he could.

Had she been hit?

He didn't feel any burning pain to indicate the bullet had struck him, but then again, adrenaline had flooded his system and could very well be masking it. Still, he was able to think clearly and move so if he had been struck, he didn't think it could be a life-threatening injury.

Already his weapon was in his hand, and he scanned the area where the shot had come from. Without shifting his body from where it kept Monique pressed into the ground, he spotted a shadow and lifted his weapon, firing off a single shot.

When no more shots came, he had to assume that he'd hit his target.

Hit that one, but there'd be more out there.

More coming.

And it was just him there to protect Monique.

Waiting another full minute to make sure there hadn't been another shooter within range, when no more shots fired he eased up an inch off Monique, just enough that he could look down at her and see her face.

Wide eyes stared up at him, and he could see her pulse fluttering in the hollow of her neck. But she was alive and breathing, and that allowed him to take a full breath.

"Are you hit?" he asked, keeping his voice pitched low. It wasn't just a guess that the shooter wouldn't be there alone. He'd dealt with the teams her father kept sending several times over, and it was never just one man. At least another five would be out there somewhere, possibly in the woods already, possibly waiting in a van hidden somewhere close by. Wherever they were, they'd have heard the shots and be coming. Could already be on their way.

"N-no, I don't th-think so. They followed you here," she said, her voice shaking, and her body joining in, he could feel it trembling beneath him.

"Yeah, they did," he agreed.

Now wasn't the time to get into a discussion on whether these men had been sent by her father. Jax knew they had, but Monique wasn't in a place where she was ready to accept that yet. Although she was getting there. She'd been willing to talk, he knew she was even though she hadn't said the words, and he wasn't going to go and die, or let her die, until they had everything between them straightened out, and had hopefully lived a long and happy life together.

"We're going to run for my car, okay?" he told her, still scanning the area so he was prepared for the next shot when it came.

"Why not my house?"

"Because there are more of them than there are of us, and I don't want us to get trapped somewhere. My car can move, can get us out of here. If they contain us in the house, they can just call in more men, and I'll never be able to pick them all off before they get to you."

While Jax knew originally he had been her father's target, since Monique had been dragged into this he had to assume that her father now viewed her as a liability who had to be eliminated. Her father had to know that he'd told her everything, but had no idea that she was so far defending him. All Samson Kerr had wanted to do all along was clean house and keep his secrets. Unfortunately, his own daughter had now become a problem that needed to be cleaned up and disposed of.

Not going to happen.

Not on his watch.

"Okay," Monique agreed, looking up at him with such a trusting expression that his heart squeezed painfully tight in his chest.

Already once before he'd let her down. In fact, he was the one to drag her into this mess to begin with. And yet she still believed that he could get her out of this alive. That trust humbled him even as he knew it didn't extend to anything other than him keeping her alive.

Still, if she could trust him to do that, he had to believe that with enough work on his part he could gain back all her trust.

"On three we're going to move. You're going to jump straight into the driver's door since it's closer and open. Then you're going to climb over to the passenger side and get down in the space between the front of the seat and the dash. Can you do that for me?"

"You can't drive and shoot back at them if they shoot at us," Monique protested.

"I can and I will." He would do whatever it took to get Monique some place safe. He'd always known that her father would have someone watching her property, and that person would report back that he was there, still in contact with her. It was a calculated risk since her father might only act if Jax was still there, but then again he might not, and there was no way he was going to leave her alone and unprotected.

"No, Jax, let me drive." Her hands gripped the front of his shirt and clung to him. She was clearly terrified, but determination also shined in her eyes.

It would make it easier to be able to focus on eliminating threats if he wasn't also driving the vehicle, but it would also put Monique in a more vulnerable position.

"I can do it," she said before he could disagree. "And we go on three, you get in first so you can get into the passenger side. One, two, three."

Since she was already wriggling out from underneath him, there was nothing else he could do but move along with her, although he stayed behind her until they reached the car, then he hurried in, knowing if he refused, she wasn't going to budge.

Little minx was going to be punished for twisting his arm like that. Keeping her safe was his top priority, she should know that. Yet she'd made it impossible for her not to get her way without delaying their departure with an argument.

"Not cool, princess," he muttered as she slammed the door closed and turned the engine on.

"I was just making the best decision for both of us," she said stubbornly as she shot him a frown before gripping the wheel.

"The best decision is whatever keeps you the safest."

"No. I might still be hurt that you weren't honest with me, but I don't want you hurt and certainly not dead. I don't ... I don't know what happens next. Between us, I mean. But I do know that a part of me would die if you did."

For a second, their gazes connected, and he felt it zing between them.

The connection he'd felt that very first second he laid eyes on her.

She felt it, too, he knew she did, could see it in the emotion that flared in the stormy gray depths of her eyes.

"I'm sorry, Monique. For everything," he murmured.

"I know. I forgive you. I don't want to die holding onto that anger. I want you to know that I think we can work things out. I don't want this thing between us to end the way it did."

Relief had the air whooshing out of his lungs in a rush. It was everything he'd wanted to hear from her, but everything he hadn't been sure he ever would.

"Thank you, princess. I swear, you won't regret it." Leaning over, he crushed his lips to hers in a quick kiss. "But you should know, that little stunt that you just pulled to get your own way, you're going to be punished for that. I'm thinking I'll keep you on the edge of an orgasm for hours, until you're begging and pleading to come, and only when I'm sure you understand that your safety is always going to be my top priority will I let you."

Monique sucked in a breath, her eyes wide, but darkened with desire. His girl didn't want to be treated like a china doll, that's what she'd told him, and he had no intention of treating his strong, sweet warrior like she was fragile when she was anything but.

"Drive, princess," he ordered gently. They'd been lucky that no one else had come yet, but there wasn't just the one shooter out there, and they'd already tempted fate long enough.

With a shaky nod, she pressed on the accelerator, and they headed down her driveway. Once they put a bit of distance between them and her property, he'd call his brothers, let them know what happened, and that they needed a flight out to Delta Team's secure compound. The Delta Team guys really did have to be annoyed with all the flying backward and forward they'd had to do for his family, but they were good men and wouldn't complain, even if they would have preferred not to have their privacy violated.

They were almost to the road when the bullets started flying, and as he opened his window and tracked where the closest shooter was, Jax prayed that Monique had what it took to drive under immense pressure.

If she didn't, if she panicked, if his decision to allow her to drive and him to shoot wound up backfiring and cost them their lives, he would die with that regret sitting heavily on his shoulders.

~

November 10th
10:09 A.M

Panic thrummed inside her.

Buzzing about like a swarm of angry hornets.

But ruthlessly, Monique beat it back.

This was her plan, and now her and Jax's lives were depending on her holding it together and driving them out of there. Not holding it together was not an option.

Especially with the promise of Jax's intriguing punishment hanging in the air.

A stupid thing to be thinking about as she jammed her foot on the accelerator and zoomed them faster down the driveway, but it helped to give her a tangible reason to keep a lid on her fears. Something small but pleasant to focus on. Something that wasn't tied up in an emotional tangle like her relationship—whatever that was going to look like—with Jax.

Being brave isn't about not being scared.

It's just about doing what you have to do in spite of being afraid.

The reminder helped, and she sped up as they approached the turn into the road, anxious to get away from the bullets she could hear dinging into the sides of the vehicle.

"Slow down a little," Jax coached as he leaned out the window and fired off a few shots. "You take that turn too fast and you'll lose control and send us flying."

With the aches and pains from the accident still present in her body, and the memories of her terror as the car flipped and twisted as it rushed down the embankment still fresh, Monique slowed a little. The last thing she wanted was to crash the car because if she did, it would all be over.

There were more of them than there were of her and Jax, so that was a whole lot more weapons that would be firing on a wrecked car than Jax could fire back at. They'd either be killed or kidnapped again, and neither of those options was at all appealing. Kidnapping was only prolonging the inevitable anyway. They were loose ends, and whoever was behind these attacks on Jax's family was determined to have them all snipped off.

While the tires squealed as she took the corner a little faster than she should have, Monique was able to keep the car on the road.

"Good girl," Jax murmured as he pulled back inside the car.

"Did you get them?"

"Some of them maybe, I doubt all."

"So they're going to follow us." It was what she'd expected, but she would love for there to be a quick fix and a happy ending to this little drama. Especially now that she knew for sure that she and Cassandra were sisters and she'd decided to forgive Jax and see if they could salvage the relationship they'd started building in the French forest.

"They will. You want me to take over driving?"

"No." That would be taking the coward's way out. This was something she could do, and it left Jax free to take out the men after them. It wouldn't be fair to put all the pressure on him while she did nothing but cower and hide.

"You sure?"

Since there was no judgment in his tone, Monique didn't feel like he was implying that she was incapable of contributing, more just that he was every bit as scared as she was, but he had the training and experience to hide it better.

"Positive. Besides, they're going to start shooting again any—" She broke off as bullets once again began to fly.

"Second," Jax finished for her as he once again shifted in his seat so he was balancing precariously out the window so he could return fire.

A glance in the rearview mirror told her that a vehicle was rapidly approaching them from behind.

Déjà vu filled her senses.

This was exactly what it had been like in France, only Jax had been the one driving. Still the small road, the trees all around them, the isolation, it was all too familiar, and her hands, which had been gripping the steering wheel with a death grip, began to tremble.

As though sensing her growing panic, even though he wasn't looking at her, his attention focused on picking off the threat, Jax's soothing voice rumbled through the vehicle. "You got this, Monique. You're okay, and you're doing a great job. All I need you to do is keep doing what you're doing. Can you do that for me?"

"Y-yes." The word came out more as a squeak, but the shaking in her hands decreased, and her panic receded to a more manageable level. Even though she'd been abducted last time they were in this scenario, they'd survived only because of Jax, and she believed he could get them out of this alive again.

The sound of the gunfire was so loud, and she wished she could lift her hands to cover her ears and scrunch her eyes closed so she could pretend this wasn't happening. But she didn't do that. Instead, she kept her grip on the wheel and drove as fast as she could while still maintaining control so they didn't go skidding off the road and into the trees.

It seemed to be working until ...

"Uh, Jax?"

"Yeah, princess?"

"There's another car in front of us on the road," she said. That fear she'd been doing such a great job of containing now suddenly burst free, erupting inside her and spewing almost paralyzing waves that had her entire body stiffening while her heart rate went haywire.

A curse fell from his lips as he looked over his shoulder to see that they were about to be sandwiched between two vehicles, both of which were firing on them.

There was no way out.

The road wasn't wide enough for her to go around them, and even if it was, the car in front could just move to block her. There were no turn-offs any time soon, it would be another ten miles before they'd reach another road. Her animal rescue was secluded, she'd chosen it for just that very reason. With all the animals she had there, it could get loud, and she didn't want to bother neighbors, plus she'd always liked the peace and quiet. It was calming and soothing.

Well, it used to be.

Now she wished there was help somewhere close.

"I'm going to have to stop," she said, already easing her foot off the accelerator. What other choice did she have? Ram the other vehicle and hope that she and Jax miraculously survived?

"No!"

Jax's shout startled her, but it had the desired result as her foot slammed automatically down onto the pedal again.

"Keep driving," Jax ordered.

"But we're going to hit them," she protested, even though she was sure he must understand that already.

"Not if we time this right."

"What do you mean?" Did Jax suddenly think he was there with one of his former SEAL teammates, or one of his brothers? Maybe there was something they could do to avoid the inevitable crash, but she was just plain old Monique Kerr. Sure, she was good with calming traumatized animals, but that skill wasn't going to help them now.

"If we get this right, we can eliminate both vehicles," Jax told her.

"Time this right?"

"They assume we're going to stop. Why wouldn't they? It would be crazy not to."

"And we're crazy?"

Jax laughed. "Yeah, princess. We're crazy. I want you to keep going, fast, don't stop, and don't let your fear get the better of you. I know I messed up, and I know I blew what trust you once had in me, but I need you to trust me now. Can you do that?"

Could she?

If this was about just freely handing her heart over once again, she was sure the answer would be no.

But this was their lives they were talking about, and she trusted Jax to know how to get them out of this alive.

"I can do that," she assured him.

"Thank you. You're going to keep driving, don't let up on the speed, then when I tell you to, you're going to take a hard right."

"Into the trees?"

"Do your best to avoid hitting them, but as soon as you turn off the road you're going to let up on the gas and go for the brake. We should lose speed fairly quickly given the terrain, and even if we hit, the slower speed means we shouldn't be banged up too badly."

"We hope."

"We hope," Jax echoed. "But with perfect timing those two vehicles are going to hit head on at full speed."

"Which will eliminate our problem." It was a risky plan but the best they had. "Okay, I can do this," she assured him. At least she hoped she could. For some reason the slowing down and avoiding trees once they turned seemed like the easier thing to do. Because driving at a high speed, toward an oncoming vehicle, was really putting her desire to trust Jax to the test.

Still, she held firm.

Didn't slow down.

Tried not to flinch as they bared down on the approaching vehicle which was zooming toward them on the quiet country road.

Her grip on the wheel tightened as they got closer and Jax didn't order her to turn.

They were going to hit.

They were too close.

It was unavoidable.

Right when she was about to break her promise to trust Jax and slam on the brakes he yelled the word she'd been waiting to hear.

"Turn!"

Not hesitating to do as he ordered, Monique yanked the wheel to the right, and they swerved off the road a mere couple of seconds before she heard the deafening boom of the two vehicles colliding.

Thankfully, the trees weren't as tightly packed together as she'd feared, and while she narrowly avoided the first few as the car slowed, it was easier to navigate, and soon they came to a stop.

They'd done it.

They were both alive.

And she hadn't even crashed the car.

Breathing heavily, she turned to watch as Jax pulled his torso back through the window and sat in his seat.

"I did it," she whispered, shocked that she managed what had seemed like an impossible feat.

"Yeah, you did. If you don't tell me not to, I'm going to kiss you, princess."

His hopeful eyes watched her, and she respected that he'd given her an option and that he didn't move a muscle until she gave a small nod of assent.

Then his hands were gripping her hips, and he hauled her over the center console and onto his lap. She didn't even have time to think before his mouth crashed down onto hers.

Melting into the kiss seemed like the easiest thing in the world, and she prayed she wasn't making a huge mistake in giving this man another chance. Because Jax Holloway absolutely held the power to crush her in his hands.

CHAPTER Sixteen

November 10th
8:13 P.M.

Jax finally relaxed as he guided Monique into the suite he'd just booked for them at a nice hotel, a short drive from the private airfield where one of the Delta Team guys would pick them up in the early hours of tomorrow morning.

Safe.

For now, at least.

He'd bypassed several other airfields that Prey would have clearance to fly in and out of at short notice, because he wanted to put as much distance between him and Monique and the men her father had sent after them as he could.

Tomorrow, once he had her tucked away safely on the Delta Team compound, he'd sit down with Monique and they'd talk. Really talk. About every piece of evidence they had pointing to her father as one of the rapists, and then they'd work through with her and see if she could come up with some ideas of where her dad might be hiding out like the coward he was.

But not tonight.

Tonight, he needed to make sure Monique ate, showered, and slept. They'd picked up some food, toiletries, and a couple of changes of clothes along the way, so she could take a nice long shower or bath, put on some clean clothes, eat something, and then fall into bed for a few hours of sleep before they had to leave for the airfield.

"You can use the bathroom first," he offered as he made sure the door was securely locked behind them. Jax had chosen a hotel where you had to use your room key card to access the lift, so if they were tracked there, it would make it that little bit harder for the men to do anything more than wait in the lobby. Something that would be obvious in the next few hours once the guests all hit their rooms.

"Are you coming with me?" Monique asked, and his heart clenched.

He hated that she was so afraid after what she'd been through these last couple of weeks that she was now afraid to take a shower alone. If he could go back and undo everything, he'd do it in a heartbeat. Find another way, any other way, to get the intel he'd needed to protect his family without hurting this sweet, brave woman in the process.

Today she'd been amazing, driving that car like a pro, and fighting the urge to slow down or turn away from the oncoming collision until he'd given her the word. She'd even managed to navigate through the trees without hitting any of them. He was so proud of her, and he admired her strength and determination, and if she needed a little coddling right now, he would give it to her.

Only when he turned to tell her he'd sit on the floor in the bathroom with his eyes closed while she cleaned up, it wasn't fear he found in the gray eyes watching him, it was something else.

Heat.

Desire.

Need.

"You did say I deserved a punishment for manipulating you back at the rescue," she said, and her voice wasn't scared or anxious, it was sultry and seductive.

Jax groaned. There was nothing more he'd love to do than take Monique to bed and take his time with her, teasing her, punishing her, making love to her. But now wasn't that time. Regardless of whether she was initiating it, it felt like he'd be taking advantage. It had been a high-stakes day, and she'd been riding an adrenaline high. Could he believe that this was what she really wanted and that she wouldn't regret it in the morning?

As though sensing he wasn't going to give her what she was demanding, Monique sidled up to him, boldly cupping the bulge in his pants and squeezing just enough to draw another groan from his lips.

"Unless of course you'd rather be the one to accept a punishment," she sassed, an amused spark in her eyes along with a heavy dose of desire.

Capturing her wrist, he spun her in one smooth movement until she was pinned against his chest, her back to his front. "Not sure it's a punishment, princess, when you're this excited about it."

Instead of answering him, she wriggled her backside against the ridge in his pants, and he huffed a chuckle. His little princess had no idea what she was getting herself into. She might have a wild streak, and an apparent kink for punishment, but she was so sweet and inexperienced in this kind of sex that he couldn't wait to blow her mind.

Guiding the hand he held into her pants, he dragged her fingers along her center. "Are you wet for me, princess?"

"Yes," she said on a moan as he pressed her fingers against her entrance and then swirled them around her bud.

"Are you excited for your punishment?"

"Yes."

When he pulled her hand free and sucked her fingers into his mouth, she gasped, and looked up at him over her shoulder, her pupils blown, her tongue darting out to swipe along her bottom lip.

Corrupting his sweet princess was going to be fun.

Releasing her, he stepped back, amused when she mewed a protest. She was going to do a whole lot of protesting before she got what she wanted tonight. A whole lot of begging, too.

"Strip and go lie on the bed," he ordered, and watched as she scurried to do as he commanded.

Only once she was naked and settled on the large bed in the center of the room did he move. Opening the bags of clothes they'd bought, Jax wished they'd been able to stop by his house instead. There he had everything he needed to make this punishment perfect, but he was sure he'd be able to improvise.

There was one thing he always traveled with that he was glad he had. Suffering from debilitating cramps in his legs as a kid, he'd gotten accustomed to carrying a deep tissue massager with him. It wouldn't be as good as the collection of vibrators he had at his house for the occasional time he allowed himself to spend a little time with a woman, but it would do the job.

"Last chance to back out, princess," he warned as he approached the bed, stalking toward his prey and more than ready to teach her a lesson. One he hoped she would never forget, because in the end, nothing was more important to him than her safety.

Although her eyes were wide as she took in the two pairs of socks he had in his hands, she shook her head. "Don't want to back out."

"Okay then, but don't forget this is a punishment," he reminded her as he took one of her wrists, touching a kiss to the sensitive skin on the inside of her wrist before he wrapped the makeshift binding around it and tied it to one of the bedposts. "Do you remember what your punishment is going to be?"

"You won't let me come for an hour." She said the words, but he could tell she didn't really believe him.

Her mistake.

Hour or not, she was going to be writhing, panting, begging, and crying for an orgasm before he allowed her to come.

"That's right. Because you were a bad girl, weren't you?" he asked as he repeated the process with her other arm, kissing her wrist before binding it just tight enough to the bedpost.

"Y-yes," she said, her eyes watching his every move with curiosity that was going to wind up killing the cat.

"What's the most important thing?" Jax asked as he moved to the foot of the bed and trailed a line of kisses along the inside of one of her legs, all the way down to her ankle. When she hadn't answered by the time he had her ankle secured to the bedpost, he smacked his fingers lightly against her bundle of nerves, making her jolt. "Answer me, princess. What's the most important thing?"

"My safety," she said obediently.

"That's right. And you'll remember this punishment the next time you think you can manipulate me, won't you?" he asked as he trailed another line of kisses down her other leg, then tied it firmly to the bedpost, leaving her spreadeagled before him.

"Yes."

"Now you'll take your punishment like a good girl, won't you, princess? Because you know you deserve it."

"Yes," she quickly agreed. Although when he moved to pick up the massager and its buzz filled the room, she jerked on the bed in surprise.

"Not as good as what I have at home, but I think this will still effectively teach you a lesson." Positioning himself on the bed beside her, Jax stroked his fingers down her cheek, then let them drift down her body. Circling one of her breasts, dipping into her belly button, then sweeping between her legs to scoop up the evidence of her arousal.

Using that, he coated the vibrating end of the massager and then moved it between her legs.

At the first touch of the tool against her sensitive bud, Monique's hips jolted off the bed, and he chuckled. So sweet. So innocent. So corruptible.

Holding the toy firmly against her, he lazily massaged one of her breasts, plucking at her nipple until it pebbled beneath his ministrations. Watching her body carefully, the second he thought she was close to coming, he removed the toy, making her whimper, her hips rocking as she sought the friction she needed to find a release.

"Nuh-uh," he reminded her. "You don't get to come until I'm ready for you."

"Jax, please, I won't put myself in danger again," she pleaded, giving him puppy dog eyes as though that was going to convince him to let her come this quickly.

Without giving her an answer, he leaned in and captured her lips, kissing her slowly, sensually, taking his time, in no hurry to end the night. He could do this for hours, the question was, could Monique?

When he knew the approaching orgasm would have receded enough to play again, he pulled his mouth from hers, and returned the toy to between her legs, playing with her other breast as he watched the orgasm begin to build.

This time, when he withdrew the toy, Monique cried out her displeasure. "Please, Jax," she begged. "Please. I'm so close."

"And you'll remain close until I'm sure you've learned your lesson."

"I have."

Touching a kiss to the tip of her nose, he shook his head. "Not yet you haven't. But you will."

Capturing one of her nipples with his mouth, he teased it, suckling lightly, then harder, flicking it with the tip of his tongue, and then scraping his teeth against it. There were still the lingering marks of the bite he'd given her when they'd first made love, and he found he liked seeing his mark on her. Maybe he'd keep one on her body permanently so she never doubted that he saw every single side of her, even the ones she hid from everybody else.

Moving away from her breast, he put the toy back between her legs, and even though the orgasm had receded, it built quicker this time. Only a minute or so later, he pulled the toy away and lavished attention on her other breast. Sucking, and licking, enjoying the way she thrust her chest forward, seeking more of his attention.

This time he moved down her body, using his mouth and his fingers instead of the massager. Featherlight kisses dotted her entrance and her bundle of nerves, and then he slid a single finger inside her, pumping it lazily in and out as he continued to pepper kisses to her bud, light enough that they wouldn't let her come even though he knew she was close.

"Please, Jax, please," she begged, tears shimmering in her eyes, but from the flush of arousal on her skin, he knew that despite her desire to come, she was enjoying every second of their play as much as he was.

"Mmm, not sure we've been at this an hour yet," he reminded her.

"But I've learned my lesson."

Adding another finger, he stroked deep, making sure the pads of his fingers caught that special spot inside her, and she moaned and rocked her hips into his touch. "I'm not sure you have, princess. If I'm too lenient on you, I might lose you."

Her gaze locked on his. "You won't."

"I don't want to," he answered honestly. "I don't want to lose you."

"You won't," she repeated. "You haven't."

Those words hit him firmly in the chest, and all of a sudden, he couldn't hold back. Withdrawing his hand, smirking as she mewled another protest, Jax stripped out of his clothes and then spread his body out over hers.

One thrust and he was buried deep in her tight, wet heat.

Touching a kiss to the fading bite mark on her chest, he then kissed her hard on the mouth. "Maybe I shouldn't let you come at all, that would really teach you a lesson, wouldn't it?" he asked as he pulled back and then thrust in hard, knowing his girl could take it, that she wasn't fragile and didn't want to be treated like she was.

"You wouldn't," Monique said, but there was a thread of doubt in her voice.

"Oh, princess, I absolutely would." Another hard thrust made her cry out, and he knew she was so close to coming she could taste it. While another time he might deny her an orgasm as he came inside her, that time wasn't today. Today, he wanted them to come together. She'd forgiven him when she had no reason to, was giving him another chance, and he wasn't going to do anything to mess up that chance.

"Please, Jax, please. Let me come. I'm begging you." Her hips rocked against him as much as they could with her bound ankles.

"Begging, huh?" Balancing his weight on one hand, his other hand touched her where their bodies were joined. "Then give me everything you have, princess."

Picking up the pace he pumped himself in and out, sinking in as deep as he could with every thrust while his fingers worked her bundle of nerves, until she was crying out his name as her internal muscles clamped around him, setting off his own orgasm.

It crashed through him with all the power of a hurricane, drenching him in emotions and feelings. And even as the storm receded, something settled in his chest, a knowledge that he was right where he was supposed to be.

This beautiful woman beneath him was his to protect, his to care for, his to see, and he was going to make sure she never doubted again that she was seen for who she was and not for her last name.

Which started with the mammoth task of convincing her that her father was a dangerous rapist who would end her life to protect his own.

~

November 11th
11:33 A.M

"Whoa," Monique exclaimed as they drove through a huge wrought iron gate and approached an enormous Gothic mansion.

It looked like something out of a movie.

It was huge, four stories high from the looks of things, with at least a dozen windows on either side of the front door. Ivy grew over parts of the building, which only added to the mystique vibe the place had going. While she had no idea what state they were in, since apparently the only way the Delta Team guys would bring you here was blindfolded, wherever they were was someplace with thick forests everywhere, reminding her a little of her home.

Although they were deep in the forest, there was a huge expanse of open lawn surrounding the Gothic mansion.

"How come there are no trees close to the house?" she asked, leaning forward in her seat.

"Safety," Lion responded with a single-word answer. Something she'd gotten used to over the last few hours.

At first, she'd been a little put off when they reached the airfield and boarded the plane, only to be told she would have to wear a blindfold for the duration of the flight and that it wasn't negotiable. It was that or Lion would inject her with a sedative that would knock her unconscious until they reached their destination.

Not willing to allow herself to be that vulnerable with strangers after the ordeal of the last few days, she'd gone along with the blindfold thing. Without her sight, her nerves had gotten the best of her, and in an attempt to ease them, she'd chattered away the entire flight.

While Jax had joined in on her random chatter, obviously sensing her need to fill the silence so it didn't feel like she was without her sight and her hearing, Lion contributed only the bare necessity. If she asked him a question, he answered with as few words as possible, but despite that she liked the big man with the wild, dark blond hair.

"You mean like if someone is sneaking onto your property, you'll be able to see them as they approach your house?" she asked. Jax had warned her that the Delta Team guys were a little ... extra, but she didn't come from this world, and she didn't really know what exactly that meant. So she'd determined to treat them no differently than she would anyone else.

"Yes," Lion replied.

"Do you think that's a possibility? That someone would try to attack you here?"

"Unfortunately," Lion answered, and a weariness to his tone made her heart hurt. What had these men gone through that made them so over-the-top about their security? Growing up as she had, with her last name, she understood being security conscious, but this was taking things to a whole other level.

Hesitating for a second because Jax had told her these men didn't like being touched, Monique went with her instincts and lightly touched his shoulder. "I'm sorry you were hurt. I hope you're able to find what you need to move on."

Lion's gaze snapped to meet hers in the rearview mirror, the intensity of his gaze unnerving. There was something about his eyes that was ... unusual, to say the least. Right now, there was surprise in them, but also respect when she didn't let her gaze skitter away, and something softer like appreciation.

Offering him a smile, she leaned back in her seat, and a moment later they pulled up outside the mansion. As soon as they climbed out of the car, the front door opened and a whole stream of people came barreling out.

Of course, she immediately recognized Cassandra, and she could see the brothers she'd met in France, so she assumed the women were all their girlfriends. There were some men she hadn't seen before, and she knew one of them had to be the other stepbrother, but she didn't know which one of them he was.

Slightly overwhelmed by the sudden rush of people, Monique found herself edging closer to Jax, who threw an arm around her shoulders and tugged her into his side like it was the most natural thing in the world, and she felt herself relax a little.

While she didn't love big crowds of people, these people weren't just any old random ones, they were Jax's family. Cassandra's family. So in a way, they were kind of her family, too, even if she didn't know them very well or at all really. Most of what she knew came from her brief interactions with Jake, Cooper, Connor, and Cole in France, and then what Jax and Cassandra had told her about them.

"I'm so glad you're here," Cassandra said, making her way through the group to come and give her a hug. "Are you okay with the results?" she whispered in her ear so no one else could overhear them.

"I always wanted a sister, and I'm glad I got you. Are you okay with the results?" Monique pulled back so she could study her little sister's expression and make sure she was telling the truth.

"Growing up with six brothers, I always wanted a sister, too. I'm glad the universe finally did something right and gave me you," Cassandra replied, holding her gaze so Monique could see the sincerity in her words.

Knowing she had two people on her side out of this overwhelming group helped even more. Or maybe it was three people on her side because she noticed that Lion had positioned himself slightly between her, Jax, and Cassandra, and all the others.

"I'm glad the universe did something right and gave me you, too," Jax murmured as he touched a kiss to her temple, and Monique was sure she must be blushing up a storm.

Images of last night flashed through her mind. The delicious torture of Jax working her to the edge but not letting her come over and over again, until when that orgasm finally did hit, it was the most powerful thing she'd ever experienced in her life. Then they'd taken a shower together and he'd made her come again, and after eating they'd fallen asleep in each other's arms.

Forgiving and making the decision to move on meant she could have a lifetime of moments just like those ones.

"I'm Essie. Are you going to marry Uncle Jax? Can I be the flower girl?" a little girl of around five asked as she pushed her way through the adults.

Monique chuckled at the earnest expression on the child's face.

"You are just adorable, I bet you would be the absolute best flower girl in the whole entire world," she told the girl, who beamed.

"My daddy is going to marry my new mommy, and I'm going to be their flower girl. And Uncle Cooper is going to marry Willow, so I gets to be their flower girl too. And Uncle Cole is going to marry Susanna, and Uncle Connor is going to marry Becca, and Uncle Jake is gonna marry Alannah, and I gets to be the flower girl for all those weddings," the child rambled.

"Actually, no one other than your daddy and I are actually engaged, cuddle bug," a woman with wild red hair and pretty green eyes told the little girl.

"Well I knows they are going to even though they haven't gotten 'ngage yet," Essie said with a huff.

The woman, who Monique knew must be Essie's former nanny and now soon-to-be stepmom, rolled her eyes and tugged on one of the child's pigtails. "You might be right, but it's polite to let the guy do the proposing. Or the girl, I guess. Hi, I'm Gabriella."

"Monique," she said as she shook the other woman's hand. "And she definitely deserves to be a flower girl as many times as she wants. She's so cute, how do you stand it?"

"It gets easier," the man who must be Essie's father said dryly. "Cade. Sorry, we didn't meet in France. I thought it was best to stay here with Essie and Gabriella." The big man's hand shifted to rest on the stomach of his fiancée, and Monique knew that Gabriella was pregnant and that so far was yet to carry a pregnancy to term. They were all praying that this time it turned out differently, and Monique would gladly join in with those prayers. The couple were clearly deeply in love, and she hoped they could add their baby to their little family.

"We're glad you're here," Cole said, stepping forward. "Sorry I didn't stick around and let Cassandra fly back here alone so it wasn't just the two of you against those men yesterday."

"We handled it together," Monique assured him. "And you were where you needed to be. I'm Monique," she said to the woman with long dark hair and pretty green eyes who was holding Cole's hand.

"Susanna Zangari. I think we might have met a few times when we were kids."

"I remember. I'm glad you were able to get away and build a life where you can be yourself and be happy," she said sincerely, then shuddered. "Your dad, he ... gave me bad vibes."

Surprise flitted through the green eyes that looked back at her. "He wasn't a good man, even though most people didn't see that. But I'm free from him now. Really free." Pushing up onto tiptoes, Susanna touched a kiss to Cole's cheek. "Now that I'm believed."

"Always," Cole said. Then caught Susanna's chin between his thumb and forefinger and kissed her properly.

"That's Cooper's girlfriend, Willow," Jax said, pointing to the pretty blonde who smiled and offered her a warm smile. "Connor's girlfriend, Becca," he continued, pointing out the stunning woman with pitch black hair and dark blue eyes, who also offered her a smile. "And lastly, Jake's girlfriend, Alannah. They only just got together, but Alannah grew up in the house behind ours, so she's always been like a part of the family," he said, pointing out the other blonde, who stepped forward and gave her a hug.

"We're all glad you're safe and that you're here now where you'll be protected," Alannah told her. "Those guys are quiet, but they're the best. No offense," she added, looking to Jake and his brothers.

"None taken," Jake quickly assured his girlfriend.

"Steel, Dragon, Blade, Voodoo, and Thunder," Jax rattled off, indicating one of the silent men with each name.

The only indication the men gave were almost imperceptible nods of their heads. Their gazes were always attentive, always roaming the area, and she got the feeling they'd rather head inside rather than stay in the open.

She was more than happy to oblige, not just because she didn't want to make the guys uncomfortable, but also because she needed to make a phone call. Monique hadn't wanted to call her dad until she had the official results of the DNA test, and then yesterday, after she'd gotten the email, she and Jax had been attacked. After that, she hadn't had a moment alone to talk to her father.

Now they were here she couldn't put it off any longer. Not only did he need to know that he had another daughter, but she wanted to find out where he was staying so she could organize a meeting for him with

Jax and his brothers. They needed to be able to eliminate her dad as a suspect as the fourth rapist so they could focus on finding the real guilty man.

She liked all these people, wanted them to be happy and free. They deserved it after everything they'd been through. She could help them get one step closer to finding that freedom, and she couldn't wait to do it.

CHAPTER Seventeen

November 11th
12:20 P.M.

For the first time in ... almost as long as Jax could remember ... things felt good.

Not perfect. They wouldn't be perfect until they had the final man who had raped his stepmom either dead or in prison, but they felt good. As close as he was going to get until then.

There was still work to be done with Monique. She was there, and she'd slept with him last night, trusted him with her body and her pleasure, trusted him to know he wouldn't take things too far but still give her what she needed, but he hadn't completely regained her trust yet.

As much as he'd love to dedicate every single second of his time trying to convince her that he wouldn't let her down again, there was still work to do. Just because she didn't believe it didn't mean that her father wasn't a dangerous man.

A dangerous man who was now backed into a corner.

It was imperative that they convince Monique that her dad was involved and then work with her to try to figure out where he might be holed up if he was desperate and not wanting to be found.

"You going to go and talk to her?" Jake asked as Jax headed for the huge staircase that would take him up to the third floor, where he and Monique would be staying for as long as they were there. She'd asked for a little time to get herself settled, and he'd needed to check in with his brothers anyway.

"Yeah. She should have her stuff unpacked by now and be making herself at home," he replied.

"Good luck."

Rolling his eyes at his big brother, Jax shook his head. "I don't need luck." A miracle maybe, but not luck. Monique was there, and she was ready to listen to him, he just needed a miracle to convince her that her father wasn't the man she thought he was.

Which shouldn't be absolutely impossible given she already had a barely existent relationship with him.

"That's what you said to me when I messed up with Alannah by leaving the hospital," Jake reminded him as if he'd forgotten that his brother had come dangerously close to ruining the best thing to ever happen to him.

"You needed luck to convince Alannah to forgive you, but Monique said she forgave me and wants to figure things out."

"But is she ready to accept the truth? We all get why she doesn't want to, but we need her. She's our best bet at ending this and being able to live normal lives."

"Normal." Jax huffed. "I don't think I even know what that is. But I do know the stakes. I'll find a way to convince her. She's not trying to be obstinate, she's just overwhelmed, and this all came at her out of the blue. You guys get that, right?"

While he didn't want to give up his family, he'd made it clear when they got home from France that if he had to choose a side, it would be Monique's. But that wasn't what he wanted. He wanted Monique to be accepted by his family the same way the women his brothers loved all had been.

"Relax. We all like Monique. She's sweet and genuine. We all get being overwhelmed, no one is holding that against her."

"Appreciate that." Driving his fingers through his hair, the pressure to convince Monique as quickly as possible of her father's guilt was resting heavily on his shoulders. Once they overcame this last hurdle, it should be clear sailing between him and Monique. Especially since they were staying together, it gave him unfettered access to her, and he was going to take advantage of that. "Better get up to her."

"Good luck," Jake said again, amusement in his voice that made Jax smile. His brother had taken on a lot of responsibility at a young age, and Jake had learned to hide his emotions behind a gruff exterior. But ever since he'd realized that love had been staring him in the face all along in the form of his best friend, he was slowly loosening up. Learning he didn't have to be in control of himself all the time.

"Yeah, yeah, luck," he muttered as he took the stairs three at a time up to the third floor. This place was like a maze. Corridors everywhere led to a warren of mostly empty rooms. The six Delta Team guys lived there together, their rooms all up on the fourth floor, and all the living areas were on the first, so the middle two floors weren't used.

Well, they hadn't been until he and his family had invaded Delta Team's peace and quiet.

The entire Charleston Holloway family would forever be grateful to these guys for giving them sanctuary when they needed it. It meant a lot, especially given that everyone at Prey knew these guys were battling something dark, but no one knew what that was exactly.

Locating the room he and Monique would be sharing—a small miracle in itself that she had agreed to share and not asked to have her own room—Jax stopped outside the door, his hand on the handle, when he heard voices inside.

Everybody else was downstairs, which meant she must be on the phone.

Who would she be talking to?

Someone from her rescue?

"No, Dad, that's not good enough. This is important. You need to tell me where you are, or you need to fly back home. That's not negotiable."

The sound of Monique's firm voice had his vision going black.

She was talking to her father?

Why would she call her dad without running it by him first?

What part about her father being a dangerous criminal was she missing?

And how could she risk everybody else's safety, including the six men opening their home to her?

Anger had him shoving open the door more violently than he should have, and it banged into the wall, no doubt leaving a mark. Monique jumped at the sound and spun around from where she was standing, staring out the window. At least she had the good grace to give him a sheepish look.

"I have to go, Dad, but this conversation isn't over," she said before lowering the phone from her ear and ending the call.

"You called your father?" he growled, aware of the menacing note to his voice even without Monique's flinch.

"Uh, yeah, of course. Isn't that why I'm here? To organize a meeting for you with my dad? I mean, that's why you came up with the whole track me to the Halloween ball in France plan, wasn't it? You wanted my help connecting you with my dad, so that's what I'm doing."

The fact that she sounded so genuinely confused as to why he'd have a problem with her calling her father didn't soothe his anger.

If anything, it did the opposite.

How could she be so blind to the danger swirling around her?

Was being run off the road not enough? Being kidnapped? Shot at?

What was going to be enough for her to take off her rose-colored glasses and see the reality that was staring her in the face?

"You shouldn't have called him without talking to me first," he snapped, making her flinch again.

Still, she jutted out her chin and looked back at him defiantly. "It was safe to make a phone call. It couldn't be tracked. I checked with Lion in the car that I could make calls without compromising anyone's safety, and he said I could."

"He said you could call your rescue to check in, not your rapist father," he spat. It wasn't really anger flooding his veins, it was fear. Monique meant a lot to him, more than he would have thought given how short a time they'd known one another. It was one thing for her to be sweet and innocent, but it was another to ignore reality.

It made her the spoiled princess socialite that everyone thought she was, because it showed she had no real grasp on the real world, and he didn't know how to combat that.

Which left him almost breathless with fear.

He couldn't lose her.

But how could he keep her safe if she was fighting against him?

"You have no proof my dad raped your stepmom," Monique told him. "And I don't need your permission to make a simple phone call. I was doing exactly what you want and trying to find out where my dad was, or at the very least, have him fly out to wherever you want to meet him so you can talk to him and then move forward, looking for the real fourth rapist."

"What you did was show me that you're like a child, willingly closing your eyes to the danger right around you," he shouted, knowing he had to tone it down but unable to stop himself. "When are you going to grow up and stop believing in fairytales, unicorns, and magical happy ever afters when life has shown you nothing but that it's a cold, dark place? When are you going to stop playing the role of spoiled little princess and enter the real world?"

November 11th
12:32 P.M

It felt like someone had flicked a switch.

Shutting her down.

Like Jax's words had been a blizzard raging through her soul, completely wiping everything away.

Child.

Spoiled.

Princess.

Monique had always hated that word.

Always.

Until Jax anyway.

Because when he called her princess, it had never seemed like an insult.

Except for this time.

This time it was definitely an insult.

He was a liar.

From the very beginning, he'd lied to her, and she'd been stupid enough to believe that a man like him could ever fall for a girl like her. What was worse, though, was she'd learned he was a liar, gotten her heart crushed, and still decided to give him a second chance because he'd seemed so sincere.

An act.

That was the only explanation.

The idea had crossed her mind that he'd only followed her back to her rescue because he still had information he needed from her. Now she had to believe that was all he'd ever wanted from her because he'd said he saw her, the real her, not the spoiled, immature, socialite princess the media always portrayed her as, but that wasn't true.

Okay, so she still believed in fairytales and tried to look for the good in life. It wasn't because she wasn't aware of the dark, she'd learned the hard way when she was fourteen that evil existed even in places that ought to be safe. Just because she wanted to have her own happy ever after didn't make her spoiled, stupid, or a child.

It just made her ... her.

Something Jax obviously didn't see.

Driving his fingers through his hair, Jax shot her a helpless look as though it had dawned on him that he'd taken his tirade too far.

"Monique ... damn ... that came out all wrong."

Actually, it was probably the first honest thing he'd ever said to her. In his moment of frustration—ironically, when she was trying to do the one thing that had led him to her in the first place—he'd let slip how he really felt.

His brutal honesty might have hurt, but now she knew. Her need to look for bright spots in life because there hadn't been a whole lot of them in her twenty-six years was always going to be interpreted as her being flaky, stupid, and spoiled.

So what was the point?

Maybe she should just accept the world was the cold, dark place Jax pronounced it to be and stop fighting against it. Stop wanting more.

"I know you don't believe it yet, but your dad is not a good guy. He *is* involved in what happened not just to my stepmom all those years ago, but to my family now. These last few months, he's helped engineer attacks on my brothers and the women they love. He is a dangerous man, and the thought of him being anywhere near you ..." Jax trailed off and stalked across the room toward her.

No.

She didn't want him near her.

Didn't want to see him ever again.

If there was any way to leave this place, to go back home and hire her own security if Jax's problems had spilled over into her life, then she would do it. But the truth was, she couldn't hire anyone better than Prey Security. They were world-renowned, the best of the best. And while she was sure Lion or one of the other Delta Team members would fly her out of there if she insisted, she didn't want to be a bother.

Didn't want to be anything really.

Just wanted to sink down into the ground and allow it to swallow her whole.

It seemed like the easiest option.

Sidestepping out of the way when his hands reached toward her, she watched as disappointment flickered across his features, and his hands dropped listlessly to his sides, his fingers curling into fists.

He was doing all the right things if he was trying to convince her that he cared, but the thing was, she no longer believed anything he said or did.

Jax was supposed to be the one who saw her. The real her. All animal-obsessed, introverted, somewhat awkward, dreamy, fairytale-wishing her.

But he didn't.

He was like all the others.

Saw only what he wanted to.

"I think I'll move my things to a different room," she said softly as she moved to collect her suitcase, which was still on the floor by the huge wooden wardrobe that dominated one wall of the room. She'd put her things inside it, and in the dresser drawers, now she'd have to put them all back in the suitcase and move, but it would be worth it to put some distance between herself and Jax.

"No, you stay here, I'll find another room if that's what you want," Jax told her.

Monique shook her head. All his brothers and their partners were on this floor, and she wanted space from all of them.

As she began to gather her items together, she could sense Jax's frustration growing. Whether it was at her, himself, or the situation, she had no idea. Nor did she particularly care.

What she needed was to get out of this place, be alone, and clear her mind so she could try to think. Maybe she couldn't leave this property, but she could leave the house, leave the room at the very least.

Abandoning her task halfway through it, with a pile of clothes lying on the bed ready to be packed into the suitcase, Monique fled toward the door.

"Stop, please, can we talk this through? Can I explain?" Jax asked.

A pleading quality to his voice made her hesitate. The polite thing to do would be to stay and see what he'd say, talk about it, let him explain, and share her feelings. But she didn't want to do that.

Right now, she wasn't feeling much of anything.

Just a dull emptiness. Kind of like when you were really hungry and your stomach felt like it was clawing at itself to find the smallest bit of nutrition that it could to soothe it. Only the empty ache wasn't in her stomach, it was in her heart. Deeper than that, it was in her soul.

All her life she'd wanted only one thing.

To be seen.

Something she'd thought she found with Jax.

When she didn't say anything, he must have taken that as an acquiescence because he moved toward her again, and she couldn't take it. There was too much anger, too much sadness, too much betrayal, and they were all lost inside a sea of emptiness that she physically hurt from the lack of anything solid to find footing on.

Shaking her head at him, she turned and ran.

Where she was going, she wasn't really sure.

All she knew was that she couldn't be there.

Flying through the house, somehow she managed to find her way through the rabbit warren of corridors back to the stairs. Several times she almost tripped as she ran down the three flights back to the ground floor, but thankfully she didn't. The last thing she needed was an injury that would force her to be reliant on people she couldn't trust.

When she threw open the front door and the cold air hit her face, Monique relaxed a tiny bit. Fresh air had always been the thing that soothed her, from the time she was a tiny girl who would sneak away from her grandmother's boring lessons and approved activities to roam the grounds of the family estate. It was where she first learned to love and care for animals.

It was only as she ran for the trees ringing the house that she realized for the first time how desperate she was to have someone care for her the same way she cared for all the animals that came into her rescue. She could take care of herself, had been doing it most of her life, but it would be so nice to have someone *want* to do it.

Maybe that's why she'd fallen so hard and fast for Jax. He gave off such an air of confidence and capability that it was hard not to fall under that spell. While he had protected her and helped keep her alive in France, and when they'd been attacked both times, he'd done it with ulterior motives.

Once the trees swallowed her up she began to slow. She felt safe, covered by a protective ring of trees, she didn't have to worry about being seen or not because nobody was out there but her. That was why she'd always gravitated toward her own company. When you craved being seen, it hurt to be in a sea of people and not have a single one look hard enough to see you. But when you were alone, you took being seen out of the equation.

Dropping to her knees in the soft dirt, Monique hung her head and allowed her tears to fall.

Jax had called her a child, and maybe in some ways she was. Because she'd always clung to the notion that one day her time would come where she'd get her fairytale ending. Find her Prince Charming, be swept off her feet, and live happily ever after.

It was time to accept that it was never going to happen.

It was time to accept that she had to change herself to fit the world she lived in.

It was time to move on and leave childish notions behind.

CHAPTER *Eighteen*

November 11th
6:49 P.M.

Everything was so wrong, Jax wanted to scream.

Ever since she came back inside from wherever she'd run off to earlier, Monique had been nothing but a shell of the sweet woman he'd been getting to know.

Now she was so polite it hurt. Her face was completely blank, her smile brittle. She responded to every question or comment posed to her, but there was no life to anything she did.

She was like a shell going through the motions.

What made it even worse were the dirty looks his brothers and their girlfriends kept shooting him. The Delta Team guys, too. If looks could kill, he'd be dead a hundred times over already.

This was killing him. A few careless words, and he'd ruined the best thing to ever happen to him. It wasn't what he'd meant, those words he'd spoken to her, none of them were true, or how he saw her. It was nothing more than his fear talking, and his frustration at the whole situation.

How did he manage to keep messing this up?

Monique was a surprise, the last thing he'd expected to find when he went to that charity gala, but she was also more than he could ever have hoped for. Looking for a girlfriend hadn't even been on his mind, not even after all five of his brothers falling in love in the previous few months. Yet from that very first second that his gaze connected with Monique's, he was hooked. He knew how lucky he was that she'd given him this second chance, and he'd managed to mess it up in twenty-four hours.

As badly as he wanted to make things right, he couldn't if Monique wouldn't give him a chance.

Not that he deserved one, he got that, but it didn't stop him from wanting one.

Desperately.

More than he'd ever wanted something in his life.

Adding scoops of ice cream to all the plates of brownies he'd just prepared, he drizzled caramel sauce on top of each and then grabbed the biggest one. This was Monique's favorite dessert, he remembered her telling him that in one of their talks while they were walking in the forest in France, and while it wasn't like he expected brownies and ice cream to soften her toward him, he at least wanted to show in little ways that he was invested in her. In them.

"I made dessert," he announced as he walked back into the large dining room where they'd all eaten dinner together.

Monique was the only one who didn't look over at him.

She just sat there in her chair, staring blankly into space. There wasn't a spark of life left in her pretty gray eyes, it was like she just wasn't in there anymore. Everything that made Monique Monique seemed to have vanished.

His words had done that.

While he didn't have many memories left of his mom, he'd only been four when she died, one memory he did have was her telling him and Jake to always be careful with their words. Words could hurt someone more than any weapon, they were the most dangerous thing in the world.

As a child, he'd never gotten that, at least not really, but now for the first time his mother's warning was sinking in with undeniable clarity.

Words hurt.

Words were dangerous.

If you wielded them in the heat of the moment, you could cause damage you never foresaw.

"Is that ice cream, Uncle Jax?" Essie piped up.

"Yes, it is, messy Essie," he replied, still standing beside Monique's chair, the dessert held out between them like a peace offering. It wasn't much, but he wanted her to know that he really did see her, even if his careless words earlier suggested otherwise. He'd listened to all the things she told him, even the little things.

"Yay! Ice cream is my favorite dessert," Essie cheered.

"These ones have hot brownies with them, and some caramel sauce on top, they're Monique's favorite."

If he was hoping to get some sort of reaction out of her, he was mistaken.

Monique didn't move at all.

May as well have been alone in the room for all the signs of life she was giving, or complete lack thereof.

"Here you go," he said, setting the dessert on the table in front of her, half expecting her to ignore it, or refuse to eat it, to yell at him maybe.

But she did none of that.

With a painfully polite nod, she offered him a smile that was nothing more than the curving up of her lips, it went nowhere close to reaching her eyes or looking real. "Thank you," she said, her voice perfectly polite with not a hint of anything real to it as she picked up her fork.

"Where's mine, Uncle Jax?" Essie asked before Gabriella could shush her.

The little girl was the only one not picking up on the tension hanging thickly in the air. It wasn't like he'd hidden the careless words he'd hurled at her in fear. As soon as Monique had gone running out of the house, he'd gathered his family and told them about her phone call and how badly he'd reacted to it.

Like he'd known they would, despite their disappointment in him, the whole family had rallied. Supporting Monique while they asked her questions about her father, and talked through every piece of evidence they had against these men. Trying to show her through their words and actions that she had a place there if only she could accept it.

Even if she couldn't forgive him, she still had a place.

This was Cassandra's family, and she was Cassandra's sister, so she was family too. Jax prayed she would come to see that. While not being able to have her in his life the way he wanted would be the worst kind of torture, if Monique at least found a place to belong where she would be accepted, then that would be something.

"Coming right up," he answered Essie, turning away from Monique and trying to fight the disappointment.

Not that he was giving up.

He'd made this mess, and it was his job to clean it up.

Whatever he had to do, however long it took, he was going to find a way to show Monique that he saw her. That he knew she wasn't the immature, spoiled, vacuous, high-society princess the media portrayed her as.

The opposite.

She had depth and substance, she was smart and compassionate, knowing who she was, what her skills and strengths were, and putting them to work in her community. She was sweet and put people at ease, even if she was a little introverted.

Honestly, she was everything, and he was an idiot for not making sure she knew that.

"You know you're an idiot, right?" Jake asked as his brother echoed his thoughts as he apparently followed him through into the kitchen.

"I know." That was going to get no argument from him.

"Why would you say that when you know she's sensitive about not being seen?" Jake asked.

"Why did you mess up and walk away from Alannah in the hospital after she asked you to move your relationship from friends to lovers?" he shot back, not to make his brother feel bad but to illustrate his point.

"Because I was terrified of losing her," Jake replied.

"Right. When I walked into that room and found her on the phone with her dad, knowing how vulnerable she is to him because she isn't ready to let herself see the truth, it was like something in me went feral. I could *so* easily lose her, and I just snapped. Words were coming out of my mouth without me realizing it. It wasn't until I saw her shut down literally in front of me that I realized what I'd done."

Only by then, it was too late to take back those words.

They were out there, and they would forever hang between them. Even if Monique was able to forgive him and give him another chance, they would still be there. Likely for the rest of their lives there would always be that tiny bit of doubt hidden in the back of her mind, wondering if he really saw her or the version of her the media had created.

"Tell me how I fix it," he ordered. Jake was his big brother, the only one who had always been there for him, looked out for him, cared for him, and guided him. Now he needed him to give him step by step instructions on how to fix the mess he'd created. "How did you fix things with Alannah?"

"By being honest. By holding nothing back. And by promising that I would never let my fears and insecurities come between us again."

That all sounded great, but how was he supposed to do that when Monique didn't want anything to do with him, and seemed intent on pretending she was nothing but the overly polite, empty inside woman the world thought her to be?

~

November 12th
10:16 A.M

If she didn't get somewhere on her own in the next few seconds, Monique was going to lose it.

Clinging to her calm, cool, polite façade was becoming increasingly difficult. It took everything she had in her, every single thing she'd ever learned from her grandmother on how she was supposed to behave, not to let everything that boiled inside her come exploding out.

Just because she was beginning to accept that the life she wanted was never going to happen for her, and she'd better become resigned to the life her grandparents wanted for her, didn't mean she wasn't angry, hurt, confused, and betrayed by Jax's words.

It seemed he regretted them. He'd apologized several times, and he kept doing little things for her like last night's dessert, that she assumed were supposed to convince her that he was sorry, but she couldn't allow herself to believe it.

A game.

That's all.

He was playing another game with her. Had to be. Although why he would bother she wasn't sure. Yesterday she'd listened to them go through everything they knew about the men involved in Carla Charleston's rape. While she still didn't see any definitive proof that her father was involved, it was more than obvious that they were convinced. So she'd made a list of every conceivable place where she thought her dad might be.

The sooner they proved his innocence, the sooner she could get away from this family and move on with her life.

Stepping into the cover of the trees, Monique was infinitely glad that this morning she'd been able to walk across the open field and not run like her instincts were driving her to do. Practicing keeping herself under tight control was imperative going forward. It was the only way she would survive without her rescue and her solitude. As soon as she told her grandparents she was ready to marry whoever they chose for her, she was sure she'd be married within the year, and her life as she'd always known it, always dreamed of it, would be over.

Tears burned the backs of her eyes, and now that she was out of sight from anyone who might be watching from the mansion's windows, she ran between the trees until she came to the little spot she'd found out there. Even though she knew she wouldn't be there for much longer, this spot had begun to feel like hers. It was just a tiny clearing, no more than five feet across, but perfectly round. In the middle was a huge rock that warmed with the sun's rays, making it the perfect place to sit and cry, allowing the woods to absorb her pain.

Cry is exactly what she did.

Letting all the pain and disappointment inside her, all the words she wouldn't allow herself to say out loud, to come pouring out.

Normally, she wasn't a big crier. After being abducted as a teenager and having her grandparents basically tell her to get over it, deal with it, and don't let anyone know she was suffering, she'd learned it wasn't worth the effort.

But these last twenty-four hours, it felt like she'd shed a lifetime of tears.

She'd just let them fall where no one could see or hear.

Thankfully, her new bedroom was on the second floor, which meant she had the entire floor to herself, so she didn't have to worry about anyone overhearing. Still she'd mostly cried in the shower, and then once she curled up under the covers in the huge antique canopy bed.

Now, alone and surrounded by nothing but trees, she didn't hold back.

All that anger at Jax flooded out of her. Her mind raged with all the words she wanted to say to him. How could he do that to her? How could he listen to her talk about her deepest pain and pretend that he understood, that he saw her, the real her, only to then throw it back in her face? Why would he do that? She'd done everything he asked of her, and that phone call had been for them, she already knew her dad was no rapist.

It wasn't only Jax she was angry with, though.

It was herself as well.

Fool me once, shame on you, but fool me twice, shame on me.

How could she not see through Jax's façade? How could she be stupid enough to give him a second chance? How could she be there alone when he had his entire family and she had no one?

Only suddenly she got the feeling she wasn't actually alone.

Glancing up from where she'd pressed her face against the tops of her knees as she wept, Monique saw a figure sitting on the ground, leaning against the closest tree. Immediately, she recognized Lion's wild mane of hair, so she wasn't afraid for her safety. She was, however, immensely embarrassed.

She'd only let go, allowed her emotions to burst free because she thought she was alone. If she'd known that Lion was nearby, she would have gone up to her room instead and prayed that Jax didn't come looking for her.

Was this Lion's special place too?

Was she intruding on it by being there?

That was the last thing she wanted to do. These guys were doing a wonderful thing by taking in the entire Charleston Holloway family, letting all those people intrude on the tranquility they'd created.

"I'm sorry," she murmured, wiping away the tears still streaming down her cheeks with the back of her hand. Not that it seemed to do any good. As soon as she wiped some away more took their place.

Lion didn't say anything, but he looked up from whatever he held in his hands and shot her a look that she interpreted as one telling her she didn't need to apologize.

For some reason, she didn't feel awkward around this man, even though he was huge and definitely gave off an intimidating vibe. Jax had told her to leave these guys alone as much as possible, but she hadn't asked Lion to sit there while she cried, and she couldn't help but notice that he'd put himself in a spot between her and the mansion, almost as though he was keeping guard.

"Is this your spot?" she asked.

His unusual eyes met hers, and again she sensed that he was seeing more than just her. That he was looking right down into her soul. "Yes."

"I didn't mean to intrude on it."

"It's fine."

"Do you want me to leave?" As much as she felt safe in this tiny little clearing with the late fall sun shining right down on her, she didn't want to take over Lion's special place.

"No."

With that single word, he went back to whatever he'd been doing as he watched over her while she sobbed. Now that the tears were finally slowing down, Monique could see that he held a piece of wood in his hand and that he was using a small knife to whittle away at it.

Curiosity got the best of her, and she slid off the large rock and took a step closer. "What are you making?"

Instead of answering with words, he lowered the knife and held up the piece of wood. It looked like he was carving it into the shape of a hedgehog. Was it because of her? Did he somehow know about Cinderella? Her heart ached at the thought of her little baby not being by her side, but she knew whoever she wound up being married off to wasn't likely to think a pet hedgehog was cute.

"A hedgehog," she whispered, and he nodded. "Why?"

"You know why."

"How do you know about Cinderella?"

"You know that as well."

Did she?

Did he mean Jax?

"He told you," she said softly. That surprised her. She knew he'd been doing little things for her, cooking food he knew were her favorites, having pink sheets delivered to her room, having her favorite music playing in the common spaces, her favorite flowers sitting in vases, her favorite perfume turning up in her bathroom.

So many little things, all based on bits and pieces she'd told him about herself while they were walking through the forest in France.

He'd remembered every single one of them.

"Why?"

Lion cocked his head, studying her. "You know why."

"I don't," she said on a sob, and her eyes grew watery again.

"Because he's an idiot, but he's an idiot who cares about you."

"If he cared, why would he say such mean things to me?"

"Because sometimes when we're angry or scared, we say or do things we don't mean."

"Are you talking from experience?"

Lion gave a single nod.

"I don't think I can let myself trust him again, believe him," she admitted. "I did that once, and it backfired. Now it feels like he's just playing nice to use me for information, like he planned to all along."

"Jax is an idiot, but he's a good guy. You don't have to trust him again. That's your choice. But believe this. If he weren't a good guy, he would have taken his revenge on your father any way he could."

Monique gulped, understanding what he was saying even though he hadn't said the words aloud. "You mean by hurting me."

"Instead of doing that, he's protected you every way he knew how. He was a jerk to say those things to you, and you should make him grovel before you accept his apology, but never forget what kind of man he is."

There was something else she understood even though he hadn't said the words aloud. "Lion, what are you going to do to the people who hurt you and your team?"

"Get revenge any way we can."

With those words, he pushed the wooden hedgehog into her hands and stood, walking away and disappearing into the thick woods.

What he'd said was true. Jax and his family believed her father was guilty. If they just wanted revenge, they could take it out on her, after all, she was alone out there with them, and she'd been alone in the forest with Jax in France. Mostly alone again when she was at her rescue and Jax was watching over her from his car.

It wasn't enough to make her let go of the hurt and anger, but it was enough to make her think seriously about her next move.

CHAPTER *Nineteen*

November 12th
2:33 P.M.

Leaving her alone was probably the best thing to do.

If Monique wanted company, there were more than enough people for her to find it. Instead, she'd chosen to sit on the front porch, wrapped in a blanket to ward off the chilly fall weather, rocking herself almost absently in the porch swing. She wasn't doing anything, just sitting there, gently rocking, staring off into space, and Jax would give anything to know what was running through her mind.

There was something slightly different about her by the time she wandered out of the woods and back to the mansion for lunch. It wasn't like she'd returned to the woman he'd first met, who he'd been busy falling in love with these last couple of weeks, but she also didn't seem to be empty inside. She'd clutched something tightly in her hands, almost as though it were a lifeline, although he had no idea what it could possibly be. When she'd noticed him trying to get a look at what it was, she'd quickly shoved it into her pocket.

But her voice had been a little more real.

Her expressions not so dead.

And Essie had even managed to draw Monique into a genuine conversation. Bless the little girl's heart, he was so glad that the child was so bubbly and full of life that she just drew everyone in whether you wanted her to or not. Since Essie was only five, she was no threat, and Monique seemed comfortable enough interacting with her.

Now he just had to figure out a way to have the same impact on her.

Were the little things he was trying to do making any impact at all?

Was he completely kidding himself that a dozen tiny gestures could undo the horrible words he'd thrown at her?

Even if he was fighting a losing battle, he wasn't going to give up.

Not when what he was fighting for was worth so much.

Worth everything.

So Jax dragged in a deep breath, feeling more nervous than he was used to, slipped through the living room where he'd been staring out the window watching Monique, and headed outside to join her on the porch.

If she heard him come through the front door, she didn't make any indication of it. Just continued to sit there, staring out at the woods surrounding the Gothic mansion. What he wouldn't give to go back in time and keep his words in check no matter how scared he was when he realized she was calling her dad with no comprehension of the danger she could be putting herself in.

Without those words hanging between them, Monique wouldn't be so intent on isolating herself. He could only imagine how alone she must feel with his entire family there and her with no one.

Not that it was true.

His family was her family, and he knew Cassandra hated the distance between her and the sister she'd just found. Plus, the Delta Team guys were definitely protective of Monique, especially Lion.

Clearing his throat, he saw Monique tense, and then it was like she was drawing in reserves of strength as she turned to face him.

A benign smile curled her lips up, and when she spoke, her voice was the epitome of polite. "May I help you?"

Tired of this little Miss Perfect routine she had going on, and desperately wanting the real Monique back, Jax strode across the porch, closing the distance between them until he was standing before her. With him standing and her sitting, she had no choice but to tilt her head back to look up at him, and he saw her visibly swallow as though affected by his presence.

Please be affected by my presence.

I'm driven crazy by yours.

"Do you mean that?" he asked.

"Mean what?" Her brows drew together in confusion, and he almost whooped in relief at the small gesture of normalcy.

"Your may I help you. Was it real? Did you mean it?"

"Uh ... yeah ... I guess ..." Monique stammered, clearly trying to figure out where he was going with this and if she could continue to maintain her air of politeness that she seemed intent on clinging to.

"Good. You can help me by dropping the act you have going on."

"There's no—" Pausing as though catching herself, Monique drew in a deep breath and schooled her features back into one of polite indifference.

"Uh-uh. You just said may you help me, and I said you could help me by stopping being someone that you're not."

A spark of frustration flickered to life in her eyes before she could cover it. "How would you know who I am anyway?" she snapped before once again smoothing away her anger and shoving it back down.

No.

He didn't want that.

Jax would gladly take every bit of anger she had. It was all well-deserved, and he wanted to shoulder it for her so she could let it go and be free.

"I know you, I see you. I messed up. I'm not denying that. But I'm fully prepared to get to my knees and beg for forgiveness."

Actually, that wasn't a bad idea.

Too bad he hadn't thought of it earlier.

Doing just that, Jax dropped to his knees in front of the porch swing where Monique was curled up, making her eyebrows jump to the top of her head.

"What are you doing?" she demanded.

"Exactly what I said. I'm so sorry, Monique. I lashed out in fear the other day. I know you don't see it because you're loyal to your father, but he's not a good man. He's dangerous, cold, and unfeeling, and will do anything to protect himself. Including hurting you. Your loyalty is making you vulnerable, and the thought of you getting hurt ..." Jax sucked in a breath because he couldn't even finish that sentence out loud. Felt like that would be bad luck, and Jake was right, he had needed good luck that day.

Now he definitely needed a miracle.

"I hurt you, and I'm so sorry. You are not spoiled, immature, or a child. You are a beautiful, brave, strong woman who lived through a horrific ordeal as a teen and came out the other side even more beautiful, brave, and strong. You know who you are, and you haven't let your family pressure you into being who they want you to be. I like the woman you are. I like your passion when it comes to caring for animals. I like how you put people at ease because you're so genuine. I like every single thing about you, and I want the real Monique Kerr back. So if you were serious about the may I help you, then please do that. Please be you again."

His impassioned speech had rendered her silent in shock, if the way she stared at him, mouth hanging open and eyes wide, was any indication.

Good.

He hoped he'd gotten through to her at least a little bit.

When she finally let loose and let him have it for the way he'd talked about her, he'd know that he'd gotten through to her.

"Can you do that for me?" he asked, resisting the urge to reach out to her. As badly as he wanted her in his arms, she didn't feel the same right now and she deserved his respect for her boundaries. She deserved a whole lot more, but this was something small he could give her right now as they built back toward bigger things.

"I ... I don't know," Monique whispered, momentarily letting her guard down and showing some of the vulnerability she was feeling.

Unfortunately, he got where she was coming from. She'd spent her whole life having her grandparents try to mold her into who they wanted her to be, and then the media portrayed her as something she wasn't. She'd told him herself that all she wanted was to be seen, and she'd allowed him to see the real her only to have it thrown back in her face.

It was no wonder she was wary about trying to be herself again.

"Can you try?" he asked.

Maybe that was too big an ask for her right now, but he couldn't stand seeing her stifle herself. She deserved to be free to be whoever she wanted to be, and to be seen for that person and nothing else.

"I can try," she said softly, and a sliver of the guilt and regret smothering him slid away.

A baby step, but a step nonetheless.

"Perfect. Because you're perfect just the way you are. Anyone who can't see you is an idiot. Myself included," he added with a self-deprecating grin, and was rewarded by a tiny smile from Monique. "I won't ever allow my fear, or any other emotion, let me speak words that hurt you. Never again."

That was a vow he intended to keep even though he didn't expect her to believe it right now.

"If you're feeling up to it, I have a surprise around the back. Something we're all going to do together," he told her. Just because he had made baby steps this afternoon didn't mean he could let up. Not even for a second.

Jax was fighting the most important battle of his life in regaining Monique's trust, and he intended to give it his all.

November 12th
3:00 P.M

I can try.

Those words seemed stuck in her head as Monique remained where she was, curled up in a blanket on the porch swing, Lion's carved hedgehog held tightly in her hands, waiting for Jax to tell her what this surprise he had planned was.

Although she'd said the words, she wasn't sure how true they were.

Right now, she didn't think she could be her real self around Jax and his family. She wasn't even sure if she could be her real self when she went back home either. But she also wasn't sure she could ever really be who her grandparents wanted her to be.

Her fingers stroked the soft wood she held, and she decided she didn't have to figure it out right now.

Maybe what she needed was to get out of her head for a little while.

Jax had apologized, and it wasn't like she'd never spoken words in the heat of emotion that she wished she could take back, in fact, she doubted there was a person alive who had never done that. There was still some anger, although it was fading a little, and there was still a whole lot of hurt, but she did believe that he was sorry. He'd told her several times, and was trying to undo the damage he knew his words had caused by showing her little things he'd seen in her or remembered.

The problem was, she wasn't sure the damage could be undone.

Of all the things he could have said in fear he'd chosen words he knew would tear her down, and that bothered her. Just because he said he'd never do it again didn't mean that he wouldn't.

How could she take the risk of handing over her trust again when she wasn't sure it wouldn't be abused?

Because Jax is a good guy.

The words whispered through her mind, spoken clearly in Lion's voice, and she tried to grab onto them and hold them.

"Well, I remember how much fun we had around the fire at night in the forest while we were lost in France," Jax said, his voice lacking the usual confidence she was used to hearing in it. "Those moments were fun despite our situation. And I remember you told me you'd always wanted to sit around a fire pit at night and make S'mores and tell ghost stories. So I thought we could build a pit this afternoon and then christen it tonight."

Another small sliver of her anger fell away. He really had remembered every single thing she'd told him about herself, and he was working so hard to prove that to her.

The thing was it was working. The more he showed her that he'd seen her, heard her, and acknowledged it by doing those things for her, she took another step toward forgiving him.

What happened when she reached that place, Monique wasn't sure yet. Forgiving and putting herself back in a position where she could be hurt were two different things. But for now, at least one of the wounds on her heart healed.

"Okay," she agreed, letting the blanket she'd tucked around her shoulders fall down.

"Yeah?" Jax raised a hopeful brow like he's mostly expected her to turn down his offer.

Not that she could blame him, she hadn't wanted to interact with him or his family for the last couple of days. But closing herself off from everyone wasn't making her feel any better, it was making her feel worse. More isolated, more alone, less unsure of her place in the world.

"Yeah," she repeated, managing to offer up a ghost of a smile, the best she could do under these circumstances.

"Perfect." His face broke into one of those full-on grins that did crazy things to her hormones.

Once he'd stood, giving her space to put her legs down, she swung them down and pushed to her feet, still holding onto her hedgehog.

"What is that?" Jax asked, eyeing the small object with curiosity as they crossed the porch.

"Lion made it for me." She held up the object so he could get a better look at it.

"A hedgehog."

"You told him about Cinderella."

"I did," Jax agreed. "Right before he went looking for you earlier when you went out into the woods."

If Lion had only learned about her pet hedgehog right before he found her sobbing on the stone in that little clearing, that meant he'd managed to carve the wood into this spectacular creation in less time than it would have taken for her to feed her little baby if she were back home.

"Wow," she murmured, impressed not just by the speed but by how good a job Lion had done. The hedgehog looked more like a photo that had a brown filter applied than it did a carving.

"Those guys are ..."

"Different," she finished for him. "And special."

"Both."

Side by side, they walked down the porch steps and then around the side of the house. They didn't talk anymore, but she didn't have any other words she wanted to say right now, or anything she wanted to hear. Maybe the only way she could heal was to allow Jax to keep proving to her with his actions and not just empty words that he didn't mean what he'd said, that he really had seen her.

Around the back of the house, she found everyone hanging around, waiting. All of them were there, Jax's brothers, their partners, Essie, the Delta Team guys, Jax's sister. *Her* sister.

As big a shock as she'd had learning she had a half-sibling, it had to have been a bigger shock for Cassandra learning that her father wasn't actually her father. Yes, her sister had had more time to come to terms with the idea than she had, but still, Monique knew she shouldn't have shut Cassandra out just because she was angry with Jax.

It was just hard for her to accept that this family wanted her there for any reason other than to try to get a location for her father.

If that was all it was, they didn't need to be out there waiting for her just because Jax was trying to work his way back into her good graces. She'd already told them everything she could think of, and her father was no longer answering her calls, so she had nothing left to offer them.

Yet there they were.

Smiling at her as she approached.

A rush of warmth flooded her system. While she was a long way away from believing these men and women would ever really be her family, she'd gotten a glimpse of what it would be like to call them that, and she liked it. A lot.

"Ready to get started?" Cooper called out.

"Are the Delta Team guys really okay with us digging up part of their yard?" she asked Jax.

"Wouldn't be doing this if they weren't. In fact, I'm pretty sure I got a nod of approval from your self-appointed guard cat."

That made a surprised laugh burst out. "Guard cat? I'd love to hear you call Lion that to his face."

Jax gave an exaggerated shudder. "No thanks. Pretty sure his claws would come out and I'd find myself shredded to pieces." The smile he shot at her slowly morphed into something more serious. "You have people in your corner, Monique. People who see you. Value you. Please try to believe that."

"I'm trying," she said, and it was true. It wasn't easy, and it wouldn't happen overnight, but she was trying.

Shutting down and trying to smother her real self wasn't the answer, and she didn't need to find that answer today. Today could just be about having fun.

"I know you are. I am, too." Jax's dark eyes bored into her, and she forced herself not to break that connection. To feel what he was trying to show and tell her. To allow herself to believe that even though things felt so hard right now, this would pass, and one day the burden would lighten.

What happened after that she could just wait and see.

"Then let's go build a fire pit," she said, heading off again toward the others.

"Here you go," Connor said, passing her a shovel when she reached them.

"We marked out the spot, and the guys said we need to dig down about three feet," Willow informed her.

"Three feet? That's going to be one huge fire pit," Monique said, taking in the marks on the ground that indicated where they were going to be digging. "Looks like it's got about a five-foot diameter."

"Jax said it had to be perfect for you," Becca told her with a grin that shifted between her and Jax.

"Perfect, huh?" Glancing up at Jax, she saw him watching her with a soft, tender expression. It felt so real, and she wanted to believe it was so badly.

"You deserve only perfection," he told her as he grabbed a shovel from Jake and together all of them began to dig.

Together. And it felt wonderful not to be alone.

November 13th
11:47 A.M.

He was gaining momentum, and things were starting to look up.

Jax couldn't be more pleased.

There was still a huge distance to travel until he was anywhere close to convincing Monique not just to forgive him but to give him a second chance, but he now had hope that it was possible.

Because he knew if he gave her time to stop and think, he could undo all the progress he'd made, Jax was ready for the next step in his plan to win Monique back.

Still, he was a little anxious as he approached the library where Monique had headed after breakfast. He'd wanted to follow her as soon as she left the huge dining room where they'd all eaten together—minus the Delta Team guys—but she needed a little space, and he needed to get things set up.

Now nerves fluttered to life in his belly as he reached for the closed library door. Dating girls had always been easy, not that he'd done a whole lot of it as a teen. He'd been twelve when his stepmom and dad were accused of being traitors, so he hadn't had a normal adolescence. Those years had been taken over by him and his siblings working with their limited resources to try to find proof that their parents hadn't betrayed their country.

But when Cade, then Jake, then Cooper and Connor all graduated from high school and left home, he had to do something to fill the empty void. So he'd taken to dating. As many girls as he could. He was loyal in a relationship, but no one could ever accuse him of being invested.

Not even once he became an adult.

Training for the SEALs had been hard, and between that dominating his attention and then his family's quest for answers, there just wasn't enough time in the day to commit to another person.

Monique had changed that.

For the first time in his life, he wasn't just invested, he was all in.

Something he just had to convince her of.

Refusing to allow his nerves to drive him away, Jax knocked on the door so he didn't startle her, and then pushed it open and walked inside. Like every other part of this enormous Gothic mansion, the library looked like it was straight from the set of a movie. For men with a skill set that involved knowing dozens of ways to kill someone, the Delta Team guys were certainly good interior designers. Not what you'd expect from them. Those six men exuded strength and a barely contained danger.

Cross them and regret it.

Not that he had any intention of crossing them. And like they'd done everything in their power for him and his family, Jax knew they would all return the favor if the Delta Team guys ever needed it.

"Hey," he said softly when he spotted Monique curled up in an overstuffed armchair by the fireplace, a book lying open on her lap.

"Hey," she returned just as softly.

Holding up her coat as though it was somehow magic and would convince her to come with him when he wasn't entirely sure that she would, he took a few steps closer. "Would you like to go for a walk with me?"

"A walk?"

"Out in the woods. I know how much you love the peace and tranquility of being surrounded by nature." As much as he'd been afraid for her life when they'd been in France, Jax was so glad that those days wandering lost in the forest had given him so much insight into who Monique was. Now he realized that maybe there were things he needed to still learn about himself. Like that he had a tendency to say things he didn't mean when he was scared.

"I ... would it be ... just the two of us?" she asked as her tongue darted out to nervously swipe along her bottom lip.

"That's what I was planning, but if you'd feel more comfortable if we brought someone else along, just tell me and I'll go and ask Cassandra, or Lion, or whoever would make you feel the most at ease." While he wanted one-on-one time with Monique, more than that he wanted to make sure she was happy and comfortable, so if she wanted company, then that's what they'd do.

"Really?" There was a slight skeptical arch to one of her eyebrows, and while it hurt to know she doubted everything, even the smallest of things when it came to him, at least she was no longer pretending she didn't care.

Those couple of days where she'd been completely withdrawn and shut down had been some of the scariest of his life.

"Of course."

Ever so slowly she closed her book and then pushed to her feet. Her hand trembled slightly as it reached out to take the coat, and her expression was thoughtful as she shrugged into it. "No, it's okay. I guess it can just be us."

Not quite the enthusiasm he would have liked, but at least she agreed to go somewhere alone with him.

Probably more than he should have hoped for.

Slipping her feet into her boots, which had been sitting on the floor beside her chair, she looked at him expectantly, and he took a moment to drink in the sight of her. While she may not be smiling at him, she wasn't looking at him in anger, or sadness either, and the trust that she offered without even realizing it warmed him. She didn't know where they were going beyond a walk in the woods, yet she knew he wouldn't take her anywhere dangerous.

Resisting the urge to reach for her hand, Jax started walking toward the French doors that opened onto a small patio. Monique followed him, and together they headed outside, across the lawn, and into the trees.

As soon as they were surrounded by the tall fir trees, he felt Monique's anxiety levels drop a little. This was where she was most at home, and if he could earn his way back into her life, he would move out with her to her rescue. It wasn't so far away from his brothers that he wouldn't still be able to see them often, and he could travel easily to join them when they were planning a mission.

"Jax." Monique gasped as they reached the spot he'd been walking toward. "How did you know? Did Lion tell you about this place?"

"I asked him if there was a special spot you went to out here, one that you'd feel safe in, and he mentioned this one." Glancing around the tiny clearing, dominated by the huge rock, he hoped he'd gotten the details as close to perfect as possible. It was a gamble given he hadn't actually seen the photo that Monique treasured, but he'd done his best.

"It looks ... it's like ... the balloons tied to the trees, the bubbles, the picnic blanket ... it's all exactly like in the photo I have of me and my mom right before she left. How ... did you see it somehow?"

"No."

"Then how did you get it just the way it looks in the picture?"

"I listened." He took a step closer, somehow resisting the urge to reach out and touch her because she looked wound tight. "To every word you said. Everything you told me."

"No." Desperately, she shook her head as she took a step back.

"Yes," he contradicted firmly, not to upset her but because it was true.

"No," she said again, taking another step away from him. "No. You don't get to pretend that you listened to everything I said, everything I told you. Not after you threw it all back in my face."

With each word that flew from her lips, her tone grew louder, shriller, angrier.

It was the explosion he'd been waiting for, and he was surprised she'd managed to keep her emotions locked down tight for so many days.

"How could you say those words to me? How could you take the thing you know causes me the most pain and use it against me? There were so many things you could have said to me in anger or fear, but you chose that. You chose to be cruel. I told you how much I hate how the media portrays me, how my grandparents want me to be, how desperately I want to be seen for me. Why would you do that to me?" Tears streamed down her cheeks, and there was a plea in her voice like she wanted some magic answer that would make everything better.

But there was none.

All he could give her was honesty, accountability, and promises not to do it again.

"I can't excuse my behavior," he told her. "But I'm owning it, acknowledging it's something I need to work on to make sure it doesn't happen again, and apologizing for it."

"Saying sorry doesn't take back the pain. I trusted you, I forgave you once already, and you still took my biggest vulnerability and exploited it. Those words you flung at me felt like knives carving into my heart and stealing away pieces of it. I let you see the real me because I thought you were different. But you weren't different. You didn't see the real me, you saw only what you wanted to see, and part of me hates you for that."

Her words hurt, but he craved her honesty, so Jax simply nodded.

"And why are you just standing there now, taking everything I'm saying? Why are you being so understanding about it all? Don't you care?"

"Oh, princess. I care. Each word you say hurts because it's your pain, and I caused it. But I deserve your anger, I deserve to hear what I did to you." Closing the distance between them in a single step, Jax did reach out this time and grab her arms, hauling her up against him. "Don't ever think that I don't care. I care, and I will spend the rest of my life proving to you that you didn't make a mistake showing me your true self. I see you, I remember everything you told me about yourself, and I want to learn everything else there is to know about you."

"I want to believe you, but I don't."

"Until you can, I'm going to keep showing you all the ways I see you," he vowed.

With a shake of her head, Monique broke free of his hold. "I can't ...

I need some space," she whispered as she turned and took off through the trees, leaving him standing, watching her go.

This wasn't how he'd planned their picnic lunch date to go, but in a way it had gone even better. Monique had broken down, shown him her pain and anger, and he had to believe that now she could start dealing with it instead of ignoring it.

Then he had to believe they could work on repairing their bond.

Because he wasn't giving up on getting his miracle.

~

November 13th
5:25 P.M

Ugh, that man was annoying.

Just who did Jax Holloway think he was being so understanding and taking her anger like he knew he deserved it?

Was he trying to make her fall harder in love with him?

Because if he was, it was working.

Monique sighed as she dropped down onto the bed in her room. She'd fled there after her confrontation out in the woods and hadn't been brave enough to leave yet.

It had felt so good to let out all her rage, to tell him exactly how she was feeling and how his words had hurt her. It was like she'd let go of a heavy boulder she'd been dragging around with her these last few days.

Actually, it was like setting down a boulder she'd been carrying around most of her life.

Just because she didn't allow her grandparents to dictate her life didn't mean she didn't have big feelings about everything they'd done to her. Denying her the love and affection she'd needed as a child, the care and comfort she'd needed after her kidnapping and rape, the support she'd needed as she built her adult life.

There was anger at her dad, too, for walking away after her mom ditched them both. For not wanting her either. And she absolutely held a huge amount of anger directed at the mother who had abandoned her so easily.

But she'd never allowed herself the freedom to tell the people who had hurt her the damage they had caused.

Maybe it was something she needed to start doing.

When her phone began to ring, she shoved herself off the bed and crossed to the dresser where she'd dropped it earlier. It was probably the rescue calling to check in. She'd asked them to keep her in the loop of any issues and any new arrivals.

Only when she reached her phone, it wasn't the rescue's number on the screen, it was her father's.

Sucking in a sharp breath, she froze. Should she answer? Get Jax? Last time she'd spoken with her dad, he'd freaked out on her. If she didn't answer now, though, who knew when she'd get another chance. This was the first time he'd called her back since she'd delivered the news that he had another daughter.

She had to answer.

She needed her father to convince Jax and his family that he wasn't a rapist so that maybe she and Jax could move forward. Maybe. If he kept showing her that he saw her.

Snatching up the phone, she accepted the call. "Dad, I've been trying to talk to you for days. Why didn't you call me back?"

"Maybe because I just learned I had another child, Monique," her father snapped in that brisk tone of his she knew so well. He wasn't doing well, knowing he had another daughter, which she supposed she could get. Cassandra was twenty-four, which meant he'd missed out on a huge portion of her life.

Although he'd also willingly missed out on almost all of her life, too.

"You need to meet with this family, Dad. You need to tell them that you're not a rapist."

Silence met her request.

Why was he being so stubborn about this? He had to know that the Charleston Holloway family worked for Prey Security. Eagle Oswald was not someone to be messed with. If her dad didn't agree to talk with Jax and his family, she had no doubt that Eagle would pull whatever strings he needed to force her father's hand.

"Dad—"

"I'll meet with you and the girl," he announced, cutting her off.

"You mean me and your daughter, not the girl," she reprimanded gently. While she understood her father had a shock, Cassandra deserved better from the man who had fathered her.

"I'll meet with you both."

"I don't think they're going to let Cassandra come without them. Someone is after their family, keeps trying to kill them. They won't just send her off without knowing she's safe." Actually, Monique doubted they'd let Cassandra or her go alone. She was starting to allow herself to believe that this family cared about her, would protect her, and wanted the best for her.

"I'll meet with you both," her father repeated in a voice that brokered no arguments.

Well, she'd warned him. If he chose to believe that Cassandra's brothers weren't going to tag along then that was on him.

"I'll text you a location once I finalize my flights."

Her dad was ready to hang up, she knew it, but there was one more thing she needed to ask him about. Something that had been niggling at her ever since she learned of her father's affair.

"Dad, wait."

"What is it?"

"About Mom ... did she ... was the reason she left ... did she know that you cheated on her? Is that why she left you?"

"Your mother had a choice when she left, Monique. She could have you go with her or leave you behind. She chose to leave you behind. She became a problem that needed to be buried, and I gave her a choice. Choices she made, and we all had to live with the consequences. I'll text you an address shortly."

With that he was gone, leaving her frozen in place.

A problem that needed to be buried.

What did that mean exactly?

And why did she get the feeling that it was nothing good?

It was a weird way to acknowledge that her mom knew about the affair and obviously wanted to take it public. Knowing her dad, he probably blackmailed his wife into leaving destitute and with their daughter, or leaving with a bag of money but no child.

But buried …

There was something about the word that had her insides churning.

What if he meant it literally?

Phone still clutched in her hand, Monique left the room on shaky legs that felt too weak to support her. Somehow, they did, though, and she stumbled down the stairs and across the huge entrance hall to the front door.

Jax would be on the porch in the swing. She had no idea why she was so certain of that, but she was. And as she flung open the door she saw she was right. He was sitting right on the porch swing where she'd been when they talked yesterday before working on the fire pit.

"Monique? What's wrong?" he asked, jumping to his feet as soon as he saw her.

When she opened her mouth to tell him, the words seemed to get stuck in her throat. It couldn't be true, could it? Her dad blackmailing her mother into leaving her behind was one thing, but if it was more than that …

Then it meant her entire life was a lie.

That all her anger had been majorly misdirected.

"Princess, you're scaring me," Jax told her, now standing before her. "Tell me what happened. I can't fix it if I don't know what the problem is."

Again, she tried to get the words out, but she couldn't seem to make her voice work.

All those words, all those emotions, all those fears were trapped inside her.

"It's all right, I'm here." Jax's strong arms closed around her, pulling her to rest against his chest, and she sagged into his hold, allowing him to take her weight.

It felt so nice.

Held like this, she felt safe and protected. There was lingering anger and hurt from Jax's words, and she knew she wasn't ready to take a leap of faith with him, but she trusted him to help her with this.

"You have your phone. Did your dad call?" Jax asked.

Keeping her face pressed against the hard planes of his chest, she nodded.

"Did you get him to agree to a meeting?"

Another nod.

There was so much she needed to say. She had to get it together because there wasn't another choice, she and Jax were going to have to come up with a plan.

"Just me and Cassandra," she managed to whisper.

"No way are the two of you going alone."

The fierce protectiveness in his voice made her smile. He'd said the two of them. Not just Cassandra. He wanted to protect her, too, and that thawed a little of the icy fear clogging her veins.

"I told him that," she said, lifting her head so she could look up at him. "If he chooses to think only Cassandra and I are going to show up, that's his problem."

"Damn right it is." Jax's large hands lifted to frame her face, the heat of his palms seeping into her cheeks and slowly spreading to the rest of her body. His thumbs swept softly across her cheekbones, and she allowed his touch to ground her, strengthen her.

Remind her that she wasn't alone.

Gripping Jax's wrists, she clung to him, regardless of everything going on between them, she needed him right now.

"What else did your dad say, princess? What upset you?"

Saying these next words aloud was almost impossible because speaking them to another person felt like making them real. But if they were real, then her father was a monster.

A dangerous one.

Just like Jax had been insisting all along.

"I think ... I think my dad might have killed my mom."

CHAPTER Twenty-One

November 13th
5:50 P.M.

That was the last thing Jax had expected Monique to say.

Seeing the fear and grief in her eyes had his last thread of control snapping away. Jax was trying to do the right thing, trying to hold back, not push Monique too hard too fast, and be restrained in the way he interacted with her.

But not right now.

Not when she was hurting.

Not when he could do something about it.

Gripping her hips, he lifted her off the ground, and she didn't hesitate to wrap her legs around his waist and her arms around his neck. Something in him soothed at the easy way she clung to him when she was hurting and needing comfort.

"Why do you think your dad killed your mom?" he asked. Honestly, now that she'd said it, he wondered why they hadn't considered that possibility already. They knew her dad was dangerous, and her mom disappeared right around the time that the rape would have occurred.

Was it possible Monique's mom had proof of her husband's crimes and threatened to take it to the police, and he'd had no choice but to silence her?

"He said that my mom became a problem that needed to be buried. It was when I asked him if Mom left because he'd had an affair. It's the phrasing, it's weird ... right?" Her storm gray eyes bored into him, begging for him to come up with a reasonable explanation that didn't involve her father murdering her mother.

"I'm sorry, princess, but yeah, it's a super weird way to say it." As much as he would love to coddle her and pretend this wasn't happening, that would only be proving he didn't see the real Monique. Because the real Monique had it in her to handle anything, especially when she had an entire family at her back.

"He also said that he gave my mom a choice. She could go on her own or with me. I thought maybe he meant he was blackmailing her, that if she kept quiet and left me behind, she could leave with money, otherwise, she'd be homeless and penniless. But I can't get over the word buried and my fear that he killed her, so that means ... it means he thought about killing me as well."

The utter horror in her voice gutted him, and he didn't hesitate to lean in and brush a soft kiss to her lips. "I want to tell you that there's no way your dad would have thought about killing his innocent two-year-old daughter, nothing would make me happier, but your dad was okay with my four-year-old niece being abducted and used as leverage, so I think we have to acknowledge that your father is capable of anything."

"Even contemplating murdering his toddler daughter," she said, desolation dripping from her words. "My mom ... all my life I've been so angry at her for abandoning me, for leaving me behind with people who didn't really love me. But ... she didn't leave me behind. At least not willingly. She must have made some kind of deal to get him to let me live. She saved my life."

Tightening his hold on her, Jax nuzzled her neck, wishing he could rip the pain inside her right out of her body so she wasn't suffering. "You had no reason to think your dad would kill your mom," he reminded her. How could she? It was only a couple of weeks ago when he barreled into her life that she'd even learned her father had been unfaithful.

"You were right about him all along." Her huge eyes shimmered with tears, and when a stray one slipped free, Jax leaned in and captured it with his lips.

"I was looking at things from a different position," he reminded her. "But now you know the truth about him and I'm so damn relieved because now I know you're not fighting against me and I can keep you safe."

"He killed my mom," she whimpered, and tears slipped down her cheeks. "He's trying to cover up his crimes by going after your family. He tried to have us both killed in France. H-he didn't c-care if those m-men killed m-me. His o-own d-daughter."

He couldn't imagine all the thoughts and emotions running rampant inside her with this revelation. While his dad had all but unplugged himself from their lives after their mom's death, there had still been good times the three of them had shared, and he and Jake both knew their dad loved them even if he didn't say the words. Even though he'd been only four when he lost his mom, he knew she'd loved him as well.

While Monique had now learned her mom hadn't left by choice, she'd also learned that the only parent she had wasn't just responsible for fathering a child through an affair, but had raped an innocent woman, committed more crimes to cover it up, and murdered his wife.

"I'm so sorry, princess," he murmured as he touched kisses to her face. "But he'll pay for what he did. To your mom, to my stepmom, to you, to all of us. I swear to you he'll pay."

His words must have sunk in because while tears continued to tumble down her cheeks, determination sparked in her eyes. "I want to help."

"You've done your part," he assured her. Once they had an address of where to meet with her dad, he and his brothers would take over, do whatever was necessary to ensure the safety of all of them going forward, even if that meant ending her father's life.

"You don't know him like I do. If Cassandra and I don't show up, he's not going to hang around and give you and your brothers free range to get to him."

"There is no way on earth I am allowing you to meet up with the man who killed your mother, who threatened to kill you, too, even though you were only two years old at the time, and who would have been okay with you dying as long as he silenced me. No way."

Arching a brow at him, she met his gaze squarely. "Did you just say you wouldn't *allow* me to do something?"

"That's exactly what I said."

"And you don't think that's a little controlling of you?"

"Not when we're talking about your safety."

"So you're not going to apologize for your alpha caveman behavior?"

"Absolutely not. I'm not going to lose you," he said simply. And honestly, it *was* that simple. He was fighting to win her back, he wasn't handing her over to a man who wouldn't hesitate to end her life to protect his own.

"You're impossible." She huffed, but he sensed she wasn't all that unhappy with his attitude to her safety. "But, Jax, Cassandra and I are going to need to be there if you want a chance to get my dad."

"Don't want you in danger," he said softly as he pressed his face to her neck and breathed in her sweet scent. The thought of using her and his sister as bait made him feel ill, even as he knew she was more than likely right.

"It'll be okay, Jax." Her fingers stroked his short hair, and he ate up the comfort she was offering, knowing what a precious gift it was given how strained things were between them.

"You're right. It will be." Lifting his head, he forced himself to pull it together. If he wanted Monique to be safe long term, he might have to make this small concession. "There is no way in hell I am letting your father take you away from me."

"I know you won't." Her quiet tone spoke volumes. There wasn't a flicker of doubt in her eyes. While she might not trust him to keep her heart safe, she definitely trusted him to keep her body safe.

Baby steps.

They'd taken a few more of those today.

"Then we'd better get inside, call the others, and work out a plan. You and Cassandra won't be meeting your dad alone. The whole family is going, and this time your dad isn't going to win. We have our entire futures at risk. Our whole lives since we were tweens and teens have been working toward this moment. We have the answers we always wanted, and now we're going to get proof from your dad that he and his buddies set up my dad and stepmom."

"Your family deserves to finally be able to move on, Jax. To be able to look forward instead of back."

"They do. Cooper and Willow, Cole and Susanna, Connor and Becca, Cade, Gabriella, Essie, and their unborn baby, Jake and Alannah, Cassandra, they all deserve to have the futures they deserve. A future I hope I might be able to have with you if I haven't already completely ruined my chances."

As he held her in his arms, her body still wrapped around his, their faces so close he could feel the warm puffs of air with each breath she took, he could see the internal battle she was having between her heart and her head. He believed he still held her heart, it was her head that he needed to win over.

"One step at a time, Jax. First, let's take down my dad, then we can worry about us," she finally said.

It wasn't the answer he'd hoped for, but it also wasn't an outright no.

For now, that was going to have to be enough.

~

November 14th
6:18 A.M

Never in her life had Monique been this scared.

Of course, she'd been scared in France, when she realized they were going to be run off the road, and when they were kidnapped, when they were walking through the forest not knowing if they'd find their way out, and when they saw the footprints.

But all of those things had just happened.

There had been no choice on her part. She was just thrust into the situation and left to deal with it.

Unlike this.

This was something she had chosen. Something she knew she had to do, not just for Jax, Cassandra, and the rest of their family, but for herself as well. For her mom.

No matter how terrified she was, this had to be done.

It was the only way to have a future without remaining in hiding and constantly looking over her shoulder, wondering when the next team of assassins was going to come after her.

Jax said he wanted a future with her, and she wanted that, too, only she was still scared of getting hurt.

First things first, though, because if they didn't take her dad down, then none of them were going to get a future, and that was something she wouldn't allow to happen.

"We got this," Cassandra murmured softly from beside her as they waited for the heavy iron gates to open so they could drive their rental car down the driveway to the house where her father had told them to meet him.

At least something had gone their way. The property belonged to her family, it was their summer estate, and while she hadn't visited since she was ten, she'd remembered enough of the layout of the building and grounds to give detailed notes to Jax and his brothers.

If her father thought he was giving himself a home ground advantage, he was going to be sorely mistaken.

"Yeah, we do," she agreed. While she hated the idea of her little sister coming with her right into the lion's den, she was also so proud of Cassandra. The woman was so strong, so determined, and it seemed like she was feeling empowered by finally having something she could contribute to the mess she believed her conception had set into motion.

"He's not going to know what hit him," Cassandra said, pure confidence ringing from her tone.

"Nope, he's not," she agreed as the gates finally opened and she drove down the driveway.

The two of them were wearing comms, including cameras. So everything they said and saw would be transmitted back to the guys. They'd opted to make it one way because if her father even caught a whiff of the fact that they were about to double-cross him, she had the feeling he wouldn't hesitate to kill them both.

Not something she would have even considered two days ago.

Now she believed it to be the truth, terrifying though that was.

Pulling to a stop outside the house, both she and Cassandra dragged in long breaths before they climbed out of the car. Then side by side they climbed the dozen steps that led to the porch and the eight-foot-tall front door. This property had always been one of her favorites, and she'd loved that the front door was rounded rather than rectangular like almost all other doors. She'd had a cute little room up in the attic as her own, and she'd loved everything about it, from the dormer window to the secret door that led to a hidden room.

Now, though, she had no warm and fuzzy feelings as she knocked on the front door.

Expecting it to be opened by staff, she was surprised when it was her father himself standing on the other side. It had been almost three years since she'd last seen him in person. He'd stopped coming to Christmas dinner, and that was the only time she ever went back home. She talked to him on the phone on her birthday and his.

If she'd had any lingering doubt about her father's involvement in all of this, it was eradicated by the cold glint in his eyes as he looked at Cassandra and the complete indifference when he looked at her.

Maybe it was only Cassandra he specifically wanted out of the way, but he also wouldn't feel an ounce of remorse if she wound up collateral damage. It shouldn't hurt because her dad had never been an involved part of her life, but it did.

"Thank you for coming," her father said as he stepped back to allow them both to enter.

"Thank you for finally arranging this meeting," Monique said, keeping her tone neutral. If her father knew that she believed what Jax's family had told her, he could very well kill both her and Cassandra right here and now. "I'm sure it must be a shock to learn you have another daughter."

"Another daughter," he echoed, his voice so hard she almost believed if she reached out and touched her father that he'd feel like stone beneath her hand.

"So, this is Cassandra," she said as her father closed the door behind them and walked toward his study, at least that was where she assumed they were headed.

"Charmed." Sarcasm virtually dripped from the single word.

"Dad," she rebuked. "It's not Cassandra's fault that you cheated on Mom, or that she left when she found out." Those words tasted bitter on her tongue, given that she believed her dad had actually killed her mom, but she was there to gather as much intel as she could so that her father paid for every single crime he committed. "That was what you were trying to tell me on the phone, wasn't it? That mom found out, and you bribed her with enough money to go and leave me behind? That's why she left. Right?"

Part of her wanted her father to convince her that it was true. That her mom had just walked away and left her behind, and wasn't buried six feet under somewhere in an unmarked grave.

Her father didn't reply until he had them both in his study, the door closed behind them. Then he turned to study her and Cassandra with the coldest set of eyes she'd ever seen. Monique was used to his eyes being void of emotion, but not like this, not deadly.

"I'm going to give you a choice, Monique. Much like the one I gave your mother almost twenty-five years ago."

She gulped. "What choice?"

"You can walk away and pretend you never saw anything, never heard anything, don't know anything. You can continue living your life, playing with your little animals, and being a complete embarrassment to this family and everyone who worked so hard to build the fortune you now enjoy. Or you can suffer the same fate as your mother."

It felt like all the oxygen had been sucked out of the room as her father confirmed her worst fears.

Her mom hadn't left by choice.

She'd been murdered.

And now her father was threatening to do the same thing to her.

"Mom's dead," she said softly, the reality of it sinking in. Along with the grief and guilt about years of anger directed at a dead woman, was a heavy shot of anger. "Mom somehow found out that you raped Cassandra's mom and she was going to bring you down, so you killed her."

Fury sprang to life in her father's eyes. "She was so smug, thought she had it all figured out. She'd been compiling evidence for years."

Cassandra gasped. "My mom wasn't your first victim."

"Your mother was nothing special," their father spat. "Certainly not worth losing everything over."

"Mom had proof, though," Monique said.

"Proof that saved your pathetic life," her father sneered. "She was dying either way, but I gave her a choice. Either she gave me all the evidence she had so I could make sure it was destroyed, or you died too. She chose you. So I let you live. Let you waste your life. But instead of being grateful for that, you're just like her. Here, stirring up trouble, sticking your nose into things that don't concern you."

That was the best compliment her father could give her.

She'd let her mom down by believing the lie that she'd abandoned her, but now Monique was going to spend the rest of her life honoring her mother's memory, her strength and bravery.

"I am like mom, only where she failed, I'm going to succeed. Cassandra and I aren't here for a little meet and greet, we're here to get justice for our mothers."

"Then you're both going to suffer the same fate," her father shot back.

The bookcases lining one wall suddenly sprang open and two men dressed in black ran in. Before either of them could react, one of the men slammed the butt of his weapon into Cassandra's temple, dropping her to the floor, and the other pressed the cold barrel of a gun to her temple.

CHAPTER Twenty-Two

November 14th
6:58 A.M.

When two men with guns ran into the study, Jax lost it.

One of the men must have hit Cassandra because the view from her camera was suddenly coming from the floor.

Monique's camera remained steady, which meant she was still on her feet, but he'd seen the other man approach her and didn't have to have a vivid imagination to know that she currently had a gun held on her.

"We have to get in there," he ground out, already heading toward the house.

"We can't, not yet," Cade said in that infuriatingly calm tone that his oldest stepbrother seemed to be a master at.

How could Cade be so calm?

How could any of them?

Even if they didn't care about Monique—and he knew that they did—their sister was in there.

"We have to," he snapped, a thread of panic obvious in his voice. "He's going to kill them."

"Not yet," Cade said, voice still even like this was no big deal.

"He can't kill them here," Cooper said.

"Not if he doesn't want to get caught," Connor added.

"He has to be smart enough to know that even if we let Cassandra and Monique come here alone, we wouldn't let them go without knowing where it was they were going. If they turn up dead, we're going to be going after him publicly, and he can't risk that. He is going to kill them, but he's not going to shoot them dead in his study at a property owned by his family, because forensics would prove where they died," Cole elaborated.

"Look, listen," Jake said, indicating the tablet he was clutching in his hands.

"What are you doing, Dad?" Monique's strained voice came through the comms. "Men with guns? Really? One of them just knocked Cassandra unconscious. What do you think you're doing? Are you really going to stand there and watch your own daughters be murdered? Your own flesh and blood?"

"My daughter and her friend are going to tragically pass in a car accident right down the street. So sad, I was going to be visiting with my daughter after her ordeal in Paris," Samson Kerr said, and from the look on the older man's face, he would feel no remorse for ordering the death of his own children.

"They know, Dad. They know that you're Cassandra's father. Do you really think they'll believe that?" Monique asked. "They're not stupid. DNA tests will prove Cassandra is your daughter, and this whole lie you've been living is going to come crashing down around you."

"They don't have any proof," her father snapped.

"Oh yeah, we do," Connor said, drawing Jax's attention away from the tablet.

"It was there?" he asked, somewhat incredulously.

On the flight, they'd all discussed Monique's mother, and what kind of proof she could have discovered that proved her husband was a rapist. They'd wondered if maybe she'd kept something hidden, or made copies of whatever she had, something that, if stumbled upon, would be enough to alert whoever had found it of her husband's crimes. Monique had come up with a spot on the grounds of this property that she thought might have held enough significance for her mother to hide evidence there.

The spot from the photo.

The picnic in the woods with the balloons and bubbles that he'd recreated for her yesterday.

Monique couldn't articulate why that photo had been one she'd clung to over the years, only that, for some reason, it had always been in her room, and she hadn't been able to get rid of it even though she was angry with her mother.

"A folder, inside a box, buried right where the picnic blanket would have been. There's a letter to Monique in here as well, along with what looks like copies of a calendar, along with a key that explains all his codes. There are a few items of bloodstained clothes, and some other things as well," Connor explained.

"So we have enough to destroy him?" Jax confirmed, because that was the only thing stopping him from running into that building and saving the woman he was madly in love with.

"I'd say that along with the footage from Cassandra and Monique's cameras we have more than enough to bury him," Cooper said.

Still, they all looked to Cade for the final say. With a young daughter to care for, the oldest of them might have asked Cooper to step in and lead Charlie Team, but they all knew that Cade was the head of their family.

Giving a single nod, Cade started for the house. "Let's go and end this once and for all."

Not needing any more urging, all six of them took off toward the house. They'd already combed the grounds before Monique and Cassandra arrived, and neutralized half a dozen threats. They knew two more, three including Samson Kerr, were inside, possibly more.

Since they knew the layout of the house, they entered through a side door that led into a pretty conservatory, close to Samson's study. The house was quiet, and while Jax would love nothing more than to just go bursting into the room, he held it together and kept his cool. Or at least as much of it as he could manage. Monique was in there, and he'd already acted rashly once and wound up hurting her, he had no intention of doing it again and risking her life in the process.

"I gave you a choice, Monique," Samson's irritated voice boomed. "You made it. You decided to side with outsiders instead of your own father."

"My own father, who had my mother killed, who used me as a bargaining chip, and would easily have killed me too. Who almost got me killed in France, and then again at my rescue, and who is currently standing there doing nothing while someone holds a gun to my head," Monique said, her voice strong and confident, and he was so very proud of her. She was holding it together, gathering every bit of evidence she could so her father would pay for what he'd done.

"I didn't ask you to side with those lowlifes," Samson spat.

"Lowlifes? They're not the ones who went around raping who knows how many innocent women, and they're not the ones who have killed to cover it up. You think you're better than them just because you have more money? You're nothing. Nothing but a run-of-the-mill criminal."

The sound of flesh hitting flesh was the last thing Jax heard before he shoved open the door and all hell broke loose.

Both the guards in there turned and moved to fire, but Connor took out one, and Cooper the other, before any bullets could come flying their way.

Samson Kerr reacted quicker than any of them could have expected, pulling out a weapon and grabbing Monique, yanking her up against his body and using her as a human shield.

"This is who you're siding with over your own family?" Samson sneered.

"Don't talk that way about them, they're good, honest men. Loyal and protective. They make mistakes sometimes, but they own them and try to fix them." Monique's gaze met his, and in them he read her forgiveness. "If you're going to kill me, then they're going to kill you. It's as simple as that, Dad, and I'll take my last breath happy knowing that you finally got what you deserved. I'm glad Mom saw the truth in you, and I'm so proud of her for doing something about it."

"You always were so much like her," Samson snarled, in what he clearly thought was an insult, but Monique smiled.

"Thank you. I'm glad I'm not like you," she told her father.

"We have your wife's proof," Jax informed Samson, and panic flared in the older man's eyes. "Plus, both your daughters were wearing wires. We have all of this recorded. There is not a chance in the world that you are getting away with any of it. You raped my stepmom, and then when you realized there was living proof you had her husband's team ambushed just so you could have her set up as a traitor."

"For once in your life, do the right thing," Monique said softly. "Tell them the truth. They deserve it."

"It's over either way," Jax said. Both of Samson's guards were dead, and there were currently six weapons aimed at him. He had no training, and while he could kill Monique if he wanted to, all it would get him was six bullets to the head.

Slowly, the weapon pressed to Monique's temple lowered. "All she had to do was abort the baby, and none of this had to happen," Samson said, the reality of his situation seemingly beginning to sink in.

"I didn't deserve to die for your mistakes," Cassandra—who had looked like she was unconscious—yelled as she snatched up the dead guard's weapon and stood, firing at her biological father and hitting him right between the eyes.

Ending a quarter of a century-long nightmare with a single bullet.

Samson dropped, and Jax was by Monique's side before she hit the floor beside her father, sweeping her up into his arms and burying his face against her neck.

It was over, Samson was dead, his words enough to clear his father and stepmom's names. They were all safe, no longer tied to the past, no longer living, looking over their shoulders, waiting for the next attack. No longer spending every waking minute searching for the truth.

For the first time in almost two-thirds of his life, he was free.

The only thing standing between him and the future he craved was his own mistake. Monique forgave him, but was she willing to give him another chance?

~

November 14th
6:18 P.M

Twelve hours.

It felt like a lifetime had passed, but in reality, it had only been twelve hours since she and Cassandra were sitting outside the gate waiting to drive down the driveway and confront their father.

Now he was dead, at Cassandra's hand, and they were all back on a plane heading for the Delta Team property to reunite with the rest of the Charleston Holloway family.

Statements had been given to the cops, evidence handed over, and Monique had no concerns that there would be any repercussions for Cassandra for shooting their father. He might have been lowering the gun he'd held to her temple at the time, but she hadn't mentioned that, and she was pretty sure that none of the guys would have either. The weapon had still been no more than an inch from her head, and even if someone saw the footage from Cassandra's camera and questioned it, it likely wouldn't go anywhere.

With her father dead, she had no parents left, but since neither of them had really played much of a role in her life—her father by choice, her mother not by choice—it wasn't like she missed them. It was more she felt so adrift, so uncertain of her place.

The guys had asked her to come with them, but offered her a choice if she'd rather go back to the rescue. Jax wanted a future for them together, and she had a sister now, which made these guys family even if she never got back together with Jax.

She wasn't alone ... so why did she feel like she was?

Hot water rained down upon her, and even though she'd already scrubbed every spot of her father's blood off her body and out of her hair, she still felt it clinging to her skin.

Just as Monique grabbed the bottle of shampoo and prepared to do another head-to-toe scrub, the door to the tiny bathroom in the plane opened.

Before she even looked, she knew who was there.

Jax.

While she'd done a quick clean-up at the house after the forensics people had gathered their evidence, he'd suggested once the plane took off that she use the shower to clean up properly. She'd half expected him to offer to come with her, but he hadn't, and she'd been torn between being relieved and regretful.

Just because she had reservations about going forward with a relationship with Jax didn't mean that her feelings for him had dimmed. They hadn't. If anything, they'd only continued to grow. He'd messed up, but he had owned it, apologized, and tried his best to rectify his wrongs by showing her all the ways he saw her.

Including not doubting her and stopping her from confronting her father and playing her role in bringing him down and getting justice for them all.

"How you doing, princess?" he asked as he stood on the other side of the glass shower wall.

"I'm ... doing," she answered, it was the only thing that seemed to sum up the storm of emotions inside her. She was doing the best she could. Nothing more and nothing less. "I want to read my mom's letter, but ... I don't think I'm ready." She wasn't sure when she would be either. Everything she'd learned was too much to deal with.

"That's okay. When you're ready, you'll know, and the letter will still be there. If you want me to leave, I will, but I'd rather not leave you alone right now."

Tears sprang to her eyes. She didn't want to be alone. She wanted to belong. Belonging felt like being with Jax, and she didn't want to overthink things and talk herself out of it.

So she reached over and pushed open the shower door.

Relief filled the dark eyes that looked back at her, filled with warmth, respect, and tender affection. Stripping out of his clothes, Jax stepped into the shower with her and closed the door. With the two of them in there it was a tight fit, but she didn't mind the small space, if anything, having it filled with Jax's presence made it feel safe.

"Let me," he said, taking the bottle of shampoo from her hands, and squirting a generous amount into the palm of his hand.

Turning her around, his large fingers worked the shampoo through her shoulder-length locks. Soapy suds slipped down her skin as he massaged her scalp until she moaned in delight and the tension drained out of her body.

Moving them both slightly so she was directly under the spray, he rinsed out every bit of frothy white soap, then reached for the conditioner. Again, he worked a generous amount through her hair, then grabbed the comb and eased out all the knots.

Once he'd washed out the conditioner, he grabbed the body wash and squirted out into his hand about three times as much as she would usually use, making her giggle.

"Do you think I'm twenty feet tall?" she asked, looking up at him over her shoulder.

In response, he merely grinned at her, then opened the bottle again and squirted more body wash on both of her shoulders, her back, and then a huge amount down the front of her chest. As the water streamed down on her, the body wash began to lather up, leaving her covered in trails of suds like she was taking a bubble bath instead of a shower.

Soapy hands roamed her body, stroking over her skin in soft caresses, and when one of those big hands settled between her legs, the other on one of her breasts, Monique sighed and leaned back into the sturdy chest behind her.

The future was uncertain, but some things she knew for certain. Jax owned up to his mistakes, he wasn't too proud to say he was sorry, he made her feel beautiful and desirable, and he made her feel like her last name could be anything and he'd still want her. He made her feel safe and protected, but also strong and free. He didn't make her feel like she had to be something she wasn't. And even though he'd messed up, she did actually feel seen with him. After all, he'd spent the last couple of days showing her in dozens of little ways that he'd taken the time and effort to remember details about her and things she liked.

"Jax, more," she murmured as his deft fingers swept along her center, teasing her bundle of nerves, but not giving her enough. Not nearly enough.

"Are you sure?"

Was she?

Sure about this moment and wanting more of his touch? Absolutely.

Sure about the future and knowing she wanted Jax to be part of it? Yes.

She was.

Today, she could have died. It had reminded her once again of the fragility of life, and while it would take some more time for her to fully trust Jax again, she knew that she didn't want to be without him. That the connection that had sparked between them that first day was something special that shouldn't be given up on.

"I'm sure."

A breath shuddered through him, and his lips pressed to the top of her head, resting there for a long moment before he pressed a finger inside her. As he thrust that finger in and out, adding another, and making sure he caught the spot inside her that already had sensations building inside her, he continued to touch kisses to her head, her temples, her cheeks, her shoulders, anywhere he could touch while his fingers worked their magic and his thumb played with her bud.

"Jax, don't tease me today, please," she whimpered as she rocked her hips against his hand. "I want to come, and I want you in me when I do."

Just like that, she was lifted, spun around, her back pressed against the warm tiles, with Jax's hands under her backside as he slid home in a single thrust.

"That feels ... it feels like ... like ..."

"Perfection?" he supplied, pulling back and thrust into her again.

"Like home," she whispered, and it did. "Jax, I don't want soft and careful, I want—"

"Hard and fast. I know, princess, I remember."

With that, he took over, not holding back as he slammed into her again and again, her back bouncing off the tiles with each thrust hard enough to leave bruises. Bruises were good, bruises meant she'd been seen, given what she asked for, what she wanted, what she needed.

His mouth found one of her nipples, and he suckled it hard as his fingers moved to her bundle of nerves, working it furiously, almost to the point of pain, and pleasure curled inside her.

When his teeth closed over her breast, biting just hard enough that she felt the pressure of his teeth break her skin, that curl of pleasure exploded into a hurricane that whipped through her, leaving a trail of ecstasy in its wake. Jax came, too, with a roar of possessiveness before his lips crashed against hers in a fiery kiss that felt like he was branding her soul.

Aftershocks were still rippling through her system, and her breathing was heavy when Jax finally pulled back, pure love shining from his eyes as their gazes met, and Monique knew she'd made the right choice.

"Thank you for seeing me."

"Always. You'll never be unseen again."

She believed that. So long as she had Jax, she would always be seen.

CHAPTER Twenty-Three

November 15th
2:44 A.M.

It was dark when they approached the mansion in the early hours of the morning, and yet it seemed like every light in the Gothic building was switched on.

It looked like the whole family was ready to celebrate.

Jax could hardly believe this nightmare was over.

More than that, he could hardly believe that Monique was there, in his arms, ready and willing to give him another chance.

After spending most of his life focusing on this one moment, on having the proof that cleared his dad and stepmom's names, it felt surreal to know it was done. Tarek Mahmoud, Akio Yamamoto, Richard Gaccione, and Samson Kerr had finally been brought to justice. They were all dead, but in the end, the evidence they'd found buried by Monique's mom was enough to prove that his father had never conspired with a teammate's wife to have their team ambushed.

His dad was no traitor, and now the whole world knew it rather than just his family.

Now they were free from the bonds of the past, it was time for all of them to look to the future, and he could think of no better way to celebrate that future than with all the people he loved.

"Looks like everyone's waiting for us," Cooper said.

"Probably can't wait to tell Cassandra how much she kicked butt," Cole teased.

Cassandra smiled, but it didn't quite reach her eyes. While she was the youngest and had been the least affected by the night their parents were dragged out of bed and arrested, Jax thought she was probably going to be the most affected by how this all ended.

She'd learned the truth about her biology and was grappling with blame that wasn't hers to shoulder. She'd also taken a life, and while none of them could fault her for doing it, that didn't mean it wasn't going to have a lasting impact.

"Just did what I had to do to make sure this is really over and we're all safe now," Cassandra said. Casting an anxious glance at Monique, she fidgeted. "You're not angry with me for killing your dad?"

Instead of offering gentle, soothing words of reassurance, Monique rolled her eyes. "Pretty sure I already told you I wasn't at least two dozen times now. Stop asking, little sister. He might have been my father, but he was never a dad to me. And he would have killed me when I was just a toddler, let me believe my mom didn't want me, and planned to kill both of us yesterday. I'm glad he can't hurt anyone else."

The answer seemed to satisfy Cassandra, at least for now, and her smile became a little more genuine when Lion pulled the car to a stop outside the mansion, and the front door immediately opened. The family spilled out, bright smiles, chattering voices, and lots of love as the women he thought of as his sisters ran into the arms of his brothers.

Cade swung Essie up into the air, tossing her and catching her, making the little girl squeal in delight. Then he set her down, curled a hand around the back of Gabriella's neck, and kissed her hard on the lips. Releasing his fiancée, he dropped to his knees before her and touched a tender kiss to her stomach, where their baby was still growing. Gabriella's smile was so warm as she ran her fingers through Cade's hair, the love she felt for him and his daughter evident on her face.

Jake ruffled Alannah's hair affectionately when she approached, earning him a good-natured punch to the shoulder. Those two were the newest relationship, and after spending almost thirty years as friends, they were still adjusting to being a couple. Whatever Alannah said made Jake laugh, and he lifted her off the ground and kissed her.

Cooper went down on one knee before Willow, who gasped, her hands flying to cover her mouth, her eyes wide as saucers. He pulled a small black velvet box none of them knew he'd had from his pocket, and opened it up. The diamond inside caught the light, sparkling like a rainbow sun.

"Willow, I know this is fast, but from the moment you bravely told me you'd wait in that underground prison until I could come back for you, trusting me not to leave you behind, and putting your life on the line to protect mine, I knew I wanted you. The more I've gotten to know you, the harder I've fallen. I love you, Willow Purcell, and I don't want to live without you by my side. Will you marry me?" Cooper asked.

A sob broke free from Willow, even as she was nodding. "Yes! Yes, yes, yes, yes, yes, a million yesses. After my dad's death, I shut myself off. It was too painful to let people get close, but nothing could have stopped me from falling for you, Cooper Charleston. I would be honored to be your wife."

Everyone cheered as Cooper slipped the ring onto Willow's finger, then stood and pulled her up against him so he could kiss her.

Jax was pretty sure that wasn't going to be the only proposal over the next couple of weeks and months. Hell, maybe they'd all be engaged by Christmas. Then they could have a big family wedding, kind of like the Bravo Team guys had done earlier in the year.

Becca tugged on Connor's arm, and when he dipped his head to hear whatever she had to say, he whooped out a laugh, then picked her up and spun her around.

"We're having a baby," he yelled at the top of his lungs, making all of them smile. If anyone deserved a second chance at parenthood, it was Connor and Becca after what had happened to them when she'd gotten pregnant while they were both in college.

"Of course the twins have to do everything together. If one is taking a huge life step, the other one has to as well," Cole teased his brothers.

"Soon as I get a ring, I'm proposing," Connor told Becca as he set her back down on her feet and rested a hand on her stomach.

"Guess that means we have to get you knocked up," Cooper told Willow, who laughed and batted at his hand.

"One thing at a time," Willow told her new fiancé.

"Cade is engaged and having a kid, Connor is having a kid, Cooper is engaged, we gotta step up our game, sprinkles," Cole told Susanna as he hauled her into his arms and dotted kisses to her face.

"I'm ready when you are," Susanna told him.

Cole's eyes about bugged out of his head. "Really?"

"The moment you told me you believed me, I was ready to commit my future to you," Susanna told him.

"Yeah, baby girl, let's start planning that future we both want," Cole said as he planted another kiss on her lips.

"They all look so happy, don't they?" Monique said as she leaned into his side.

"What about you, princess?" Jax asked as he turned her so they were facing each other. "Are you happy?"

The smile she gifted him made him feel like he'd just won the lottery, it was so warm, sweet, and directed at him. "I'm happy, Jax. You make me happy, and while we still have some trust to rebuild, I'm sure by the time you're ready to propose, I'll be more than ready to say yes."

"Be careful with your words, princess," he warned as he touched a kiss to the tip of her nose. One of his hands gripped her hip, anchoring her against him, while the other brushed across the bite mark on her breast that was covered by her sweater, making a breathy moan tumble from her lips. "I might be ready to propose sooner than you think, just to make sure you can never leave me."

Monique giggled and pushed up onto her tiptoes to touch a kiss to his stubbled jaw. "I think I could handle that."

"Get a room, lovebirds," Cassandra teased from beside them.

When he looked over at his little sister, he noticed that her gaze kept darting between their siblings and the Delta Team guys who were all hanging around looking distinctly uncomfortable with all the emotional displays.

Well, Cassandra was looking at one Delta guy in particular.

Dragon's unusual violet eyes kept darting Cassandra's way as well.

He'd suspected there was something brewing between Cassandra and one of the men who had been watching over her, and it seemed like Dragon was that man.

"You two?" he asked, nodding over at Dragon.

Cassandra's cheeks went bright red. "Maybe. I'm not sure. Those guys are hard to get close to, and ..."

"What?" Monique asked.

"And I think they're about to do something stupid. Something they won't be able to come back from," Cassandra said softly. "Something that might turn them into the monsters they're afraid they are."

Before Jax could ask what Cassandra meant by that, Alannah spoke.

"We'd better go inside," Alannah told them. "While you guys were off slaying dragons to keep us all safe, we cooked up a storm."

"It's like a Thanksgiving feast in there, guess we're a little early this year," Becca added.

"I helped make dessert," Essie piped up.

"Then let's go eat," Cade said.

As everybody headed inside, Jax kept Monique beside him. This year, he had a lot to be thankful for. Not only did his family finally have the answers they'd needed to move on, but they'd all fallen in love, and he couldn't wait to see what the future held for all of them.

Steel and his team have waited a long time to get their revenge in the first book in the action packed and emotionally charged Prey Security: Delta Team series!

Perfect Revenge (Prey Security: Delta Team #1)

Also by Jane Blythe

Detective Parker Bell Series

A SECRET TO THE GRAVE

WINTER WONDERLAND

DEAD OR ALIVE

LITTLE GIRL LOST

FORGOTTEN

Count to Ten Series

ONE

TWO

THREE

FOUR

FIVE

SIX

BURNING SECRETS

SEVEN

EIGHT

NINE

TEN

Broken Gems Series

CRACKED SAPPHIRE

CRUSHED RUBY

FRACTURED DIAMOND

SHATTERED AMETHYST

SPLINTERED EMERALD

SALVAGING MARIGOLD

River's End Rescues Series

COCKY SAVIOR

SOME REGRETS ARE FOREVER

SOME FEARS CAN CONTROL YOU

SOME LIES WILL HAUNT YOU

SOME QUESTIONS HAVE NO ANSWERS

SOME TRUTH CAN BE DISTORTED

SOME TRUST CAN BE REBUILT

SOME MISTAKES ARE UNFORGIVABLE

Candella Sisters' Heroes Series

LITTLE DOLLS

LITTLE HEARTS

LITTLE BALLERINA

Storybook Murders Series

NURSERY RHYME KILLER

FAIRYTALE KILLER

FABLE KILLER

Saving SEALs Series

SAVING RYDER

SAVING ERIC

SAVING OWEN

SAVING LOGAN

SAVING GRAYSON

SAVING CHARLIE

Prey Security Series

PROTECTING EAGLE

PROTECTING RAVEN

PROTECTING FALCON

PROTECTING SPARROW

PROTECTING HAWK

PROTECTING DOVE

Prey Security: Alpha Team Series

DEADLY RISK

LETHAL RISK

EXTREME RISK

FATAL RISK

COVERT RISK

SAVAGE RISK

Prey Security: Artemis Team Series

IVORY'S FIGHT

PEARL'S FIGHT

LACEY'S FIGHT

OPAL'S FIGHT

Prey Security: Bravo Team Series

VICIOUS SCARS

RUTHLESS SCARS

BRUTAL SCARS

CRUEL SCARS

BURIED SCARS

WICKED SCARS

Prey Security: Athena Team Series

FIGHTING FOR SCARLETT

FIGHTING FOR LUCY

FIGHTING FOR CASSIDY

FIGHTING FOR ELLA

Prey Security: Charlie Team Series

DECEPTIVE LIES

SHADOWED LIES

TACTICAL LIES

VENGEFUL LIES

CORRUPTED LIES

TRAITOROUS LIES

Prey Security: Cyber Team Series

RESCUING NATHANIEL

RESCUING TOBIAS

RESCUING MICAH

Prey Security: Delta Team Series

PERFECT REVENGE

Christmas Romantic Suspense Series

THE DIAMOND STAR

CHRISTMAS HOSTAGE

CHRISTMAS CAPTIVE

CHRISTMAS VICTIM

YULETIDE PROTECTOR

YULETIDE GUARD

YULETIDE HERO

HOLIDAY GRIEF

HOLIDAY LOSS

HOLIDAY SORROW

Conquering Fear Series (Co-written with Amanda Siegrist)

DROWNING IN YOU

OUT OF THE DARKNESS

CLOSING IN

About the Author

USA Today bestselling author Jane Blythe writes action-packed romantic suspense and military romance featuring protective heroes and heroines who are survivors. One of Jane's most popular series includes Prey Security, part of Susan Stoker's OPERATION ALPHA world! Writing in that world alongside authors such as Janie Crouch and Riley Edwards has been a blast, and she looks forward to bringing more books to this genre, both within and outside of Stoker's world. When Jane isn't binge-reading she's counting down to Christmas and adding to her 200+ teddy bear collection!

To connect and keep up to date please visit any of the following

Made in United States
Cleveland, OH
12 August 2025

19363428R00146